About the

Andy Heaton grew up on a council estate in 1970s Bolton. The middle child of five, he faced a challenging early life. His career journey included roles as a delivery driver, pallet maker, second-hand car dealer, and estate agent. At the age of twenty-four, a horrific personal tragedy changed his life, ultimately leading to the breakdown of his marriage many years later.

Everything changed in 2008 when Jo entered his life, helping him to live again.

Inspired by their partnership, Andy decided to pursue acting at the age of fifty, igniting a passion for writing and storytelling. After several years of development, the first seeds of *Mirra* were sown. Two years and many drafts later, *Mirra* is ready for readers.

Mirra

Andy Heaton

Mirra

Pegasus

PEGASUS PAPERBACK

© Copyright 2025
Andy Heaton

A CIP catalogue record for this title is available from the British Library

ISBN-978-1-80468-075-9

*Pegasus is an imprint of
Pegasus Elliot MacKenzie Publishers Ltd.*
www.pegasuspublishers.com

First Published in 2025

**Pegasus
Sheraton House Castle Park
Cambridge CB3 0AX England**

Printed & Bound in Great Britain

Acknowledgements

I want to take a moment to thank everyone who has supported me on this journey. I appreciate Jenny Penrose for her honesty and for always being available on the phone, despite us never having met. A big thank you to Graham Morris for his support and to my good friend Stephen Bradshaw (TV Cops) for his valuable assistance with police procedures.

My wife, Jo, deserves acknowledgement for her steadfast support and courage by still sharing my bed after reading *Mirra*. My life and *Mirra* wouldn't exist as they do without her.

Dedications

For Jo X

Thanks for your help and patience throughout this
process.

Chapter 1

The moon hangs high above the outskirts of Manchester, casting a silver glow upon the sprawling landscape. It's 1978, a year shrouded in whispers and secrets, yet for five-year-old George, the world is as simple as the blanket that covers him on the back seat of his father's beloved Ford Cortina. The crunch of the gravel beneath the tyres wakes him from a deep sleep. He blinks sleepily, clutching his best friend, a knitted rag doll called Raggy.

"Where are we Daddy? Are we nearly at mummy's?" He mumbles, his soft voice barely filling the confines of the car. "Not yet, love. Just doing an errand for Uncle Jack," Graham replies, his eyes fixed on the winding driveway ahead. Graham is a man of sturdy build, in his early thirties, with a face that wears the responsibility like a well-worn pair of shoes.

As the car rolls to a stop, George's gaze falls upon an imposing Victorian manor house. The red bricks loom like a fortress, intricately carved stonework framing the windows and doors, whispering secrets from bygone times. Graham turns off the engine, half turning to meet his son's curious eyes.

"George, I need you to be a good boy and wait here for a few minutes," he instructs in a soft voice. George nods, his attention shifting to the grandeur of the house. He tosses his blanket aside. "Look, raggy, isn't it big" he exclaims with his small voice filled with wonder.

Graham steps out of the car into the cool night air, striding purposefully towards the massive double doors. He reaches for a long black chain with a loop on the end, hanging beside the door. The doorbell chimes through the quietness of the night, echoing like a distant bell tolling.

Inside the car, George watches through the windscreen, his heart thumping with the thrill of the unknown. A man clad in a black cassock, a bit like his mum's dress George thinks, greets his father with a handshake before they both vanish into the shadows of the manor, the door slamming shut behind them.

"Do you think mummy is feeling better?" George whispers to Raggy, his voice trembles slightly as he cradles Raggy close to his ear. "Yes, I know she said she fell, but it was Errol, I saw him... No, we can't tell daddy. Mummy said."

Suddenly, the rear car door creaks open, startling him. A dark- skinned girl, breathless and wild-eyed, quickly gets into the car. "Hey, what are you doing in my daddy's car?" George shouts, bewildered.

"I need to hide from the bad man. He's chasing me" the girl, Gina, gasps, her eyes darting nervously everywhere.

George thinks for a second, remembering his mummy and the bad man. He passes her the blanket. "Me and Raggy use this to hide from the bad man sometimes."

Gina takes the blanket, sliding into the footwell under George's feet. "What are you doing?" George asks." This is the best place to hide. He won't look for me under your feet," she whispers, curling up tightly, wrapping herself in the blanket.

A loud knock on the window startles them both, making George jump. Pressing his sweaty face against the glass is Father Reid, his expression urgent. "Hiya, little fella! have you seen a girl with long brown hair run this way?" He asks, his eyes searching.

George stares for a moment, then nods, a mix of fear and curiosity swirling within him.

"Did you see which way she ran?" His voice low and intense. George points towards the trees that border the driveway. Father Reid glances back, his expression shifting to one of determination. "Thank you. May God be with you." He declares before darting off into the shadows.

As Father Reid disappears into the night, George turns to Gina, who pokes her head out from under the blanket, her smile brightens the dim interior of the car. "The naughty man has gone now," he said, trying to sound brave.

"Thanks. What are you doing here?" She asks, her voice laced with concern.

"I'm waiting for Daddy, he's gone in there." George gestures towards the house, his heart racing at what lies beyond its darkened doors. "He's not leaving you here, is he? "replies Gina. "no, daddy is taking me to my mummy's. house."

"Good, this is a horrible place," Gina replies, shuddering at the thought.

"Are you running away then?" He inquires, his young mind struggling to grasp the thought of escape.

"No. I'm going to see my friend up the canal. Anyway,

my names Gina. What's yours?" Her voice was soft and reassuring.

"George, this is my best friend Raggy," he says proudly, holding him up for her to see.

"Nice to meet you," Gina smiles, shaking his hand

and then Raggy's too. She leans in, kissing George on the cheek. A fleeting moment of warmth amidst the chill of the night.

"Thanks for helping me, George. You never know, I may be able to pay you back one day." George stares at her, wondering what she means. "Take care, you two. Bye-bye!" she says glancing outside before gently opening the door. In a flurry of movement, she slips out and dashes towards the gates, her silhouette fading into the shadows.

George kneels on the back seat, watching Gina run, a mix of admiration and concern bubbling within him. "Yes, Raggy, she is a fast runner," he whispers, turning back to his doll. "I don't know. Shall we tell Daddy about the bad man?... Okay."

The doors to the manor house open, the light in the background casting elongated shadows of Father Willis

and Graham shaking hands on the gravel driveway. Father Willis returns to the house, closing the doors behind him. Graham walks down the gravel driveway.

"Hey Graham" Father Reid calls out, his voice tinged with urgency as he approaches from the other side of the trees. "You ain't seen a young girl, dark-skinned with long hair, knocking about?"

Graham raises an eyebrow, a teasing smirk tugging at the corners of his mouth. "You've not lost another one, have you?"

"No," Father Reid snaps, his brow furrowed as he looks around. "She's gonna get it when I catch the little bitch."

"Why?" Graham asks, curiosity piqued.

"Doesn't matter," Father Reid replies, brushing past him, gravel crunching under foot. "If you see her on your travels, let me know."

The priest continues on his way, dragging his feet with an air of defeat. Graham sighs and heads to his car, opening the door and sliding into the driver's seat. Glancing in his the rearview mirror, George stands on the back seat, his small frame silhouetted against the dim light.

"Hiya, why are you standing up, son?" Graham asks, a hint of concern creeping into his voice.

George remains silent, a frown etched on his young face as he points at Father Reid in the distance. "You were talking to the naughty man."

Graham chuckles softly "He's not a naughty man, George, he's a priest."

George is adamant, his eyes wide with conviction. "He is a naughty man, daddy. The girl told me."

"What girl?" Graham inquires, his heart racing slightly, sensing the weight on his son's words.

"Gina," George replies, pointing down to the floor where his blanket lays crumpled. "She hid under my blanket there. The naughty man came to the window. I told him she went into the trees, then he went away."

A wave of pride washes over Graham; George has done the right thing. "Good lad, that was the right thing to do. Where did the girl go?"

"She went to see her friend," George says, a hint of innocence still lingering in his voice.

"Right, let's get you home. Your mum will wonder where we are." Graham leans over kissing George on the forehead. He starts the engine, the sound echoing in the stillness. Unbeknownst to them, the shadows of the night held secrets, and the playful innocence of a child would soon collide with the darker truths lurking beyond the trees.

Chapter 2

A mixed group of fifteen and sixteen-year-olds are playing football down a cobbled back street, nestled between two rows of 1920s terraced houses in Aigburth, Liverpool. The sound of laughter and shouting fills the air until an upstairs window swings open, and the Old Fella pokes his head out. "Oy, you lot!" he yells. The kids stop playing, glancing up at the old man. "Do me a favour and fuck off, will ya? I'm up for work at five!" he shouts.

Alfie, always the cheeky one, shouts back, "Come and make us, you old git!" "Right you! You cocky little bastard, you're having it!" the Old Fella replies, slamming the window shut with a bang.

The kids look around at each other, unsure of what to do next. "Come on, Alfie, let's go," Emma urges, tugging at his arm. "Nah, what's he gonna do?" Alfie scoffs, unconcerned. Just then, they hear the rattling of a gate as it swings open.

The Old Fella lumbers into the street, dressed in slippers, pyjama bottoms, and a dirty string vest, clutching a cricket bat. Jimmy edges away from him, picking up the football. "Right, smart arse! What did you say?" the Old Fella snarls, pointing the bat at Alfie.

Emma tries to pull Alfie away by grabbing his hand, as the Old Fella menacingly advances. In a moment of impulsive mischief, Alfie snatches the ball from Jimmy and kicks it straight into the Old Fella's face. The old man reels backward, stunned. "Run!" Alfie yells, and they all bolt down the alley, leaving the Old Fella tending to his bleeding nose.

The kids are all standing together, catching their breath around the corner at the top of Liverpool Road "What about me ball?" Jimmy asks, a worried look on his face. "I'll get you another tomorrow, Jimbo. Did you see his face when it hit him?" Alfie laughs, the others join in, their giggles echoing in the cool night air.

Emma checks her watch. "I have to be home by ten." "It's nearly five to, Em," Jane replies, glancing down at her own wrist. "Shit, I've gotta go! See you lot tomorrow!" Emma calls, waving as she turns to leave. "Alfie?" she calls back, pausing. "Go on then, girl. What do you want now?" he asks, turning towards her. "Walk me home, soft lad," she says, reaching out to grab his hand. "See you later, guys!" Alfie says to the rest, as he and Emma walk up the hill towards her house.

"I'm out with the girls tomorrow night," Emma mentions casually. "Do you want me to meet you?" Alfie asks, excitement lighting up his face. "No, it's a girls' night, but I could do with some of that stuff you got me last time," she replies, a cheeky smile spreading

across her face. Alfie pulls his hand away, taking a step back. "No, no way." "Please!" Emma presses, her eyes wide with charm. "Em, I've just signed for Tranmere Rovers. Do you know what'll happen if they find out?" concern creeping into his voice. Emma tugs him back towards her. "Pretty,

pretty please! I'm your biggest fan!" With a smile, she leans in and kisses him softly on the lips. Alfie, smitten, sighs, "For God's sake, Em, this is definitely the last time." "Thanks, Alfie," she says, hugging him tightly. "I best get in; me dad's stood on the doorstep waiting."

As she turns to go, Pete, her father, stands in the doorway with arms crossed, a stern look on his face. "Emma, in now!" he shouts. "Coming! See you tomoz!" she calls back, hurrying towards her house. "Yeah, hurry before your dad has a dicky fit!" Alfie teases, watching her run inside. Pete taps his watch as Emma reaches the door. "Who's that then?" he asks, narrowing his eyes. "Just a friend, Dad," Emma replies, trying to sound casual. "Make sure that's all he is. Now get upstairs and tidy your room; it's a tip!" Pete orders, watching her hurry inside.

As Emma races up the stairs, Pete stands at the door, casting a glance down the road at Alfie as he walks away. A smirk creeps onto his face. "Just a friend, my arse," he mutters to himself before stepping back into the house and closing the door with a firm click

Chapter 3

A slick coat of frost shimmers on the deserted docks in the headlight beams of the light blue Ford Transit. The engine is idling roughly in the chilly night as the group waits quietly by the stack of cargo containers.

Errol grips the steering wheel as the trawler comes into view in the distance, nothing more than a dark silhouette, like a ghost on the water. A demon, more like it, Errol sneers. He watches as it pulls up to the dock, and a handful of shadowy figures get busy mooring her. Aboard, someone flashes a torchlight, signalling to him.

He glances at Tweak beside him, then turns to Arthur and Tony, who are busy loading sawn-off shotguns in the back of the van. "Right, boys, get ready. We're on."

Arthur shoulders the shotgun he's holding. "Ready when you are, boss."

Errol nods. "Tweak, jump in the back. Keep your head down." He puts the van into gear, flashing the high beams as he drives slowly towards the trawler, pulling up to a stop beside it.

The three men jump out the sliding door on the side of the van, their shotguns ready. Arthur makes his way to the back of the van, whilst Tweak and Tony stand, aiming their guns at the group of men standing on the trawler deck.

Cloaked behind the van's tinted windows, Errol pulls

a small velvet pouch from his pocket. Tipping the bag into his palm, he smiles darkly. The diamonds shine in the dim light coming in through the windshield as he moves his hand to make them sparkle. Why shouldn't he take one, he thinks? He's earned it, and Brayden isn't paying him anywhere near enough for this job.

He pulls a glass diamond from the inside pocket of his jacket and drops it in with the priceless loot, picking out a large gem for himself. The idiots will never be the wiser. Putting the stones back in the bag, he pulls the string and slips it back into his pocket. He's about to drop his loot in his pocket as well but thinks better of it at the last second. Wrapping his treasure carefully in his handkerchief, he tucks it under the driver's seat before stepping out of the van.

As he slams the door behind him, he watches the burly Irishman in a three-piece tweed suit join his comrades on the trawler deck, stopping at the side of the gangplank. Brayden. He was as put together as ever, with his dark hair flawlessly in place, long beard oiled to perfection. Errol flexes his jaw, grinding his teeth against the wave of envy that fills him, as Brayden smiles down at him – a smile that doesn't reach his eyes.

"Top of the morning to you, lads." He looks at each man in turn, his cold eyes finally locking back onto Errol's. "I think we can lose the guns, yeah? We're all friends here, aren't we?" *More like middle of the night, you daft Irish prick*, Errol thinks, looking at the men surrounding Brayden, built like brick shithouses, dour-faced, semi-automatic rifles at the ready. His hands bunch into tight fists in his pockets; they're quite obviously out-manned and out-gunned. Expressionless, without taking his eyes from Brayden's, he nods slightly. "Put 'em down, boys."

Tweak and Tony lower their guns to their sides, keeping their fingers firmly on the triggers.

Arthur, still out of view behind the van, keeps his at the ready, aimed towards the main gate.

Brayden smiles, widening his stance, slipping his hands into the pockets of his finely pressed wool trousers. "*Ah,* that's much better, isn't it?" His smile fades as his eyes narrow in on Errol's, unblinking. "Now, show me the ice."

Errol pulls the velvet pouch from his pocket, dangling it from a loop in the drawstring. "The stones are in this bag." He flips it back into the palm of his hand. "Need to see the merchandise before I hand 'em over."

Brayden nods, eyes flashing his unspoken frustration as he keeps his cold smile frozen immaculately in place. "Come aboard, then."

"No, thanks." Errol shakes his head. "I'll stay down here, thanks. Send your boys down with the gear."

Brayden's smile falters briefly, but he quickly composes himself. "If that's how you wanna play it, fine by me." He turns to his men, speaking too low for Errol to hear. "Right, let's get this done quick, yeah? We need to catch the tide back out of this dump." He motions with his head towards Errol. "This guy's a prick, so keep your wits about you."

He turns to a tall, broad-shouldered redhead with a

nasty scar across his right eye. "Frank, you go set yourself round the back of the wheelhouse. Keep that prick in your sights. Any funny business, blow his feckin' head off."

Frank nods once, moving into position behind the wheelhouse. He squats behind a barrel. His gun aimed squarely at the side of Errol's head.

Errol watches closely as two of Brayden's goons walk off the trawler towards him, each carrying five brown, paper-wrapped packages. Tweak and Tony step forward, taking the packages and placing them down on the floor of the van, inside the open back doors.

Brayden's guys hover, watching as Tweak slices through the top package, bringing the powder-covered blade to his tongue, nodding.

"Check them all, Tweak," Errol calls back from where he stands at the bottom of the gangplank, never taking his eyes off Brayden. "All ten of 'em. Should be two kilos a piece."

"Yeah. Sure, boss." He proceeds to continue until his knife has been coated with the contents of all ten packages.

From the deck of the trawler, Brayden chuckles at Errol. "Not very trusting, are you, son?"

"Nope. And I'm not your son."

Brayden cocks an eyebrow at Errol's quick answer. "You know, I've been doing business with your boss for more than fifteen years. Everything runs nice and smooth. Works well for us; it's all about trust, and that goes both ways... son."

Errol shrugs casually, his blood boiling at the blatant disrespect. He'd like nothing more than to turn this prick's brains into fish food, but that won't get him paid, will it? He grits his teeth, forcing a tight smile. "That's all well an' good if you're the boss. I'm not. If I fuck up, I'm a dead man. So, sorry if I don't jump to take you at your word. I don't know ya any more'n you know me, mate."

Tweak shouts over to Errol from the open van, pushing the powder-coated knife back into his pocket. "Everything's good, boss."

Brayden smiles again, spreading his hands, palms up. "Happy now, son?" He doesn't wait for Errol's reply, his smile disappearing. "Now, if you don't mind, I'm in a bit of a rush. So get your arse up here, and let's get this deal done. The tide waits for no man, and I don't wanna get stuck in this fecking shithole."

"Right." Errol walks to the gangplank to follow him as Brayden turns away, making his way to the wheelhouse.

One of Brayden's goons points his gun behind Errol as Tweak comes running up the gangplank behind him.

"Tweak, man, what the fuck?" Errol stops, turning to his friend with a scowl. "Get back down there. Stay with the gear. It's cool."

Tweak stops, staring at the barrel of the gun pointed at his face, and lifts his hands up, showing he's unarmed. "Sorry, boss." He runs back down to the van. Brayden's man lowers his gun slightly but keeps it aimed in the direction of the van, his cold eyes locked on Tweak.

"Pat 'im down," Braydon instructs. Errol is infinitely glad he wasn't stupid enough to keep the diamond in his pocket.

Satisfied their guest isn't armed, the goon nods, letting

Errol follow Brayden into the wheelhouse.

Brayden looks at him, smirking. "Looks like you're not gonna get dead tonight, then, yeah? Now, enough pussy-footin'. Where're my diamonds?"

Errol pictures the perfect, shiny diamond snuggled safely under the driver's seat as he pulls out the velvet pouch and drops it into Braydon's greedy palm. The other man just slips it into his own pocket without so much as glancing at it.

Errol's permanent frown deepens. "Not checking them?"

Brayden zips up his pocket. "No need, son. Jack knows the consequences of fecking me over. He says they're good; that's good enough for me." He winks, sending an unwelcome chill down Errol's spine. "Right, piss off, then. I've got five minutes to set sail or be stuck in this cesspool."

Errol doesn't need to be told twice. He makes his way off the trawler quickly, avoiding eye contact with any of Brayden's men, who, in turn, stare daggers into his back until he reaches the van. "Arthur, Tony, get in the back. Let's move out."

Tweak shuts the door once the guys are in and makes his way around to the passenger side as Errol watches the trawler pull away from the dock, a gap-toothed smile spreading across his face. Turning the key, he lets the van rumble to life and turns off towards the gate just as a security guard steps out of the gatehouse, motioning for them to slow down.

"Shit." Tweak curses under his breath. "Quick, Tony,

gimme a gun."

"Calm down, you prick." Errol berates. "It's only Cousin Pete." He cranks the window down as he comes to a stop beside Pete.

"Cheers, Pete. How's Emma? She's on the mend?"

Pete nods, smiling widely. "She is, yeah, doin' just fine now. Thanks for the cash, mate. Really helped us out; you did."

"Eh, that's what family's for, innit? Catch you later. Give Emma a kiss." He winds the window back up as he drives away.

Chapter 4

Errol unlocks the old warehouse's rusty door, dropping the key into his pocket. He wrinkles his nose at the dank, musty smell as he makes his way towards the lone figure, tied to a chair in the middle of the space. The Tranmere Rovers tracksuit is stained and torn in a few spots, and not smelling much better than the rest of the room.

At the sound of Errol's footsteps, the captive's head snaps up, blinded by the black cloth bag over it. "H-help me, please!" The young man's voice is trembling as much as the rest of him.

Errol stops in front of him, a satisfied smile on his face as he examines the array of instruments laid out on the table beside the boy. He has everything at his disposal: a hammer, pliers, tin snips, a hacksaw, and his favourite toy, a blowtorch.

He runs his fingers lovingly over the handle of the torch. "No one can hear you, son, so quit your whining. You and me, we're gonna have a little chat. Alfie, is it, yeah?" He rears back, landing a backhand across the lad's face that sends his head spinning, his cry echoing across the concrete and steel.

"W-what do you want?" Alfie tries, and fails, to hold in the sob.

Errol calmly picks up one tool, setting it back down,

picking up another. "A friend of mine called me. You see, his little girl was given some shit recently. Shit that put her in a coma for two fucking weeks. Nearly died, she did. Lucky for the cunt who gave her the drugs, she came around. Back home with her mum and dad."

Alfie's fingers gripping the arms of the chair as he pulls at the restraints. "What the fuck has that got to do with me?"

Errol picks up the hammer, examining it as though he's never seen a hammer before. "One of her mates told her dad it was you who scored her the stuff. So, I'd say it has everything to do with you."

Alfie struggles, nearly tipping the chair over. "She's a fucking liar!"

Errol puts the hammer down, picking up a pair of pliers instead, taking hold of Alfie's hand. "It wasn't me!" The desperation drips from every word.

"You've just signed a contract with the Rovers. Are you a goalkeeper?"

"N-no." Alfie's breath hitches as he tries to fist his hand. His attempt is futile. "Defender."

"Good."

Without hesitation, he grips Alfie's index fingernail and rips it off as the boy's cries of agony bounce off the steel rafters. "Did. You get. The drugs. For Emma?"

Alfie's racking sobs muffle his words. "Y-yeah, I did. I got them. Emma asked me to. She… I didn't know they were dodgy!"

Errol tosses the pliers back onto the table, the bloody fingernail still stuck in their grip. "We know all that. What you're gonna tell me, is the name of the skank who sold it to you."

"I can't." Alfie sniffs in between the sobs. "He's a fuckin' nutter. Came and saw me when he found out 'bout Emma, said he'll kill me if I grass!"

Errol grips the top of the bag, ripping it off Alfie's head and tossing it to the dank floor. Bending, he brings his face close to Alfie's, the boy's face swollen from the hit and the tears, blood and snot still pouring from his nose.

"Look around, kid. D'you think you're walkin' out of here if you don't tell me?" He smiles, his face inches from Alfie's, as he motions to the room around them with both arms. "Tell me his name, and you're free as a bird. You get to walk outta here and go live your life."

Alfie shuts his eyes, barely nodding as he licks the blood from his lips. "Tweak. They call him Tweak." Errol looks up into the rafters of the unit, squeezing his hands into fists before he cuts the ropes from the boy's hands with his pocketknife. His jaw clenched so hard, he thinks he might break a tooth. He watches as Alfie bends down to free his ankles.

"Fuck! Fuck, Tweak, you fucking idiot!" Errol rages, picking up the claw hammer from the table.

Alfie's hands are still on the rope as he raises his eyes to Errol. "Do you know him then?"

In a single swing, Errol brings the hammer down hard on the back of Alfie's head, his own cry piercing the air as the boy falls in silence. Alfie crumples face-first to the floor, the hammer lodged firmly in the back of his skull. He never did manage to untie his legs.

Errol drops his shaking hands to his sides, staring down at the dead teenager as a pool of blood grows around him. "Fuck, I'm sorry. You should've just shut your mouth, you dumb twat. Shit. Tweak, what the fuck have you made me do?"

Chapter 5

Jaw set tighter than his grip on the steering wheel, Errol shook the memory from his mind as the van lumbered along. The headlights were the only break in the darkness on the backcountry road, as they headed back to the builder's yard to dump their gear before converging at the pub.

Arthur slaps a hand on Errol's shoulder from the back seat. "Drop me and Tony at the Nag's Head on the way past."

"Yeah, sure. Tweak, you're staying with me." He slows the van as they approach the Nag's Head, pulling up by the sidewalk.

Tweak jumps out, opening the sliding door to let out Tony and Arthur. "See you, lads, in a few."

Arthur nods as he and Tony walk into the pub, and Tweak jumps back into the passenger seat.

Errol squeals the tires as he pulls away from the curb onto the nearly deserted road. "Did you get rid of that body?"

"Yeah." Tweak sniffs, wiping his nose on the back of his sleeve. "Weighed him down with chains, dumped him in the canal. He won't be poppin' back up any time soon."

"Right." Errol frowns, eyes scanning the road. "Good.

Good. When we get to the yard, you know the drill. Same as last time." He glances at Tweak to make sure he's listening. "Just a bit out of each package, tape it up. Make sure they all weigh the same."

Tweak shrugs. "Yeah, sure. Jack's never noticed the last couple of times, sure he won't now." Errol takes a corner tightly, sending Tweak slamming against the door, grumbling as he rubs his shoulder. "Jack's not stupid. We need to be clever, yeah?" He takes another corner, easier on the accelerator this time. "This is our last time. After this score, I'm out of here before the shit hits the fan. I suggest you do the same."

Tweak wipes his nose again, nodding. "Yeah, whatever you say, boss."

Chapter 6

The floorboards creak as Billy leans back in his chair, extending the phone cord to its limit from the corner of the oak and leather desk.

"Yeah, so we're meeting here tomorrow then." He tucks the phone between his ear and shoulder as he picks at a thread on his sleeve.

"Yes. We need to sort out the new club in Leeds. Find girls to work it."

Billy nods. "Right. Willis will be here in a minute, I expect. We'll talk tomorrow." He hangs up the phone as he reaches under the desk, pressing a button and opens the office door.

A good-looking muscular young man walks in, not a crease in his expensive black suit. "Yes, boss?"

"O'Leary, nip down and get us a large whiskey. See if Willis is down there when he's supposed to be up here."

O'Leary nods curtly. "Right away, boss." He closes the door softly behind him as he leaves the office.

Downstairs, he weaves through a scattering of tables and booths where men – mostly middle-aged – flash their money while chatting up girls no older than eighteen, loosening them up with drinks and drugs. At the end of the bar, he spots Willis, arm firmly around the waist of a young girl.

The head barmaid waves at him, calling out as he walks up to the bar. "What can I get you, Feargle?"

"Whiskey for the boss. And don't call me Feargle, Francine. How many times have I told you?" Francine grins up at him, bright blue eyes flashing under the dim bar lights. "That's your name, you big galoot." She pulls a bottle of deep-golden liquid from the top shelf, pours two glasses and hands them to O'Leary. "I'm off at nine."

He takes both glasses in one large hand. "Sorry, love. On a late night, won't be home 'til two.

She shrugs, blonde curls bouncing as she smiles mischievously up at him. "I've still got the key to your flat." She winks. "Could keep your bed warm, if you want."

He purposely looks her up and down, eyes visibly lingering on her ample cleavage before slowly meeting her eyes again. "I've got an electric blanket for that, love." He winks back at her before shooting back his drink, watching her rounded backside sway in those painted-on black trousers as she walks away to serve another punter. He licks his lips. "Hey, Francine." She looks at him, eyebrows raised.

"Don't forget to feed the cat when you get in." He hears her chuckle at his back as he walks towards Willis. *"Oy,* Willis. Boss is waiting for you. C'mon."

Willis looks up, not loosening his grip from the girl's waist.

O'Leary's stomach lurches as he recognises the young kitchen helper. Grabbing her arm, he pulls her out of Willis' grasp. "Frankie, I've told you before. Stay away from this fucking creep. Get back in the kitchen and do your job; I don't want to see you out here again. Got it?"

Frankie pouts. "Sorry. I was just bringing out clean glasses, and Father Willis stopped me."

He lets go of Frankie's arm and sends her in the direction of the kitchen as Father Willis stands up from his stool, a deep crease between his brows.

"You can't speak to me like that, you disrespectful little sod."

O'Leary stares down the older man, outraged. "I can, and I will. She's fourteen fucking years old."

The priest's eyebrows rise, along with a barely noticeable smile. "And?"

O'Leary leans in close to Father Willis' face, lowering his voice. "Just stay away from her, and there won't be any problems. Now c'mon. You've kept the boss waiting."

The older man merely puts up his hands in mock surrender as he follows O'Leary. Opening the door, O'Leary shoves the glass of whiskey into Willis' hands.

"Give this to the boss. Tell him I'm staying down here; it's starting to get busy."

"Right. Sure." Willis climbs the narrow, carpeted stairs as O'Leary shut the door firmly behind him.

At the top, he raps his knuckles against the thick, carved wooden door.

"Come in," Billy's muffled voice calls out.

He lets himself in, closing the door behind him before walking over to Billy and handing him the drink.

Looking around, he takes in all the framed photographs occupying every inch of wall space.

Everyone, from the best boxers, film stars, even a previous prime minister who's been enthralled in some sex scandal or another.

"Well, sit down then."

Billy's voice pulls him out of his reverie, and he takes the seat across the desk from him.

Leaning forward, he puts his hands on the desk, his gold signet ring flashing in the light. "What can I do for you?"

Billy lifts his glass, savouring the dark amber elixir, his matching ring clinking against the crystal as he puts it back down. "I'll be talking to Jack in the morning; we're expanding. Another club in Leeds. We're going to need more girls." He looks at Willis pointedly.

Willis nods, licking his lips. "Right. We have a couple who might do, depending on how quickly you want them."

The leather chair creaks quietly as Billy casually leans back, brows drawn into a slight frown. "Next week."

"Most of the older ones are working the streets. We can pull them off and put them in the clubs."

"Mm." Billy takes another sip, staring at the liquid as he twirled the lowball tumbler… "Good. Get the pretty ones ready for next week." He puts his glass down. "Any other news?"

Willis looks up at him, cocking his head to the side in affirmation. "One of your boys offered some gear to one of the girls last night. Told her not to say anything."

"Did she say who?"

"No, I got it second-hand. Was one of the other girls, said it was one of your boys, she said she'd find out tonight."

"Right." Billy's frown deepens as he leans forwards onto the desk. "Ring me as soon as you know anything. This bastard is stealing from me, and I need to know how."

"Right. I'll ring you tonight."

Billy tosses back the last of his drink, shaking his head as he smacks the empty glass down on the polished wood, sending it spinning. "No, ring Jack. I'm taking the wife to the pictures tonight."

"Oh, that's nice. What're you going to see?"

"Endless Love."

Willis sniggers. "Right up your alley, that, Bill."

Billy grins, chuckling. "Just make sure you ring tonight, you snarky git."

Willis gets up, turning for the door. "Yeah, no problem. Might stop down and have a chat with one of the girls, if that's okay."

Billy raises his eyebrows. "Speak to O'Leary, and for fuck's sake, Willis, play nice, will you?"

"Eh?"

"Don't play daft; you know what I'm talking about."

Willis gives Billy a little captain's salute as he walks out of the room, grinning, closing the door behind him.

"Fucking freak," Billy says to the closed door, shaking his head before turning back to the wall of pictures.

Chapter 7

Parking the van in the builder's yard, far away from prying eyes, Errol and Tweak carry the ten packages of powder into the Jack's office under the cover of darkness. They make sure to reseal each of the bundles with double the tape before weighing them to make sure they're all on point.

"You can do one now, mate. I'll take care of the rest." Errol motions at Tweak with a nod towards the door.

"Right, then. I'll see you in a bit." Tweak slams the door shut after him, making sure it's closed tight. Errol carefully stacks all the packages safely in the office safe. One can never take too many precautions. Satisfied, he then turns to his little lifted stash. "He'll never be the wiser." He chuckles to himself in the empty office as he wraps it up in an old duffle coat. Errol turns the light out in the office before leaving and locking the door behind himself, he walks across the yard into an old storage shed. Glancing around out of habit, even though he already knows he's alone, he stacks a few loose pallets on top of each other just high enough so he can reach into the old heating duct where he keeps his little stockpile hidden away, making sure it's pushed back far enough not to be noticed from below, then replaces the pallets back to their original position.

Locking the gate, he decides he can't be arsed with the pub and its congregation of morons opting to head home instead. Under the bright moon, he pulls out the stolen diamond from his pocket, raising it up to catch the light. He laughs as it reflects, sparkling like a star between his fingers. Happy as a dog with two dicks, he slips it back into his pocket as he steps into a red telephone box.

Two pence in the slot, Jack is on the line before the first ring is through. *"Hello."* His voice is gruff like he's been woken from sleep, although Errol doubts that's the case. Most likely caught him mid-act with some two-bit tart.

"It's me, boss," Errol speaks into the sticky receiver. *"Job's done."*

"Good." The click in his ear sounds before Errol can say another word.

"Prick." He slams the receiver down with excessive force, cracking the plastic cradle, then puts his fist through one of the square glass panes of the telephone box, slicing his knuckles in the process, kicking the door open nearly off its hinges. "Fucking cunt could've said 'well done'. Thanks for nothin', fuckin' arsehole." He mutters as he jogs down Kenilworth Road. He needs to get this thing out of his pocket and tucked away somewhere nobody will ever think to look.

Coming up to the dilapidated terrace house, he frowns at the cracked and chipped red brick and dirty boarded-up windows. *What a dump!* he thinks, imagining Jack in his fancy house, with his fancy bed, and his fancy women, drinking fancy champagne out of fancy glasses. Errol deserves all that more than that prick does, doesn't he?

He lets himself in as quietly as he can, shouldering the heavy door. Spotting a dirty pair of small trainers in the corner, an idea creeps into his mind. As quietly as he can on the creaking stairs, he makes his way up to the third-floor attic bedroom, pushing the door open to find George asleep, tangled up in a dingy blanket. Even from where he stands in the near darkness, he can see the yellow stains on the caseless pillow from decades of use, and the sweat of its many previous owners.

Looming over the sleeping boy, Errol carefully pries the tattered knitted doll from his grasp and backs out of the room. Back downstairs in the kitchen, he slices a small hole in the doll's neck, jumping and nearly dropping the knife as something creaks behind him.

"Fuck me. Man, get a grip, it's only the wind."

Tossing the knife into the sink with a clatter, he pulls the diamond back out of his pocket. Examining it again for a moment, in the dim, yellow light from the outside lamp post, he wraps it in a strip of cloth ripped from a tea towel to soften the edges then shoves it into the hole he's cut, and up into the doll's big head. Making

quick work of it with Val's sewing kit, he patches up the hole as good as new returning the doll where he's pulled it from, never waking George.

Back on the second floor, he sheds his clothes, leaving them in a pile on the floor as he gets into bed beside a sleeping Val, shaking her awake.

"Mm?"

"Glad you're awake. Fancy a bit of fun?"

Val tries to turn back over, rolling away from him. "Mm-mm. Not tonight, babe, I'm too tired."

He grips her shoulder roughly. "I don't give a fuck if you're tired, sleepin', or dead. Get your kit off and get on top. Don't make me tell you twice."

"Errol, please, I don't want to." She tries to swat at his hand weakly, half-asleep.

Grabbing a fistful of sleep-matted blonde hair, he pulls her over onto her back. Straddling her, he backhands her across the face, then grips her jaw in an iron fist as he brings his face close to hers, spittle flying onto her cheeks as he warns her through gritted teeth. "You don't get to say no to me. Not now, not ever. You're mine, and you'll do as I say when I fuckin' say. Is that understood?"

Val squirms under him, trying to fight him off. Arms flailing, she manages to scratch his face but is quickly rewarded with a fist meeting the side of her head. She bucks and twists, but it's no use as he's more than twice her size and three times the weight. The cotton of her knickers cuts into her skin as he rips them off, forcing her legs apart with his knees. He grabs her slim wrist, spinning them above her head with one hand while the other grips her throat in a warning just firm enough to get her to keep still as tears stream down her face.

George grips his doll tightly as he sneaks to the wardrobe, the only bit of furniture in his room apart from the old, rusty iron bed, which looks like it used to be white. Behind it, in a space only big enough for a six-year- old boy to fit, is a small door leading to an open space beneath the rafters. Inside this secret hideaway is where George feels the safest. It's also where he hides his only happy memory – a photo of his mum and dad, smiling wide, holding him when he was a baby.

Scuttling back against the chimney breast, he gathers up an old, tattered blanket around him and presses Raggy, his beloved doll, close to his chest as he covers his ears with his hands to block out the noise from downstairs. His mum and Errol are screaming again, and making other strange noises he doesn't like. Disgusting, grunting noises, like the ones that came from the TV sometimes, when Errol is in the living room alone.

Spent and dripping sweat, Errol rolls off a sobbing Val. Wiping himself off on her torn nighty, he rolls over and promptly falls asleep.

She pulls the thin sheet over her battered body as she turns carefully onto her side, curling up into a ball as her tears and the blood from her busted lip stain the pillowcase. It's been nearly a week since he's last raped her, she'd let herself believe it wouldn't happen again.

Wishful thinking, she thinks, bringing a trembling hand to her throbbing head. Maybe she should just stop fighting him; she'd at least save herself the bruises.

Chapter 8

Jack trudges through the gates just as the sun begins to lighten the sky behind a grey cover of clouds. Another dreary day. He closes and locks the gate behind him, breathing hot air into his hands, rubbing them together for warmth.

A man of habit, he goes through the motions; putting the kettle on, brewing tea strong enough to lift tar off the road, then locks himself in his office, flipping the blinds closed to prying eyes.

Setting down his steaming cup on top of the large, floor-mounted safe, he bends to turn the dial, clicking in the combination, smiling widely as the door flings open to reveal the twelve neatly stacked packages inside. Content they're all there, he pulls one out, slamming the safe shut again.

At his desk, he pierces the top with a penknife, tasting the white powder with the tip of his tongue. Pure. Beautiful. Joe's been true to his word, as always.

Satisfied, he downs his scalding tea before putting the package back in the safe, then opens the blinds to find some of the workers assembled outside the gate.

Hands in his pockets, he struts out of his office and towards the gate. "Makes a change, doesn't it, you lot waiting for me instead of the other way 'round." He unlocks the gate. "Right, let's be havin' you; got a lot of work booked in for today.

He walks back to his office, his charge hand, Jimmy, following behind like an eager pup. "Mornin', boss." Jimmy nods when Jack raises his eyebrows in question. "You got the job sheets?"

Jack picks up the sheets and hands them to him.

Jimmy flips through them, frowning as he pulls one out. "Boss, you've got one here for the Brass house in town, but no description, what's–"

"It's for next week." Jack interrupts. "Gotta go have a look at the roof today."

"Yeah, all right." Jimmy nods again, tucking it back in with the others. "Was talking to Billy last night. He never mentioned it."

"Musta slipped his mind." Jack shrugs. "Right, get the boys to work." He motions towards the door with his head. "Right." Jimmy leaves the office and walks out to the yard where the rest of the crew are waiting for him to hand them out their jobs for the day.

From the window, Jack shakes his head as he watches a bronze Cortina pull up outside the gates. *How much is he gonna ask for this time?*

He sits down behind the desk as Graham walks in. "How's it going, Jack?"

"You know, busy busy, the usual. You've seen Mum this week?"

Graham sits – or more like slouches – in the faded vinyl chair across from him. "Nah. Takin' George to see her on the way back to Blackpool. That's why I called."

"How much?" Jack sighs, interlacing his fingers on the desktop, tipping his head as Graham avoids meeting his stare.

"Couple hundred should do me. Been a bad week on the road."

Jack snorts. "Told you double glazing was a fad. Come work for me, earn some real money." Graham meets his eyes, shaking his head. "Can't. Tryin' to get my life sorted so I can get George with me full-time. I have to get him out of that dump, I'm trying to convince Val to get out, too. Covered in bruises again, she was, wanting me to believe she fell hangin' out washing like I'm some kinda retard."

Jack exhales loudly. "Yeah, I can understand that. That's no place for the lad. But Val's made her bed, mate. She's a grown woman; she can leave if she wants to." He clears his throat. "I need you to do me a favour, whilst you're in Blackpool, brother." He continues when Graham starts to protest. "Drop a parcel for me at Tony,, the Greek's place in Southport. It's on your way; you can save me a trip."

"Fuck's sake, Jack. I told you I've finished with all that."

Jack knows his brother has a price. "There's five hundred nicker in it for ya."

Graham huffs, frowning as he stares at his brother. Five hundred could really help him out. "Right, fine. But it's definitely the last time. I gotta think of George."

"That nephew of mine is exactly who I'm thinkin' of, little brother. You need the money if you're gonna have him with you.?" He stands, shoving the chair back. "Why don't you bring him 'round on your way back? Barbara's always asking about him." He walks to the safe, blocking its contents as he pulls out a padded envelope.

"Yeah, can do; need to get going though; can't wait to see George's face when he meets Nipper."

Jack turns back to his brother, frowning as he slams the safe shut. "Who the fuck is Nipper?"

Graham stands, smiling like a kid. "Little Jack Russell pup I got a couple weeks ago; George doesn't know yet; he'll go mad for him."

"Right, well, Barbara likes dogs about as much as she likes kids. Might as well bring them both for tea on Sunday. She'll make shepherd's pie, George's favourite." He pulls out a bundle of twenty-pound notes from the envelope, counting out five-hundred quid onto the desk and handing it to Graham.

Graham accepts the cash, nodding as he folds it, tucking it into his shirt pocket. "Cheers. Yeah, sounds good, he'll be excited to see you."

Jack calls out to him as he walks out of the office. "Open your boot when you get to the car. One of the lads will put Tony's stuff in."

"Right."

"Have a great weekend," Jack calls from the doorway. "See you Sunday."

Graham waves over his shoulder as he walks to the car, popping the boot open before getting into the driver's seat. He watches, frowning at the rearview mirror as one of Jack's crew starts loading things in. What will he be

46

transporting this time, he wonders.

The worker slams the boot shut, smacking it as he gives Graham a thumbs up in the mirror, the noise startling the sleeping pup in the back seat sending him into a barking frenzy.

"All right, little one." Graham grabs the wriggling fur ball from the back, dropping him into his lap as he puts the car in gear. "Let's go pick up George."

Chapter 9

Detective Doonan stands, arms crossed over his chest, frown deep between his brows as he stares intently at the evidence board. It looks like something out of an episode of 'The Sweeney', he thinks as he follows the red thread pinned from bit to bit. Mugshots, crime scene snapshots, reports. His murder squad has been working this case for what feels like forever.

Politicians, business owners, even a damn priest, all caught on camera with various members of the gang they've been tracking. All have one thing in common – a gold signet ring engraved with an X.

He looks at every photograph again, as if by some miracle, he'll see something he hasn't seen yet. Jack, the crime lord. Top dog, or so it seems. But on paper, he's squeaky clean. Jimmy, whiskey in hand, ogling a naked, busty brunette on a stripping pole. Billy, the strip club owner, sat beside him. Then a series of mugshots marked in felt tippen. Tony, Errol, Feargal O'Leary, Ponytail Pete, Eddie Valentine, Jack Harrison, and Tweak.

He turns to address his detectives. "Right, lads, let's get crackin'. We need to get this bunch of shithouses behind bars."

Jackson clicks his pen, as he has an annoying habit of doing. "Easier said than done, boss. They're always two steps ahead of us. It's like they know our next move. If I didn't know better, I'd almost believe we had a mole on the crew."

"This squad's been vetted. If there's a mole, it's not one of us. And the fact they're always ahead of us is precisely why this team's been set up. The only ones who know what we're doing are us lot, and the chief."

"Who's the flat foot?" Jackson asks, pointing at Mercy.

"He's with me, for now," Doonan tells him. "Orders from upstairs."

"Why?" Morrison pipes up.

Doonan shrugs. "Don't know too much, yet, but it's come from the top, so we're not to question it."

Monroe rolls his eyes, tossing back the dredges of his tepid coffee. *"Ahh,* one of them." Mercy frowns, insulted by Monroe's tone. "What'd you mean, one of them?"

Monroe smirks at the younger man. "Fast-tracked public school boy."

"Monroe, shut it." Doonan rolls up his sleeves. "Right, we have a job to do, so let's get on with it, yeah?" He points to Errol and Tweak's mugshots. "Jackson, you can focus your attention on this dirtbag, name's Tweak, and I don't have to wonder how he got it. Heard it through the grapevine, he's been knockin' 'round with Errol; must've been moved up the food chain."

Jackson makes note of their names on his scratchpad, shaking his head. "It's gonna be a right bastard keepin' tabs on both of 'em."

"Morrison." Doonan points at the bald man. "You

49

partner up with Jackson for a couple weeks, see what you can find out. And for fuck's sake, don't get seen this time!"

Morrison shakes his head, staring at the floor.

"That weren't my fault, boss." Jackson mumbles, having the wherewithal to look embarrassed about it.

"Water under the bridge," Doonan tells him, nodding. "Just be careful, yeah? These two are nasty bastards."

Jackson nods.

"Peters." Doonan points at Mercy, standing at the back of the room. "You're with me. You do as I say, we're gonna get along just fine. Fuck this up, you'll find yourself back on parking tickets.

"Yes, sir, boss," Mercy acknowledges, his mouth set and cheeks colouring as Doonan gets to work on the board, moving around a couple of pictures.

Chapter 10

Graham pulls up in front of the imposing, three-story red brick Victorian house, his 1976 metallic bronze Ford Cortina looking slightly out of place. The house has definitely seen better days; that was being generous, he thinks, shaking his head at the boarded-up front bay window, the corrugated steel rusting around the edges.

The difference between this house and the neighbouring one never ceases to shock him; how that nice old couple put up with it, he'll never understand.

He gets out of the car and starts walking slowly up to the door, covered in old band posters, weathered and peeling. As he approaches the stairs, the door opens, Val walks out, holding George's hand. He lifts a hand to her, frowning at her appearance. She looks pale, almost sickly, under a worn, short white dress that looks to be no more than a rag. Her blonde hair seems to have not been brushed in days, hanging in long matted strands over the right side of her face, but doing a poor job at hiding the swelling of fresh purple bruises.

She clings to George's hand, avoiding Graham's eyes as she lifts a hand in return greeting, licking her split lip, and praying he won't ask about it. God, how different this woman is from the one he'd married. She'd been beautiful once, full of life, her blue eyes always smiling. Now, she's nothing more than a shell of who she used to be. Or more, a pincushion, he thinks, noticing the track marks on her arms.

Clearing his throat, he forces a smile as he looks at his son. He has his mum's blue eyes, Graham's dark hair; he's looks like an urchin in his tattered hand-me-downs. "Hiya, son. Come here and give your dad a hug."

George runs down the steps, wrapping his arms around Graham's waist, but when he squeezes him back, the boy winces.

Graham frowns. "What's up, son? Have you been hurt?"

"Calm down, Gray. He tripped comin' down the steps and banged his shoulder. Nothin' to get worked up about." Val crosses her arms in front of her chest as though daring him to rebut.

"That right, son?" Graham tips up George's chin. The boy nods, pressing his lips together, but his eyes tell Graham there's more to this tripping.

"Right, let's get you in the car. I need a quick word with your mum." George runs back to Val for a quick hug and a kiss.

"Don't forget Raggy Doll, love." Val hands George his doll before he runs back down the stairs, going with Graham to the car. Climbing into the backseat, he immediately breaks out in a fit of giggles as the squirming pup jumps all over him, licking at his face and nibling at his ears.

Graham smiles at the sight. "Meet your new puppy, Nipper. I'll be back in just a minute."

"What?" Val asks, arms still crossed defiantly, as Graham reaches her.

He points a finger at her, frowning. "If I find out that rag-headed twat or his mate have touched George, I'll—"

"He's not touched him. Now go, before you wake him up!" She hisses, looking over her shoulder nervously.

Graham steps up the stairs, reaching to move her hair from her face, revealing the full extent of the blue, swollen bruising. "Fuck's sake, Val. What are you doing with that scumbag?"

She swats his hand away, backing up a step. *"Shh!* It wasn't him. I tripped, hanging the washing out in the yard." Graham nods. "Hanging the washing. Right." He looks away, taking a deep breath, before meeting her eyes again. "Look, I know we're not together any more, love, but I can help you. Just let me!" "I'm fine, Gray. Just go."

He raises his hands, surrendering. "Right, I'm going. But when I get back Sunday night, have a bag ready. You, me and Georgie, we're getting away from this place. We'll start again somewhere new. He won't find you."

Val shakes her head sadly. "Let's just see, shall we?" "I mean it, Val. I still love you, never stopped." He grabs for her hand. "Come with us now. You don't need to stay here."

She pulls away, blinking back the tears. "You had better go. Make sure you have him back here by two o'clock on Sunday."

Graham backs down the steps, knowing he won't get her away just now, but is resigned to try again on Sunday. "It'll be a bit later. We're going to Jack and Barbara's for tea."

"Right, okay. Have a nice time." She walks back in before he can say another word. He stands staring at the door, wondering what the hell happened for her life to go so far down the wrong tracks. Exhaling heavily, he walks back to the car, the smile reappearing on his face as he sees George and Nipper playing in the backseat.

"Right, Georgie, you ready?" he asks as he gets in the driver's seat. "Ready!"

"Blackpool, here we come!"

"Blackpool, yay! Can we go to the funhouse again? And ride the donkeys on the beach?" He's bouncing up and down with excitement.

Graham laughs along with him as he turns the ignition. "We can do whatever you want, son."

From George's third-floor attic window, Val watches them drive away as she wipes her tears, wishing she'd been brave enough to take Graham up on his offer.

Chapter 11

John throws hook attached to rope into the canal as he walks the length for the hundredth time. He's been at it all day, like usual, he's only found a few bits to bring to the scrap-man, hopefully, it'll be enough for a few quid. Maybe he'll be able to eat tonight.

Never did he imagine, back when he was Captain of his SAS Squadron, that he'd end up discharged for shell shock, sleeping on the streets, and fishing for scraps. At least, most other street folk have the mind to keep away from him; it pays to look intimidating, bending his bulky, six-foot-four frame to pull at the rope again, tossing it back in a little further down and immediately hooking on to something hefty.

Pulling it up, he smiles as his loot breaks the surface – a tarnished brass headboard. This will surely earn him a few quid from the scrapman. Leaning it against a crumbling brick wall which used to house some coal or cotton factory or other, he pulls his trusty Zippo lighter out, striking it with grubby fingers until the cigarette burns cherry red.

Inhaling deeply, he stares at the glistening canal water, deciding if he'll give it another try, or count his blessings for the day.

"Hey, John! What're you doin'?"

He turns, smiling as he pulls the cigarette from his lips. "Hey, G, they let you out? Or have you escaped again?"

Gina closes the distance between them, the late afternoon sun catching on her long black hair. Only ten years old, but already standing at five-foot-four, she's a tall girl and often gets teased as much for her height as for her mixed race. Both things she has no control over.

"Nah." She shrugs. "Jumped out the kitchen window. Father Reid tried to follow me, but he's too fat and couldn't get through."

John chuckles at the mischievous twinkle in the girl's big brown eyes. "Bet that was a sight. Anyway, to what do I owe the pleasure?"

Gina grins proudly, pulling a crumpled tin foil bundle from the pocket of her oversized jacket. "Brought you some chicken legs. I nicked them from the pantry. Nearly got caught, luckily, the window was open."

He frowns, accepting the bundle. "You need to be careful, G. That place ain't right."

She sticks her hands in her pockets, kicking at a pebble. "Nah, that's the older kids. They just have me scrubbin' floors all day like I'm Cinderella or somethin'." She motions to the packet he holds with a nod that makes her seem much older than her ten years. "Anyway, that'll keep you going for a few days."

"Thanks, love. I appreciate it."

She's about to answer, but catches sight of Father Reid half walking, half jogging towards them down the towpath.

"Gina, come here, now!" He calls, out of breath. Even

from this distance, she can see the sweat glistening off his fat, bald head. She looks up at John, wide-eyed. "Bye, John. See you tomorrow." John watches her run off in the opposite direction from the approaching priest, who starts running just as he passes him. Anger rising in him, John grabs a discarded piece of lumber and throws it in front of the bumbling man, tripping him, he lands him face-first on the cracked concrete.

With a few steps, John is over him. Grabbing the back of his cassock in a fist, he pulls him back up to his feet as though he weighs nothing. With a firm grip on the smaller man's top, he brings his face close. "If anything happens to that girl, priest or not, you're a dead man. Understood?"

Father Reid's eyes widen, but he says nothing, stumbling back as John lets go of his top. Shrugging, he walks back off in the direction he'd come from, towards the children's home. John watches him disappear around the side of the building, then stuffs the chicken into his duffel bag. Maybe he'll save the scrap for tomorrow.

Chapter 12

Graham walks a lazy donkey carrying a giggling George back and forth along the beach, Nipper tucked under his arm until the boy gets bored.

"Can we get an ice cream, Dad?"

Graham smiles as he hands the donkey's lead back to the attendant and lifts George off its back. "Of course, we can. We can stop on the way, go through the hall of mirrors, yeah?"

"Can Nipper come in, too?"

"Don't see why not." Graham winks down at his grinning son, dreaming of a day when he won't have to cram all the fun in a few days at the weekends.

He offers the lad manning the ticket booth a twenty-five pence bribe to let the pup go in with them, but the ratty-haired youth cons him out of fifty. Shaking his head, Graham follows a giggling, skipping George through the myriad of trick mirrors.

Later, Mr Whippy ice cream van, Graham ties Nipper's lead to the bench nearby while he orders. "Can we get a Ninety-Nine, and a Funny Feet, please?"

"That'll be seventy-seven pence, mate."

Graham hands the man a pound note. "Can I get the change in two-pence pieces?"

"Yeah, no probs, pal."

George hops up onto the bench as Graham hands him his Funny Feet, sitting down beside him to eat his ice cream. An excited Nipper jumps at them, tangling his lead in Graham's feet, then knocking his ice cream to the ground as he bent to free him, immediately lunging for the cool treat.

George bursts into laughter, Graham quickly following suit managing to pick up the chocolate flake as Nipper licks the melting treat from the sidewalk. "Come on, then. Let's make a move." He stands, untying Nipper's lead. "Shall we go to the arcade and play Penny Shove at the Funhouse before we head back to the B&B?"

"Yes, please, Daddy." George smiles up at him, his face covered with pink ice cream. "And then, can we go fishing for ducks?"

"You got it, son."

George takes his dad's hand, pulling him along excitedly, stopping when he sees the bumper cars. "Daddy! Daddy! Can we, pleeeaaaase?"

Graham can't help but laugh at the boy's eagerness. "Right, then. Let's see if they'll hold Nipper. I don't think he'll like the bumping very much."

George squeals and laughs as Graham bumps and crashes their little car into everyone around until the timer stops. "Again, again!"

Graham laughs. "I don't know, love." He rubs his neck. "I think one might be as much as your old dad can handle. Let's get on to the arcade."

Out of coins for the arcade games, they make their way out of the amusement park. "Daddy, I'm hungry."

Graham laughs. "You're always hungry. What'd you fancy, then?"

George smiles up at him, bright-eyed. "Fish and chips, and a sausage for Nipper."

"Right. There's a chippy right 'round the corner."

Sitting at a little table outside, Graham ties Nipper up to the leg of his chair as the waitress comes up to get their order.

"Raggy, are you hungry?" George listens intently as he stares at the doll. "Raggy says he'll have one of my chips, Daddy."

"All right, son. He can have a bit of Nipper's sausage, as well."

George's smile lights up his entire face as he grabs Graham's hand on the table. "I love you, Daddy."

"I love you too, son."

With George fast asleep in the back seat, Nipper tucked into his side, Graham drives them back to B&B, the boy doesn't bat an eye when he's pulled out of the back seat and tucked into his dad's shoulder.

Graham let's Nipper do his business on the patch of grass in front of the big house, before heading in tucking George into the big bed on the second floor. He sits at the window a while, Nipper dozing at his feet, watching the funfair lights dancing in the distance.

Chapter 13

George and Nipper are playing with Raggy Doll in the backseat, chattering quietly as Graham drives into Southport on Sunday afternoon. The sun is unexpectedly bright in the noon sky as he pulls up behind the Greek restaurant, pipping his horn.

He rolls down his window as a man he vaguely recognises as Dion comes out the back door, scowling. "What do you want?" The man eyes the car suspiciously, white-knuckled fists at his sides as though trying to appear menacing.

"Tell Tony I have a package from Jack." "Right. Wait here."

Graham gets out of the car, lighting a cigarette as he watches Dion disappear back inside. Within minutes, a small bloke, about five foot six, saunters out, looking even less menacing than Dion with his bald head, sandals, white T-shirt and matching pants. Looks as though he's ready for a day of sailing, Graham thinks, trying to suppress his grin.

The man walks over to him. *"Ah,* so you're Jack's little brother. It's nice to meet you. I'm Belin." He pulls Graham into an overzealous hug, catching him off-guard.

Quickly stepping back, Graham makes for the back of the car. "Got your package in the boot." Belin follows him, snapping his fingers at Dion who's still standing by the door, as Graham pops the boot. "D, take this inside." He turns back to Graham. "Tell your brother I need more product. It's moving fast, I'll need three times this much next month."

Graham nods once, shaking Belin's hand. "I'll tell him. Nice meeting you, mate."

Belin waits until the Cortina disappears around the end of the alley before going back inside.

Chapter 14

John launches his hook and rope as far into the canal as he can, wondering if he's already managed to get everything out and if he's now only fishing for wishes. But when he starts to yank on it, he gets excited as he's snagged something heavy. Maybe the rest of that bed he fished out before.

But the more he pulls, the more he thinks maybe he's hooked onto a pipe or something stuck to the bottom. He works at it for five minutes before needing a rest and a cigarette. Tossing the crumpled empty cigarette pack into the canal, he watches it sink slowly before grabbing at his rope again and pulling with everything he has.

Finally, as it begins to give way, he sees something coming up out of the water. But just as quickly as his loot breaks the surface, he lets go of the rope and spits his lit cigarette into the canal, frozen for a moment. He runs down the towpath of the canal towards the road. Without looking, he runs across the road in front of a Ford Commer van, barely avoiding being hit as it swerves to miss him, he continues to the telephone booth. Out of breath, he grabs the receiver and dials 999.

"Manchester Police, state your emergency."

"I've just pulled a body out of the Manchester ship canal."

"A body; are there any signs of life, sir? Have you checked if there's a pulse?"

"He looks very dead to me."

"And can you tell me how you know he's dead?"

"Because he's got a hammer sticking out the back of his head. I know a dead body when I see one. I'm a veteran; I've seen my fair share."

"Right. Where are you now?"

"Corner of Marsh Street and Greaves. I'll wait here. How long before someone gets here?"

"I've dispatched a car. You should see them in about five minutes."

Leaning on the side of the kiosk, John pulls out a chicken leg from his duffel bag, discarding a dirty tissue that has gotten stuck to it, and takes a bite. If it tasted a bit off, he didn't mind – better than not eating anything at all. Maybe he'll troll the alleys behind the pubs later. They always have pretty decent scraps at the weekends.

It isn't even five minutes later when he hears the sirens approaching. He watches as the Rover Metro Police car comes to a stop in front of him and two officers climb out.

"Sir, did you make the call about the body?"

John nods at the constable whose name tag reads, PC Lewis. "Yes, that was me."

"Can you show me?"

John motions for the constables to follow him. "Yeah, this way." He leads them back to the canal where he'd dropped his rope. "There, at the end of the rope."

PC Lewis looks at the rope dangling in the water, whatever it's hooked to, has sunk back beneath the surface, Lewis looks at his partner. "Williams, call this in, will you?"

PC Williams nods, frowning as he jogs back to the car. *"Williams to base,"* he speaks into the mouthpiece.

"Receiving." The response comes immediately.

"The body is submerged in the canal, we'll require assistance."

"Received, Stand by." There's a short pause before base comes back on. *"Assistance on route. ETA seven minutes."*

"Copy." He puts the mic back on the hook and jogs back to his partner. *"Seven minutes, Lewis."*

"Right. I'll just nip back to the car for some gloves, stay with the witness."

Out of sight, PC Lewis quickly sneaks into the phone kiosk and dials out.

"Hello."

"Jack, it's me. We've just been called to a suspicious death in the canal. Know anything about it?"

"Nowt to do with us, but thanks for the heads-up, son."

"It's right outside your lockup."

"Right. Keep me informed, yeah?" "Right. Got it."

Hanging up, he pulls out two pairs of gloves from the boot and heads back to his partner.

65

Chapter 15

Father Reid walks in the front door, hands clasped behind his back as he makes his way down the corridor, looking in each classroom as he goes by.

At the third door, he stops, tapping on the glass of Father Willis' classroom, and waits for the other man to open the door.

"What is it, Reid?"

Father Reid clears his throat, keeping his voice low. "Gina's run off again. She's been chattin' to that tramp on the canal."

Willis frowns slightly, shrugging. "And? What do you want me to do?"

Reid lowers his voice even more, speaking through clenched teeth. "He threatened to kill me." Willis sighs. "Grow up, Reid. Wait 'til she gets back, put her in solitary for twenty-four hours.

She wants to run off, she can stay by herself for a while."

"Right. I need a brew." Reid turns to walk down the hall. "You want one?"

Willis chuckles. "I'm teaching Latin; I need a whiskey." He moves to close the door but stops. "Go and sort the staff room out. We need a meeting with everyone later on, need to sort out more girls for the club."

Reid turns. "Send Gina, will you? Get her out from under my feet."

"She's not old enough yet. Right, bog off." He steps back into the classroom to a group of screaming children, closing the door behind him.

"Back in your seats, the lot of you. Next one of you to speak gets a caning!"

Chapter 16

The coroner kneels over the young boy's bloated body, half covered with the generic blue plastic tarp. He pulls off his gloves, standing as Detective Doonan approaches. "It's definitely murder."

"No shit, Sherlock," Doonan sneers. "I think the claw hammer in the back of his head might be a dead giveaway."

"No need for sarcasm, Doonan," he frowns, pointing down at the boy's face and arms. "The putrefaction of the skin hints that he's probably been in the water about four days. Five, at the most."

Doonan nods, staring at the boy's vacant eyes and noting they look to have been nibbled on. "Doesn't look very old, does he?"

"I'd say fifteen, sixteen maybe, give or take a year or two. Hard to be sure, from his condition. Looks to have been tortured; one of his fingernails is missing, and the bruising tells me it happened premortem."

Doonan squints as he looks up, thinking the sun is just too bright for such a morbid day. "We found blood splatters on the other side of the canal." He points across the water, where a locksmith is cutting the padlock to the unit in question. "They lead to that unit."

He frowns, calling out as the locksmith drops the padlock and Constable Lewis was about to step inside.

"Oy! Lewis! Keep your flat feet out of that unit! Wait for Forensics!"

Lewis mutters under his breath as he sends a thumbs-up across the canal to Doonan. Self-righteous prick, Lewis thinks as he pokes his head inside.

The unit is dark, slivers of light pierce through the corrugated tin roof and walls, where asbestos boards hang, cracked and broken.

Near the centre of the space, an old chair lies on its side by a long, narrow table covered in greasy tools. Even in the dim light, he can see the trail of dried blood leading from a dark spot near the chair, smeared across the dirty concrete floor and past where he stands, to another large, dried puddle by the side of the canal, where the body apparently lay for a while before it was pushed over the edge.

Once the forensics team arrives, Lewis and Williams back off, giving them the space. Knowing he needs to provide an update, Lewis tells his partner he needs to check on his wife, as she's expecting and ready to give birth any day. "Hang around here, yeah? I'll be back in a few minutes. Keep these people away." He motions to the small crowd that has begun to gather down the towpath. "Nosey bastards."

Back across, at the telephone kiosk, Lewis dials the number he's long ago memorised.

"Jack, it's me again. Shit's about to hit the fan; don't know who the kid is, but he's young."

"How young?"

"I'd say no more than sixteen or seventeen.

69

Bludgeoned to death in your unit, blood everywhere.
Whoever did it is a butcher, didn't bother cleaning up after
themselves."

"Shit. Right, stay there, find out as much as you can.
I'll do the same on my end. Someone's gonna pay."
"Roger that."

Hanging up, he heads back across to the unit, where
Williams is trying to keep the gathering civilians off the
perimeter. Lewis arrives back at the scene out of breath
after the run back. "Gonna hang 'round a bit, get some
overtime in. Wife's doing fine, going to the pictures with
her sister, so no need for me to rush home."

"Good call, mate. This crowd's getting bigger. We
need to cordon it off or they'll rampage through."
Williams motions to more people coming down the
walkway, rubbernecking.

"I'll see if Forensics has any tape on hand."

Doonan looks up as Lewis walks towards him.
"Lewis, what're you doing?"

"We need to cordon this off, crowd's gatherin' pretty
quickly."

Doonan glances at the towpath and nods. "Yeah, right
then, do that. Then get Smelly John back to the station,
sharpish. Give him a cuppa and a buttie, stick him in an
interrogation room and stay with him 'til I get back. I
won't be long."

"Yes, boss."

Within minutes, Lewis and Williams have the area
cordoned off, to the aggravation of the crowd of
busybodies, Lewis heads back to John, who's sat waiting

on the towpath wall, staring at the commotion.

"Mister, I'm going to need you to come to the station with me."

John looks up, a deep frown creasing his already wrinkled forehead. "Why? I ain't done nothin' wrong!"

"We need you to make an official statement; you're the closest thing we've got to a witness at the minute. There's a cuppa and buttie in it for you."

John stands, towering over the other man by at least half a foot. "Okay. But you bring me back here when I'm done, and I want some cigs, as well. I've run out."

Lewis nods, leading John down the towpath, away from the crowd towards the Rover Metro parked at the end. "Yeah, we'll get you some cigs."

John folds himself into the backseat, his head brushing the roof as Lewis drives off. "You live pretty rough up there, then."

John stares out the window as they drive away from the canal. "Yeah, since the Mrs kicked me out."

"Why's that, then?"

John meets Lewis' eyes in the rearview. "Just stuff."

Lewis nods, turning the corner. "So, did you see or hear anything, when the kid was killed?"

"You're asking a lot of questions, son." John crosses his arms over his broad chest.

"Just passing time."

John huffs. "Sounds more like fishin' to me. If you're going to question me, do it at the station. Not the back of a car, okay?"

"Sorry, mate. Was just askin'."

Chapter 17

Graham pulls up outside the old Victorian house on Sunday afternoon, a sick feeling in his gut. The same one he always gets whenever he has to leave his son at this disgusting place. He's already figured out Val won't be ready and waiting to be taken away, but he'll try again next time. He'll keep trying until she gives in; she's bound to give in at some point.

"George." He turns, smiling as he sees the boy sleeping in the backseat, Nipper in his lap. "Georgie, wakey wakey, love. We're at your mum's house."

George's eyelashes flutter as he opens his eyes. *"Aw, already?"* He yawns, pushing himself up.

"'Fraid so, son. You nodded off when we left Uncle Jack's." He turns so he could look fully at him. "I need you to do me a favour."

George sits up, alert and eager. "What is it, Daddy?"

"I want you to look after Nipper for a couple of days.

I'm going away on business for Uncle Jack, and I can't take him with me. You think you could do that for me?"

A smile spreads across George's face, lighting it up. "Yes, Daddy! I love Nipper, he's my best friend!"

Graham smiles back at his son. "Good lad. You try to keep him away from that nasty Errol, yeah?"

"I'll keep him up in my room. Errol never comes up there." He lets George out of the car, walking him up to the door which had been left ajar. *Probably Val's doing,* he thinks. *So the boy could come in quietly.* "Right, then, Give us a kiss. I'll see you in a few days."

"Love you, Daddy!" "I love you too, son."

Chapter 18

Lewis hands John over to WPC Cooper as he arrives at the station, WPC Cooper leads John into an interrogation room, giving him a cup of tea and ham sandwich.

"Sir, I don't mean to be rude, but you stink. Would you like to have a hot shower? I'm pretty sure I can dig some clean clothes that'll fit you, out of the lost and found."

John nods. "Mind if I have these, first?" He bites into the sandwich before she can answer. "Yes, love. I'll leave you to it then, and get a colleague to take you to the showers whilst I find you some clothes."

"Thanks. Want my clothes back, though."

WPC Cooper smiles and nods as she leaves the room, John wonders if he would get them back, or if they'd find an excuse to pin this whole thing on him. Better enjoy the food while he can.

Chapter 19

Waving goodbye from the door, George closes it as softly as he could, then, holding Nipper with one arm, and Raggy with the other, he tiptoes past the living room where his mum is passed out on the couch.

"Come on, Nipper," he whispers into the pup's ear. "Let's go upstairs, we can make you a den."

Upstairs, he crawls into his safe space under the rafters. "This is your home for a couple of days until Daddy comes back. It's safe here." With his tattered blankets, he makes a makeshift bed for Nipper, laying him in it and tucking his doll in beside him. "Raggy will keep you company when I'm not here. I'll go find you something to eat."

Muffled scratching and whining sounds come from inside the rafters as George shuts the access door behind him. Closing his bedroom door, even though he normally doesn't, he hurries down the stairs to find some food before Errol gets back. He knows he has to keep the pup quiet, or there'll be trouble.

In the living room, George tries to wake his mum but then sees the empty needle on the coffee table. He's seen those before and knows he won't be able to wake her. Not when there's a needle. She always says it's her medicine, but he doesn't believe her.

Fending for himself is something he's done for some time, so it's nothing new. In the fridge, he finds bits and pieces. Pulling one of his mum's big pots, he fills it with everything he can carry. A lump of corned beef, a few cooked sausages, some of those cheese slices wrapped in plastic and a nearly empty bottle of milk.

Back upstairs, George carries his loot into his safe place and shares his dinner with Nipper, dim light from the open door behind the wardrobe illuminating them as they fall asleep, side by side, curled up together on the little tattered blankets with Raggy.

Chapter 20

Back home, Brayden watches closely as Saul examines the diamonds, holding each one up to his loupe as the perfectly cut facet catches the light of the roaring hearth fire, casting stars on the dark, oak-panelled walls. He can see the Atlantic from where he sits, the full moon shining down on angry white caps.

Saul puts the last of the small gems down on the velvet cloth spread out between them. "Well, they all look good at the moment. Only the two big ones left."

Brayden leans back with a smile, taking a slow pull on his honey-coloured whiskey. "I didn't have any doubts. Jack is a good man; he's never done me wrong."

Picking up the first of the large stones, Saul brings it up to the loupe, immediately pulling it back, rubbing his eye, and pulling it up again. *"Ah…"*

Brayden leans forward, putting the crystal tumbler down on the desk with a loud thud. "What is 'ah' supposed to mean?"

Saul smiles, light catching in his green eyes. "This diamond is nearly flawless. An absolute beaut!" He puts it down and picks up the last and biggest one, bringing it up to examine.

"Shlock."

Brayden frowns. "What the fuck does that mean?"

Saul puts both the stone and his loupe down slowly, looking Brayden in the eyes as he shakes his head grimly. "It means it's crap. A piece of shit. It's a fake."

"Look again."

Saul sighs loudly. "I don't need to; it's a fake. This diamond is worthless, Bray. I'm sorry."

Brayden pushes back from his chair, leaning forwards with both hands on the desk. "Are you absolutely certain about this, Saul? I've dealt with this man for a long time; I've never had a problem."

Saul shakes his head, picking up the fake diamond. "Everything else is good. Top quality product. This?" He reaches over, dropping it into Brayden's palm. "This is a piece of shit. In fact, it's an *insult* to shit."

Brayden's eyes darken as he nods his head, lips pressed into a tight line as he walks around the desk and shakes Saul's hand. "Thank you, Saul. Frank will pay you on your way out," he picks up Saul's jacket from the back of the chair and handing it to him. "Frank!"

Frank opens the door, poking his head in. "Yes sir?"

"Please pay Saul, and make sure he gets home safe. In fact, why don't you drive him? Shut the door on your way out."

Frank nods curtly. "Yes sir." He follows Saul out of the room, closing the door softly behind them.

Back in his chair, Brayden takes a long, calming breath, then another, before picking up the receiver and dialling.

"Hello." "Hi, it's me."

"Hi. Is everything okay?"

"No, everything is not okay. We have an issue with one of the pieces of glass you sent."

"What do you mean, a problem? I had my glazier check all the pieces. They were perfect when they left me."

"Well, then, seems you have a problem. The most expensive piece of glass has a major defect and is not usable."

"What sort of defect? Is the size wrong?"

"No!" Brayden nearly yells, then takes a deep breath.

"No. The size is not wrong. The glass is wrong."

The line goes silent for a long moment, and Brayden can practically hear the steam coming from Jack's ears before the other man speaks again.

"It can't be."

"I'm afraid our friend, Saul, says it can."

"Fuck! Right, leave it with me. I'll get the driver and his mate picked up and interviewed."

"I'll be there tomorrow. I'd like to personally interview this driver. Make sure he's available."

"He will be. He'll be waiting for you at the usual place."

"Right."

"Is there anything else we can do to make up for the inconvenience?"

"Let's sort out the problems with this order, first. We'll discuss compensation after."

Chapter 21

Raised from sleep by pounding music, Nipper finds his way out of the open attic nook and out of George's room, as he's forgotten to close the door. Led by a puppy's curiosity, he makes his way down the three flights of stairs, one difficult step at a time.

In the hallway, he looks into the living room, where Errol and Tweak were passing Val back and forth between them, dancing to some tempo-less drivel. Used syringes lay tossed in a heap on the table where they've been discarded, bits of blood still wet on the needles.

Shoving Val towards Tweak, Errol turns and stops short, staring down at the little fur ball. "Hello, little puppy. What's your name?"

Tweak and Val both turn at the unexpected question, seeing the white and brown spotted critter yapping at them. "It can't speak, it's a dog." Tweak slurs, grabbing at

Val's waist.

"You don't say," Errol replies, just as high. "Anyway," he takes a step towards the pup, picking it up and bringing him up to his face. "Where've you come from?"

Val half-heartedly slaps at Tweak's groping hands. "George must be home. His dad probably gave it to him.

Errol turns on her, sneering. "I don't want anything to

do with that cunt in my house. I already barely put up with that fucking kid; I'm not looking after his fuckin' dog as well." With that, he throws the dog across the room where it lands on the side of the sofa, yelping out in pain, the sharp sound waking George.

Hurrying, he runs down as fast as he can, but nearly trips at the landing just as Errol tries to pick Nipper back up, getting bit in the process and crying out. "Right, you little fucker, you're dead! Tweak, hand me the hammer and some nails. It's in that blue bucket by the TV."

Tweak throws up his hands, shaking his head. "Nah, you can't do that, boss. It's only a pup, nothin' but a baby."

Errol turns on him, lip curled like a feral cat. "Hand. Me. The fuckin' hammer. Now!"

Val tries to stop Tweak, but Errol shoves her out of the way, sending her crashing hard into the table, needles and ashtrays flying as she lands in a whimpering heap.

Before Nipper can run off, Errol grabs him, bringing him up to his face. "Where the fuck do you think you're going, you mangy little bastard?" Nipper only whimpers in response before Errol slams him hard to the floor, stepping on him so he can't get away, just as George makes it to the bottom of the stairs.

"Leave him alone, he's mine!" The boy runs at him, but Errol easily sends him flying back into the hallway with a backhand to the face.

Val tries to run to him, but Tweak grabs her.

"Pin her down," Errol growls. "Make her watch what happens to anyone who crosses me."

Across the hall, George is too afraid to move, but can't

tear his eyes away from the terrifying scene as Errol picks up the hammer and nails Tweak dropped when he grabbed Val. Without a second thought, he plants a six- inch spike on top of Nipper's back leg and swings the hammer.

Wailing cries echo through the house as all – pup, boy, and woman – scream out, just as a second nail pins Nipper's tail to the floor.

George covers his ears with both hands, bawling as Errol picks up a third nail. "Let's put you out of your misery, ya little fucker." With one more swing of the hammer, the last nail pierces the pup's tiny skull, impaling him to the floorboards as George and Val cry out. No more sounds come from Nipper.

Errol points the hammer at George, who stares back at him, cheeks burning red and tear stained. "Tell anybody about this, and I'll do the same to your mum and dad. Understood?"

Terrified, George barely nods as his mum crawls over to him and picks him up, carrying him upstairs to his room. "Georgie, go hide in your safe place, love." She

kisses his head as she sends him scampering beneath the rafters and closes the little door after him. Then, pushing his bed against the door so nobody can open it, she curls up on the dingy mattress and cries.

Downstairs, Tweak stares at the dead dog, trying not to gag. "That was a bit over the top, don't you think, mate? I think you might–"

"Shhh!" Errol rounds on him, raising the hammer again. "You're on thin ice already. I asked you to do *one* thing, and you fucked it up."

"What?"

"The kid, Tweak!"

"What the fuck are you on about? He's in the canal!"

"Not any fucking more! He got dredged up by some fucking tramp this morning. Coppers have taped up everything, including the units."

Tweak drags a hand through his greasy hair. "Fuck! All that shit is still in there."

"Well then, you had better see if you can get back in tonight and sort it, yeah? This'll come down on both our heads, and come down hard!"

"You comin'?"

Errol shakes his head. "Nah, I've got stuff to sort out here, first. I'll meet you at the docks in two days."

"What about the stuff?"

"Don't worry about it. I'll get it later." "Right, then. See you later."

Stepping over the dead dog in the puddle of blood soaking into the floorboards, Errol picks up one of the half-full needles from the carpet and heats up a hit. Injecting the heroin on the first try, he leans back and lets himself fall into oblivion.

Chapter 22

In the hallway, Jack hooks the receiver into the cradle and leans against the wall. Brayden isn't a man to be messed with. He's done business with the man for years, without a hitch. The difference now is Errol and Tweak, and obviously, one of them has fucked him over.

He walks into the kitchen to put the kettle on, just as the telephone rings again. "For fuck's sake, who's ringing' now?"

"Jack, no need for that language," Barbara calls from the lounge.

"Sorry, love." He stalks back into the hallway, yanking the receiver from the wall. *"Hello."*

"Jack, it's Willis."

"What'd you want; it's late."

"Billy told me to ring you with the name of the double dealer."

Jack switches the receiver to his other ear, frowning. *"Yeah, he did mention that earlier. What's the name, then?"*

"Tweak."

Jack's grip tightens on the receiver, his blood boiling. *"Right. Get hold of Tony and Arthur; tell them to take him to the hotel."*

"Will do."

As calmly as possible, Jack puts the phone down, makes his tea, then sits in the lounge with Barbara.

"You're looking a bit pale, Jack," she frowns at him. *"Just got some bad news about one of the lads at work, love."* He puts his feet up on the ottoman. *"Nothing to worry about."* He takes a sip of the steaming brew, leaning back to watch Coronation Street.

Chapter 23

Climbing up onto the coal bunker, Gina reaches for the window she escaped from earlier. Peeking through into the kitchen, she holds her breath until she sees the room is empty – the coast is clear. She exhales, relieved, as she quietly pushes up the glass, climbing through as her heart pounds erratically in her chest as she nearly trips on her landing, coming into an awkward crouch on the tiled floor.

She holds her breath again, listening for anyone who might have heard her. Silence. The only sounds reaching her ears are the soft ticking of the clock and her own stuttered breathing. Somehow, she manages to drag a stool over so she can close the window again, all without making a sound. She's secretly proud of how good she is at being sneaky, but the adrenaline still rushes through her as she puts the stool back and creeps to the door, peeking out.

Still nobody. Good. She wipes her sweaty palms on her thighs as she doubles back to the refrigerator, prying the heavy door open, her eyes landing on a half-full bottle of milk.

Parched, she brings it to her mouth, swallowing in big, loud gulps as some of it escapes, dribbling down her chin and onto her already dirty shirt. So intent on her delicious treat, she doesn't hear the footsteps.

Father Reid, walking past the kitchen, notices the light

from the refrigerator and immediately knows who he's going to find thieving on the other side of the open door. Pausing quietly on the other side, he waits for her to finish, listening as her swallowing echoes throughout the kitchen until she replaces the now empty bottle on the shelf and shuts the door, wiping her mouth on the sleeve of her shirt.

Shock freezes her on the spot for a moment too long as her eyes lock with Father Reid's. "Gotcha, you little shit!" he seethes through his teeth.

Gina tries to run, but the older man is much faster than she is in her surprised state and manages to grab hold of her hair, twisting a fist painfully through the long black strands as he yanks her back and spins her around to face him again.

She cries out in pain as his other hand makes hard contact with the side of her face, the stinging causing annoying tears to pool as he drags her over to the large wooden dining table, pushing her face down onto it as he reaches for his belt.

"Naughty girls get punished," he huffs in a gruff whisper.

"No! No, no, get off me!" she shouts, squirming in vain under his unyielding grip. "Nobody can hear you down here. I'm fed up with your antics, you've disobeyed me for the last time, you little tart."

Father Willis is walking by, doing his rounds, and overhears the scuffle in the kitchen. Walking in just as Reid raises his arm over his head holding his looped-up belt; he grabs his arm before he can land a blow on Gina's rear.

"What the hell are you doing?" he growls, roughly pulling the belt from Reid's hand as the other man turns his scowl on him. "I told you to put her in the punishment room when she came back, not beat her."

Reid's scowl deepens as his face flushes, as much from anger as from embarrassment at being reprimanded in front of the child. Still holding her firmly pinned down, he lifts his chin in defiance. "She deserves it. Needs to be taught some manners."

"And you" – Willis slaps the belt roughly into Reid's chest – "need to learn to follow orders. Put your belt back on. Billy has other plans for our gobby little friend here."

Reid reluctantly releases Gina and puts his belt back on as the child runs to Willis. "Yeah, you prick, leave me alone."

Willis lands a backhanded blow on the same cheek Reid had just moments before, connecting knuckles to cheekbone so hard, it sent her sprawling across the hard tiles with a whimper.

"Pick her up and take her down to the punishment room, as I instructed."

Without another word, Reid grabs a fistful of Gina's shirt, dragging her up and backwards out of the kitchen as she tries to keep her feet on the floor, screaming and fighting the whole way across the long hallway and down the basement stairs, where he shoves her roughly against the wall by the heavy metal door to the room.

Inside, the small room is nothing more than a glorified dungeon. Dampness clings to every surface. The only thing in the space is an old wooden bed without a mattress. It sits in a corner under a tiny window, high up near the ceiling, covered in frosted glass and rusted wire bars.

Keeping her pinned to the wall by the throat, Reid pulls a chained key ring from his pocket, unlocking the door and pushing it open with an ear-splintering creak.

He brings his face so close to hers; she can smell the hot foulness of his breath and feel the spittle as he speaks. "I'll have my time with you soon, little girl," his eyes glint, his mouth curving up into an ugly, crooked-toothed smile, leaving no doubt as to the meaning behind his words.

"Don't think so, you old perv." Gina manages through constricted airways as she lands her boot hard into his ankle, causing him to lose his grip long enough for her to get free and run into the room, shoving the heavy door closed behind her as he grunts in pain.

Looking through the sliding peephole, Reid sneers at her as she lifts both middle fingers up in defiance. He slams the slider shut, locking the door and pounding his palm hard on the metal surface as he leaves, the sound thundering in the small space as Gina sits on the wooden slats of the bed frame, covering her ears.

She let herself cry then, rubbing her tender scalp where some of her hair was pulled out, the tears stinging as they flood the cuts on her swollen cheekbone and split lip, tears mixing with blood, staining the pale yellow of her shirt.

Chapter 24

Tweak is eyeing the blue-striped ball, trying to figure out his next move when Arthur and Tony walk into the pub about twenty minutes after him.

Arthur walks up behind him as Tony goes to order a round of pints, just as Tweak's taking aim; Arthur nudges the pool cue, causing him to scuff his shot.

Tweak spins around, ready for a brawl, but then his scowl turns to a smirk as he sees Arthur. "What're you doing here?"

Arthur moves to let Tweak's opponent take his shot. "Jack wants us to nip down to the unit in town and put summat in the container." He raises his eyebrows as the bloke gets two balls in the pockets. "Nice shot, mate."

Tweak frowns, chalking his cue as he waits. "How come he's using that one, and not the canal one, then?" He can't let on he knows what's happening down there.

"Because the canal unit is covered in some kid's blood. Plod's all over it like a rash, seems someone managed to get in there and do this kid in, then threw him into the canal."

Tweak's palms get sweaty as he grips the cue tightly, raising his eyebrows in mock surprise. "Fuck me, do we know who?" His heartbeat is tripping into overdrive; he's suddenly gagging for a hit in the worst way.

"Not yet, no. Should soon, though. Jack has an inside man on the case, hoping to have some answers before the night's out."

"Right, good. Bloody gits. We havin' a quick pint first?" Arthur nods. "Yeah, Tony's getting them in, pal."

On cue, Tony walks up with three pints, sloshing foam over the edges as he hands them over to Arthur and Tweak.

"Careful, mate, you're spilling half of 'em." "Sorry." Tony lifts his in a cheer before taking a long
pull.

"What've you been up to tonight?"

"Ugh, don't ask. Just left Errol's – I think he's losing the plot."

Arthur frowns. "What'd you mean?"

Tweak waves a hand, swearing under his breath as his opponent sinks the last of his balls and wins the round. "Nah, it's nothin'. Forget I said anything."

"Right," Arthur cocks an eyebrow at him. "Come on lads, drink up. Time waits for no man."

As they walk out, Tony motions to the van. "You get in the back."

Tweak follows him, frowning as Tony pulls the back doors of the van open for him to get in. "I thought we were dropping something off at the unit. There's nothing in here."

From behind, Arthur smacks him on the back of the head with a cosh, knocking him unconscious. "There is now," he smiles at Tony. "Grab his legs."

Together, they lift up the unconscious man and shove him unceremoniously into the back of the van.

"Never trusted that prick," Tony mutters as he slams the door shut. "What'd you think he's done?"

"Who the fuck knows? Better him than us, though." He looks around, making sure nobody's spotted them. "C'mon, can't be late."

Chapter 25

Brayden and Frank step off the boat at the docks to find Jimmy – one of Jack's men – leaning back on his car, waiting for them. He stands as they walk up to him and pulls a set of keys from the pocket of his jacket.

"Here you are, then, courtesy of Mr Harrison." Jimmy doesn't wait for a response as Brayden takes the keys, but simply nods and turns around, getting into his car and driving off.

"Right." Brayden tosses the keys to Frank, who catches them mid-air. "Let's get on with it." He gets into the back as Frank gets in the driver's seat, and they take off towards their destination.

Brayden steps up to the container, arms crossed in front of his chest. "Frank, go get that double-dealin' piece of shite out of the container. Sit him over here for a nice little chat."

"You got it, boss." Frank rattles the door loudly before opening it, trying to intimidate the loser inside. Prying open the rusty red metal door, he goes in to retrieve Tweak, not expecting to find him awake. After a bit of a tussle, he half pulls, half pushes him out, a fistful of the gaudy purple shell suit in his fist.

"Let go of me, you – " Tweak begins to struggle, only to receive the full force of Frank's fist in the gut, dropping him to his knees.

"I'll let go of you when I'm damn well ready." He lifts him by his clothes and drops him dismissively onto the stool they've put out for him and makes quick work of zip-tying his hands behind his back and legs to the stool.

As he stands back up, Tweak spits in his face, earning himself another beating. This time, Frank's fist crunches against Tweak's cheekbone, sending him – and the stool – flying backwards, landing hard on the cracked concrete floor. Not waiting for him to try and get up, Frank brings his foot down hard on his head, then rears back and lands his steel-toed boot in his stomach.

"Fuck, Frank! How're we supposed to question him if you kill him first?" Frank turns to look at Brayden. "Sorry, boss."

"Pick him up, get him some water."

"Yes, boss." Frank grabs him under the arms and hauls him back up to sitting, righting the stool under him by the table, where he nearly falls onto it.

Blood pours from his mouth and nose as he struggles to stay upright, barely conscious, his face looking like he'd fallen in a woodchipper. The imprint of Frank's boot on it covering half his face and neck, his left eye already swollen shut.

"Sorry 'bout that, Tweak. Frank tends to get a bit cranky after a long journey over the water." Brayden apologises, drumming his fingers on the table.

Tweak manages to open his right eye enough to look up at him across the table, his gaze then dropping to the small camp stove sat between them on the tabletop. Beside it, a butter dish, clove of garlic, and a gleaming butcher's cleaver.

Brayden reaches for the cleaver, picking it up slowly as Tweak suddenly becomes extremely alert, sitting up straight on the stool, shaking his head. "Whatcha gonna do with that?"

Brayden raises his eyebrows, smiling. "Calm down, Tweak. Just makin' ya some breakfast." He picks up the garlic, crushing it under the knife's wide blade, his smile widening as Tweak's good eye never leaving the knife.

Calmly, Brayden strikes a match, lighting the stove, putting a small frying pan over it that he pulls out of a box beneath the table, then dropping a knob of butter into it, letting it sizzle and melt before throwing in the crushed garlic.

Tweak tries in vain to free his arms, twisting and turning to see behind him.

"I hope you enjoyed your night in our exclusive, five-star container, Tweak," Brayden continues, stirring the fragrant, buttery garlic. "Service isn't what it used to be, but times are tough. We normally only use it for druggies and grasses, but for you, we made an exception."

"You got the wrong guy!" Tweak half shouts, half spits. "If Jack finds out about this, you're both dead men walkin'."

Brayden's hand stills as he looks up at Tweak, then at Frank, laughing.

"Tweak, Tweak, Tweak, my boy, who do you think had you put in the container?"

"What'd you mean?" Tweak attempts a frown, but it

only serves to make him look even more comical.

Brayden simply raises his eyebrows in answer, until Tweak understands. "No. No, this ain't right!"

"I agree, son. But if you steal from me—"

"I haven't stolen anything from you, or from Jack!" "Oh, but you have, haven't you? You've lifted

product from Jack, and a nice, shiny three-carat diamond from me."

"This is bollocks! I wanna speak to Jack!"

Brayden goes back to stirring the garlic, shaking his head. "Mm-mm. Not going to happen, I'm afraid. You see, he wants you dead. Me? I'm giving you a chance to come clean. You and your mate, Errol, stole from me."

He leans back in the chair, tilting his head to the side as he stares at Tweak, unblinking. "I want what's mine. I've made the trip over here, personally, for retribution. See, when you want somethin' done right, they say you should do it yourself. So that's what I'm doin' – sends a message, don't you think? Though I'm sure, Frank here would love the opportunity to break a few more of

your ribs. But that won't do, see, I need you to be able to swallow."

He tosses the pan a bit, swirling the nearly crispy garlic bits. "Have you ever heard the saying, cutting your nose off to spite your face?"

Tweak nods, confusion washing over his face as he stares from Brayden to the pan, and back again.

Brayden nods back in turn. "Good. Because that's what I'm going to do to you. Let me explain." He picked the cleaver back up, motioning with it. "For your starter course, I'm gonna cut off your nose, fry it up with this delicious butter and garlic, then, Frank here is going to feed it to you. After that, if you're still not forthcoming with the exact location of my diamond, or Errol, who helped you fuck me over, then it's the meat and two-veg course. I think you can figure out what I mean by that, can't you?"

Tweak shakes his head violently, blood splattering. "I don't know anythin' about a diamond. It's fuck all to do with me, must've been Errol. He had them the whole time, wouldn't even let anybody look at them."

"Fuck, lad, at least let me start torturing you before you squeal like a pig!"

Tweak's voice rises to near soprano pitch as Brayden stands. "I didn't see any diamonds! It's Errol, he's done it!"

Brayden paces back and forth along the wall, dangling the cleaver from his fingers. "What'd you think, Frank?"

Frank chuckles. "He's gone and pissed himself. Normally a good sign, we got the truth."

"Right then." Brayden stabs the knife into the top of the table, bending to look Tweak in the face. "Where's your little matey boy?"

"I dunno, he's on the run."

"From who?" Frank shouts, grabbing a fistful of Tweak's dirty hair.

"Old Bill, Jack, I don't fucking know!" "Old Bill from the club?"

"No, you thick Irish fuck, the police!"

Fed up, Braydon grabs the back of Tweak's head,

pushing it down into the burning hot frying pan, the tortured man's screams piercing the air like the gates of hell had opened.

"I think he likes his face well done, boss," Frank laughs.

Brayden smirks at Frank's quip before turning back to Tweak, pressing his face down harder into the pan as he thrashes as best he can with his hands zip-tied. "Where. The fuck. Is Errol, you lyin' bastard?"

He lifts Tweak's face off the pan, the skin bubbling and blistering, his left eye hanging on his cheek by a thread.

"He's... at the... docks."

"Which docks? There's dozens."

"Th-the one you met us at. His cousin Pete works security there. Ask him." Brayden drops his head, walking back a few steps as he nods at Frank.

Smiling, Frank pulls out his Smith & Wesson, presses the barrel to the back of Tweak's head. "No! No, don't shoot! I know where he hid the drugs!"

Brayden stops in his tracks, walking back with his head tilted, a frown creasing his forehead. "What drugs?" Tweak is shaking, staring. "Th-the drugs we sk-skimmed of your shipment to J-jack."

Brayden glances at Frank, motioning to put the gun away. "Jack's never said the shipments were light."

"It was Eroll's idea. W-we get the drugs back, t-take a little out of each package, then add a b- bit more tape. Jack trusts you, so he never weighs them, and the extra tape makes up for it anyway, just in case. It all p-pans out."

Brayden strolls over, standing directly in front of Tweak. "This Errol's a greedy little fucker, ain't he? If he hadn't swapped the diamond, none of us would be the wiser."

"I knew nothing about any diamond," Tweak cranes his neck, looking up at him with the one eye that isn't hanging halfway down his cheek.

"He's playing for time, boss. Let's finish this, yeah?" "I'm not! Please! Let me go and I'll take you to the drugs. It was all Errol's idea!"

Brayden looks at Tweak, disgust plain on his face as the other man blubbers, snot running down his blistering face, the seared eyeball barely hanging on. Reaching over, he grabs it and yanks quickly, ripping it out completely and tossing it in the still sizzling frying pan, Tweak's renewed screams filling the room.

"If you're lying, I'll get Frank here to take you apart, bit by bit, while you watch. Took the last guy five days before he died. I don't think you've got the balls."

"I swear, I ain't lyin'." Tweak can barely hold himself up, leaning against the table, his entire body convulsing from the pain.

"Where are we going, then?" "Jack's yard."

Brayden nods, walking back towards the door. "Frank, gag and bag him. He's riding in the boot."

Taking the cleaver from the table, Frank cuts the bindings from Tweaks legs, leaving his arms bound at his back. "You reek of piss, you nasty fuck." He stuffs an oily rag into his mouth. "Don't you fucking dare spit it out!" he hisses before pulling a cloth carrier bag over his head and dragging him up by the shirt.

Having to practically hold him up, he pushes Tweak in front of him as they follow Braydon out of the unit and wait for him to open the tailgate. He shoves Tweak into the boot roughly, headfirst. "Get the rest of yourself in there, I ain't touching your piss-covered legs."

Tweak twists and squirms, muffled moans coming through the oily rag as he manages to get himself into the boot completely, then Frank slams it shut.

"I'll be right back," Braydon tells Frank as he walks over to the red phone box he sees down the street. "I need to make a call."

"All right. I'll lock up."

Chapter 26

Time moves in slow motion. George clings to his doll, Raggy's rough burlap skin scratching against his cheek, as he watches his dad's car pull up to the curb.

As Graham walks towards his son, he frowns and walks faster. The side of George's face was purple and swollen, his lip split. "Who did that?"

"Errol, because Nipper bit him." George sobs.

Graham kneels down to George's height, grabbing him by the shoulders. "Where's Nipper?"

"Dead." The boy cries louder. "Errol killed him." Graham's vision grows dark. "And your mum?" "Asleep."

George watches, wide-eyed and open-mouthed, as his dad shoulders the heavy wooden door. He pushes his weight against it until it gives, slamming into the cigarette smoke-filled haze of the entrance. It's as though he's in a dream. A really bad one. The kind that would make him pull the dingy comforter up over his head and hum himself back to sleep. Only this isn't a dream.

He follows his dad inside just as Errol and his mum rush out of the living room, Errol bellowing like a madman.

"What the fuck do you want? Get your fucking arse out of my house!"

George clutches Raggy tighter as he watches his dad's fists vibrating with anger, taking a step closer to Errol.

"Where's my dog?"

Spittle flies from his dad's mouth, barely missing Errol's red, contorted face as the larger man rages. "The mangy thing bit me, I did you a favour." He points to the floor where poor little Nipper lays, impaled in a dried-up puddle of blood, flies already buzzing all around. "You're lucky it didn't bite that fucking waste-of-skin kid of yours!"

Graham looks down at the pile of fur that used to be Nipper, fury surges through him as he turns to Errol. "You're a dead man walking, you useless piece of shit. Val, get yours and George's things, you're coming with me."

Errol laughs, humourlessly. "I don't think so, pal. She's staying with me. But you can take your rotten kid and get the fuck out of my house."

"I—"

Errol rushes Graham, sinking his fist into his stomach, followed by a kick to the head as Graham doubles over, sending him flying backwards towards the door and crashing into the wall.

Regaining some of his balance, Graham runs at Errol. Gripping the taller man by the shoulders, he brings his knee up hard, crushing it into Errol's groin, sending him crumpling to the cracked parquet floor. "You killed my fuckin' dog!"

George takes the opportunity to run past the men, and to his mum, who's standing a way back in the hallway. Clinging to her leg, he squeezes Raggy tightly, so tightly, the doll's eyes are almost bulging out of its little burlap

102

head.

Graham sneers down at the grunting man, lips curled in disgust. "You're already dead, you cunt. Jack knows what you've done. Skimmin' off the boss, not too clever, are you?" He motions to Valerie, without taking his eyes off Errol. "Val, take George upstairs. He doesn't need to see this."

Errol swings his arm out towards Valerie and George, an inhuman growl sounding from his throat. "You stay put, bitch, if you know what's good for you!" He manages to push himself up off the floor, charging Graham, burying his fist into his stomach again.

Graham doubles over, the breath knocked out of him, then immediately flies backwards as Errol's foot connects with his head again, landing him into the already cracked plaster wall. Blinded by the blow, he spits the blood from his mouth onto the parquet, a tooth skidding across the floor and landing near Nipper's decomposing form.

Valerie pulls George towards the kitchen as he clutches Raggy in a death grip. "Errol, stop, you're gonna kill him!" She pulls George's face up away from the gruesome scene and whispers to him. "Quickly, get upstairs. Hide in your secret place until I tell you to come out."

George doesn't need to be told twice. He runs past the wrestling men, jumping over Nipper as Errol reaches for him – thankfully missing him by inches–and scampers up the stairs as fast as his shaking legs will take him.

Graham, disoriented, takes a shot just as Errol turns back to him, knuckles meeting jawbone in a painful crunch, sending him sprawling backwards into the doorway to the living room. Valerie runs to the kitchen as Graham gains his footing and sways towards Errol. With hands shaking as much from fear and adrenaline as it is from the latest hit of smack still rushing through her veins, she takes hold of the dirty carving knife left on the kitchen bench with the remnants of last night's dinner.

She stumbles back into the hallway just in time to see Errol jump back to his feet and charge at Graham, tackling him with a shoulder to the gut, backwards and into the wall. Once again blinded by the blow, Graham doesn't move fast enough to block Errol's next attack. Gripping him by the ears, Errol smashes Graham's head back against the coat hangers on the wall.

A shocked, strangled gasp falls from Graham's lips as he stares at Errol, eyes wide and unseeing, the base of his skull impaled onto the coat hook. Realising what he's done, Errol smirks, rears back, and lets one last blow land squarely on Graham's throat, making sure there's no way he's getting off that hook.

Limp and lifeless, Graham hangs like a slab of meat at the butcher's, dead eyes staring accusingly at Errol's yellow-toothed, crazed smile.

Valerie's delirious screech fills the small space as she rushes towards Errol, swinging the knife clumsily, somehow managing to bury it into his bicep.

With a vicious snarl, Errol spins around and backhands Valerie across the face, sending her reeling and tripping over what's left of Nipper and into the bottom of the stairs.

"You stupid fucking bitch! You're lucky I don't finish you off as well!" Biting down hard on his lip, he pulls the knife from his arm.

Val sobs, wiping the tears and snot from her face on the back of her bare arm. "You killed him! You killed Georgie's dad! You're a monster!"

"Oh, shut up, you're doing my head in. Where's that little runt; I need that fucking doll." Errol steps over Val on the stairs, determined to drag George out from whatever hole he's hiding in. "Georgie Porgy, puddin' and pie, give me the doll or you're gonna die."

In a last-ditch effort, Val launches herself up after Errol, trying to get by him on the stairs to protect George. But he takes up most of the width of the staircase, and grabs her, swiping the knife and slashing right through her Achilles heel, cutting it straight through.

She screams as her ankle collapses, trying to grab onto the bannister but tumbles down the stairs; her femur snapping in searing pain as she lands in a crumpled heap at Graham's feet. Errol stares down at them both thinking the pair of them deserve each other, and he's not sorry to see the last of them.

"Well, that wasn't too clever, was it, you stupid cunt?" He walks down the stairs, standing over her, a wide smile spreading across his face. "Oops," he shrugs casually.

With every ounce of effort she can muster, she screams. "Help, he—"

But as fast as she started, she stopped as Errol's hand covered her mouth viciously.

"Shh, now, it'll soon be over, love." With his other

hand, he plunges the knife into her side, her eyes growing wider, the deeper the knife dug in. He lets go of her mouth, and she tries to scream again, but only gurgling sounds come out before his hand wraps around her throat, squeezing until her body goes completely limp.

"Don't worry, love. George will be with you again real soon." He rips off what's left of her top and carves the letter X on her forehead, blood oozing out and covering her face and chest as he stands back proudly, observing his work of art as he wraps the ripped shirt around his bleeding bicep.

Tipping his neck, he cracks it left, then right, shouting up at George as he stared unblinking at the boy's mother.

"George! Get down here now, or you're gonna get a right good beatin'!"

George shuffles himself deeper into the darkest corner of the attic crawl space, trembling so hard his teeth are chattering. Raggy pressed close, he hugs his knees to his chest, trying to make himself as small as possible. Raggy is crying now, so he must be terrified, too.

George frowns down at the doll's wet face – dolls can't cry. It must be raining outside. The roof always drips in here when it rains; he swipes absently at his eyes as the heavy pounding of feet on the old creaky stairs thunders through the paper-thin walls. Errol is coming for him.

"Come out, come out, wherever you are, ugly little fucker." The gravelly voice sends chills through George's body as he holds his breath for fear that Errol will hear him through the wall and find his hiding spot behind the chimney breast. "Your mum and dad are downstairs now, waitin'. Asked me to get you."

George hugs Raggy tightly and squeezes his eyes shut as Errol's dragging footsteps come closer to the wall. "Get out here, before I rip your head off!"

George tries to squeeze himself into an even smaller ball. Maybe if Errol comes in here, he'll be so small, he won't even see him.

"Fuck!" Errol spins around as the sound of distant sirens breaches the swelteringly hot room. Did those nosy neighbours call the police? He'd like to bash their heads in, old fuckers. He turns, hurrying out of the room and down the stairs two at a time, holding on to the busted bannister.

Valerie, somehow still breathing, tries weakly to grab his ankle as he steps over her, but he kicks her brutally to get her out of his way, prying the door open as much as he could with Graham hanging behind it. He manages it, and it slams shut again from the dead weight pushing against it from the inside. Listening to see which way the sirens were coming from, he takes off running in the opposite direction.

The house is dead quiet for a few minutes before George hears Valerie's strained voice calling him from downstairs. It's almost like she's trying to shout, but it's coming out more like a whisper. "George! Georgie! It's okay, he's gone. Come down!"

Still clinging to Raggy, he crawls on all fours to the secret entrance to his hideout, peeking out to make sure Errol's really gone. There's no movement in his empty room, except for the dust specks floating in the single beam of sunlight coming through the grimy windowpanes, where he rubbed away a spot with his sleeve so he could look out.

Tiptoeing onto the landing, he sees his mum and dad at the bottom of the stairs. "Mummy?" Valerie's eyes flutter open. "Its okay, love. He's gone. Come, help me. My leg's broken."

George's eyes fly back up to his dad who's just staring at nothing. "Why isn't Daddy helping'?" He runs the rest of the way down the stairs when Valerie only shakes her head slowly from side to side, her eyes fluttering shut again. He stops short on the bottom step as he sees the dark red puddle his mum's sat in, the big X on her blood-covered face, and the knife sticking out of her side.

His belly flips as something sour fills his mouth. That always happens when there's blood, and there's so much of it now. Covering his mouth with his hand, he swallows hard, the bile burning his throat, as he steps down and over his mum's extended legs, his eyes lingering on the right leg. It's bent funny and looks like bits of bone are poking through where more blood is coming out.

Tearing his eyes away, he looks up to Graham, grabbing his limp hand and tugging. "Daddy." But Graham just keeps staring off into the hall. "Daddy, Daddy, speak to me, please, Daddy!"

Daddy says nothing, and he smells bad like he'd gone to the toilet in his pants.

George wrinkles his nose against the stench, going back to Valerie. "Mummy, what's wrong with Daddy?" But Mummy doesn't answer, either. Her eyes are closed now, her arms limp at her sides, but George can see her chest moving up and down a little as she's slumped over the bottom stairs. Maybe she's too tired and needs to take a nap.

Hugging Raggy, George presses up against his mum's side – the side without all the blood and lays his head on her arm, drifting off to the slow beating of her heart.

Chapter 27

"Jack!" Barbara calls from the bottom of the stairs. "Jack, there's someone on the phone for you!"

"I've just got in the bath, Barbara. Get their name and tell them I'll call back later."

She goes back to the kitchen, picking up the receiver. "I'm sorry, he's indisposed at the minute. Can I get your name and have him call you back?"

"Can you just tell him it's Joseph and it's important."

Barbara shakes her head, exhaling in a small huff. *"All right, but he gets rather cranky if I myther him."*

"Thank you."

Back at the bottom of the stairs, Barbara calls up again. "Jack, I think it's important. It's someone called Joseph."

She hears the water sloshing around as Jack gets up out of the bath. "For fuck's sake, Barbara. Why didn't you tell me it was Joseph in the first place? Tell him I'm coming."

She goes back to the kitchen again. *"Joseph, can you hold on just a minute? He's coming down."*

"Yes, thank you, Barbara."

She waits at the bottom of the stairs for him, listening as he messes about, stomping around. Wrapped in a towel from the waist down, he comes running down the stairs, right past her and into the kitchen, picking up the telephone, out of breath.

"Sorry about the wait, Joseph. I take it you got what you needed?"

"Not exactly, no. We need to meet."

Jack frowns. If Braydon didn't get what he needed, it means trouble. *"When?"*

"Now. Your yard in fifteen minutes. Come alone."

He runs his fingers through his damp hair. *"I just got out of the bath. I'll be there in twenty minutes."*

"Right. See you then."

Jack hangs up, then goes back to the stairs where Barbara's still standing, looking at him with a worried look on her face.

"Is everything all right? You look like you've seen a ghost."

"Leave it, love. Something's gone wrong. I have to get to the yard."

Her hands flutter to her chest, her eyes widening at the thought of something having gone wrong. "Do you want me to come with you?"

"No, love, it's all right." He runs up the stairs to get dressed, Barbara still looking on from the bottom of the stairwell, seeming frozen in place. He comes back down minutes later in jeans and a woolly jumper, going to the door to put his boots on. Barbara follows him this time.

"Make sure to lock up, love. I don't know what time I'll be back."

"Jack, you're scaring me." She wraps her arms around her own waist, anxiety plain on her pale face.

Jack walks back towards her, pulling her into a hug she burrows into.

"Don't worry, love, it's fine. Everything's okay. Just have to fix a problem with Joseph's order before he catches a boat back to Ireland in a couple of hours, there's been a problem with his order. It's a big deal for us so can't let it go tits up." He pulls back, smacking a kiss on her cheek.

"Okay, well, be careful."

"'Course. I'll be home later, don't wait up." He closes the door behind him, waiting to hear the click of the lock before leaving.

Barbara watches through the curtain as he pulls out of the drive, then goes back to the living room. The theme tune for *Tales of the Unexpected* comes on, but she's too busy worrying to pay attention to the television.

Chapter 28

John stares at the ticking clock on the wall. He can't tell what time it is because the needle has been stuck in the same position for what feels like hours, ticking obnoxiously but not moving. He knows it's been hours because his tea's gone cold, and he needs a piss.

Standing, he pounds a fist on the door. "How long do I have to wait in here?"

Muted footsteps approach from the other side, and he steps back towards the dented metal table as the door swings open.

"Sorry about the delay, sir," Detective Morrison walks in, followed by a young police constable. "I'm afraid we've been dealing with a few things all at once."

"Can I get another buttie and a cig? And I need to use the men's."

"All in good time." Morrison motions to the chair across from him. "Can you have a seat, please?"

A deep frown creases John's forehead. "Good time? I've been sittin' here for two hours, if not more. How's that for a good time? Where are my clothes?"

Unfazed, Morrison stares pointedly at him. "I'm the one asking the questions. Faster you answer them, faster you get to leave. Now, sit down."

Snapping his mouth shut and swallowing his knee-jerk retort, John sits.

Now that the big man is closer, the stench reaches Morrison's nostrils. "Peters, wedge a chair in that door, will you? Get some air in here."

Peters nods, doing as he's told, before standing as far away from the smelly man as he possibly can, arms crossed in front of his chest.

Morrison sits, opening up a notebook and pulling the cap from his pen with his teeth. "Right, then." He stares at John again. "What were you doing by the canal this morning?"

"I live there." John mirrors the solid stare right back, unflinching. "So, you're a vagrant then." Morrison makes a note.

"If you say so." John sniffs loudly, wiping his runny nose on the sleeve of the white S.O.C.O. suit as Morrison watches, unable to hide the disgust on his face.

He clears his throat. "Can you tell me what you were doing when you found the body?"

"Dredging for metal to sell to the scrap man. Gotta eat somehow."

Morrison nods, almost imperceptibly as he continues to scribble notes on the page. "And you ended up pulling the body out of the water, instead of scrap."

John folds his arms in front of him on the table, leaning forwards slightly. "About sums it up, yeah. Do you know who he is yet?"

"Working on it." He scribbles some more. "Did you see anybody else at the time?"

"One of the kids from the home, she brought me some

chicken. Then the priest came past."

"What time was that?"

"About half an hour before I rang you."

He shifts on the uncomfortable metal chair. "Look, I need a drink, a fag and a piss before I say anything else." Morrison sighs, turning to Peters. "Fetch him a brew, will you, son?"

Peters nods, flinching slightly at the 'son' remark, before leaving the room. Pulling a packet of cigarettes from his pocket, Morrison shakes one out handing it to John. "The piss will hold." He flicks his lighter, waiting for John to lean forward.

"For a bit. Thanks." He lets out a cloud of blue smoke with a contended exhale. "Right, lets carry on then?"

John nods, flashing a yellow-tooth smile. "So, you live on the canal."

John nods. "We've already established that."

Morrison ignores the sarcasm. "Did you see anything strange over the last couple nights on the canal? People that seemed out of place, strange noises, anything of the sort?"

"Anything strange." John chuckles, raising both eyebrows. "Are you taking the piss? Strange is what we call normal, when you're living rough Drunks, prossies, gayboys, you name it, I've seen it. There's always some fuckin' weirdo doing something to someone down there." Morrison sighs. "So, you didn't see or hear anyone going into the unit near where you found the body a couple nights ago." It's more of a statement than a question. At this point, he figures he's not going to get a

115

stitch out of this smelly bastard.

Peters walks back in, handing the steaming cup of tea to John before returning to his sentinel post by the door.

John blows on the scorching liquid before taking a satisfying, slurping sip. "Nah, I didn't…" He stops, frowning into the cup before looking up at Morrison again. "Hang on a mo…"

He puts the cup down and grabs his head with both hands, rubbing hard at the sides as if it might drum up a memory. "You know, I did hear something, yeah. Someone woke me up, making a noise, throwing something into the canal on the other side. I didn't take too much notice as I was pissed, but thinkin' back now, yeah." He nods, frowning deeply. "I saw a black fella with fuzzy hair. He was running away towards the phone box I rang you from."

Finally, Morrison thinks, scribbling as fast as he can. "Could you make out his face?"

"Don't think, I coulda made my own face out that night. But he was defo black, with frizzy hair."

"Any other details you can think of?"

"Nah, sorry. Went right back to sleep when I saw him running off."

"Right. That's all for now, then. We might need to speak with you again. Make yourself available."

"You got my address." "I don't, no."

John pushes himself up off the chair. "Green tent next to the pallet of shit – care of the canal. You can't miss it, best shithole in the neighbourhood."

"Funny." Morrison stands, barely reaching John's

shoulders. "Do you need a lift back, then?"

"Yeah, and you promised me some cigs and another buttie."

Morrison shakes his head, pulling his wallet out of his trouser pockets. He pulls out a crisp five-pound note and slaps it into John's palm. "That should do ya."

"Thanks." He shoves the note into his pocket. "Can I get my clothes and a lift back?"

"Peters, fetch a pool car and drop him off at the Canal. His clothes should be ready. Maybe dig something out of lost and found while you're at it.

"Yes, sir." He turns to John. "Wait here, I'll be a minute."

Sighing loudly, John falls back into the chair as the two men leave the room. Waiting seems to be all he ever does these days.

Chapter 29

Errol wrinkles his nose as the stale scent permeates the small security room – dead fish and black tea definitely aren't the most mouth-watering combination. He discards the two-of-hearts onto the pile of cards in the middle of the table, picking up the chipped cup, lifting it with a small nod at his cousin Pete.

"Cheers for this, mate. It's only for a couple days. Just need to let some shit blow over."

Pete nods in return as he picks up a fresh card. "Yeah, no probs, cousin. Anyone else know you're here? Don't wanna draw any attention to this place."

Errol folds, tossing his cards onto the table. "Nah, just Tweak. He's pickin' me up in a couple days, when the shit dies down."

Pete shows his cards – a Full House – he scoops the small pile of five pence coins with stubby fingers. "I've got that unit over there set up for you," he motions behind them. "It's not been used for a couple years, so it's clean, and there's a bog in there.

"Sounds like the Ritz," Errol laughs.

"More like the Pitz," Pete chuckles as he stands. "Here, take this stove, and there's a bag of bits there for you. Some tea, beans, tin of biscuits, etcetera. It'll keep you going until I'm back on shift tomorrow." He hands Errol the small stove. "I'm off in twenty minutes. You'll have to keep out of sight. Don't want any of the other lads spottin' you, or they're sure to call the boss."

Errol takes the stove, hooking the bag of bits and bobs over his arm. "I'll keep my head down, no stress." He turns and pushes the door open with the scuffed toe of his shoe. "I owe you one, Pete. Big time. Catch you tomorrow." He walks off towards the unit Pete set up for him as he hears the soft click of the security room door closing. A good man, that Pete.

Chapter 30

The security lights are on when Jack pulls up to the builders yard. He turns in slowly, scanning the scene he's about to walk into. A Range Rover is parked on the right side of the entrance gate, and from the security lights shining through the glass, he can make out two people sitting up front.

Pulling up beside the vehicle, he frowns as the two blokes step out. Brayden walks around to him as Jack gets out of the car, his eyes glued to Frank, who's making his way to the back of the Range Rover.

His frown deepens when his eyes meet Brayden's. "Hi. What's this, then? Where's he going?"

Brayden's face splits into a Cheshire cat toothy grin that bears no trace of humour. "It's a surprise. You like surprises, don't you, Jack?"

"Can't say I do, no." He watches, shifting uncomfortably as Frank pulls someone out of the back, dropping him hard onto the packed gravel track. Muffled screaming, as though through a sock, comes from beneath the makeshift sac hood.

Frank shuts the boot and yanks the man up by the back of his bright purple jumper. From the short distance where he stands, Jack can clearly see the purple is stained with globs of sticky blood and other disgusting fluids. Frank shoves him forwards a few steps until they're standing in front of Jack and Brayden.

"Take the hood off, Frank." Brayden's grin borders on maniacal, turning Jack's blood to ice. Frank pulls off the hood, tossing it to the side.

It takes a few seconds of staring at the barely recognisable man before realisation hits Jack like a sucker punch to the gut.

He plasters a cold, neutral look on his face as he clears his throat. "I thought you'd found Errol for a minute."

"No. This is an even better surprise than that," he winked, nodding his head towards the imbecile in front of them. "Tweak here's going to show you where you're missing drugs are." He turned to Tweak. "Aren't you, son?"

"Missing drugs!" Jack's blood pressure instantly spikes. "What the hell are you on about? Brayden's grin disappears. "Frank, ungag him. Let the fucker speak for himself."

Frank rips the oily rag out of Tweak's bloody mouth, tossing it with the hood onto the ground. Free from the gag, Tweak immediately rambles off. "I'm sorry, boss. It wasn't my fault, honest! It was Errol's idea, he made me do it. He said you'd never notice."

Jack feels the blood boiling up his neck as he squeezes his hands into fists at his sides. "Wouldn't notice what?" The words are slow, concise.

"Us skimmin', boss. He said you'd never notice if we took a bit off the top."

Confused, and with fury quickly mounting, Jack turns

to Brayden. "What's he on about? I thought you called me here to talk about your diamond."

Brayden shakes his head slightly. "Looks like your boys have been helpin' themselves, Jack. Guess they figured you weren't paying them enough attention. Our one-eyed wonder boy, here, says they've got some of it stashed in there." He jerks a thumb behind him, motioning to the builder's yard.

Jack leans over to look behind Brayden as though he's never seen his own yard before, then looks back at him. "This is all very confusing." He rubs both hands over his face in an attempt at calming his rising temper. It wouldn't do to lose his shit in front of his most important business associate. "Where is your diamond, then?"

"Errol swapped it out," Brayden steps aside to let Jack walk up to the gate. "We have a lead on him – Frank will sort it out later. Come on, then. Open up and see if this cunt's lying to buy himself time, or if he's a thieving sack of shit like he says he is."

Buzzing with anger, but keeping a cool, composed demeanour, Jack unlocks the gate and pushes it open, leading the others in towards the building.

Inside, he flips on the office lights and stumbles back a step as he turns back towards the men and sees Tweak. The skin on half his face is practically hanging in oozing, burnt slabs, a gaping hole where an eye should be.

Jack swallows the bile that rushes into his mouth. "Fuck me! What did you do to him?" Brayden doesn't miss a beat. "He was disrespectful, so I taught him some manners."

Jack presses his lips together, nodding curtly. "Fair enough," he turns back to Tweak. "Right, where are my drugs, then?"

Tweak limps and shuffles forwards as best he can, stopping when he reaches the duct of the decrepit old shed. "In there," he points up to the grate. "He wraps it up and stuffs it in there, where you won't find it."

Frank shoves Tweak to the side, grabbing a couple of old pallets and stacking them on top of a rusted barrel. For a man his size, he jumps onto his makeshift ladder with surprising grace, pulling the Zippo from his pocket as he moves the loose grate and reaches into the duct with the lit lighter.

"I think I see something," he cranes his neck, squinting. "Don't know if I can reach it."

Jack grabs a yard brush leaning against the wall and passes it up to Frank on his perch. "Will this do?"

"Should do, yeah." Frank stuffs the Zippo back into his pocket, pushing the brush into the duct. No light makes it harder, but after a few tries, he's able to carefully hook the end of the brush onto the bundle he'd seen and pull it to the edge. He tosses it down to Jack and jumps off the precarious stack.

Unwrapping the bundle, Jack clearly sees that it holds a decent amount of product he's paid dearly for. His eyes bore into the one Tweak has left, where the coward half leans and half squats against the pile of pallets, unable to keep himself upright.

"Please. Please don't kill me, boss. I swear, it was all Errol's idea."

Jack rolls the bundle back up. "I'm not gonna kill you, Tweak. He is," he points to Frank, who then looks to Brayden for instructions.

"No, he's not," Brayden disagrees. "This is your mess, Jack. You clean it up." He reaches his hand, takes the bundle Jack is holding, and places it on Frank's barrel and pallet stack.

Frank pulls a gun from the waistband of his pants, holding it by the barrel as he hands it over to a wide-eyed Jack. "It's loaded. All you have to do is pull the trigger." "Boss, boss, please." Tweak falls to his knees, begging, as he shuffles forward, tugging at Jack's trousers, his voice rising to an unearthly sound, snot covering his face. "Please don't kill me!"

Cold, with a steady hand, Jack levels the gun at Tweak's head. "Not the head, Jack. We need that. Aim lower."

Without taking his eyes off the miserable little cunt, Jack lowers the gun and pulls the trigger, sinking two rounds into Tweak's chest, cutting the last scream short as he falls limp onto the ground.

Jack doesn't move for a moment, still holding the gun in mid-air as he stares at the dead man until Brayden's voice shakes him out of it.

"Frank, you know what to do."

Frank nods. "Jack, where can I find an axe?"

Jack points numbly to the workshop behind Frank. "In there, workbench against the far wall. What are you gonna do with an axe? He's already dead."

Nobody answers him, but he doesn't have to wait

long, as Frank's already back, swinging the heavy axe as though it weighs nothing more than a pencil. With his free hand, he grips Tweak by the jumper, slumping him over so that his head's resting on a pallet, then in one smooth motion, brings the axe down over his neck.

Jack nearly loses his dinner as Tweak's head rolls away from his body, coming to a stop between his feet, looking up at him with one dead eye and one gaping, empty hole. "For fuck's sake, look at this mess!"

Frank tosses the bloody axe aside, pulling the plastic bag he had tucked into his pocket. Apparently, this has all been carefully planned, Jack thinks, watching as Frank grabs the severed head by a fistful of blood- matted hair and drops it into the plastic bag with a sloppy, crinkling sound.

"What're you gonna do with it?" Jack hands the gun back to Frank.

"We're going to send his good friend Errol a message." Brayden wipes the dust off his suit jacket. "He wants to play hide and seek, he's gonna find out I made the rules to that game. Gonna flush the little fucker out." "Clever," Jack nods. "What about him?" he nods towards what was left of Tweak, bleeding out on the yard floor.

Brayden lifts a shoulder casually as he walks away towards the Range Rover. "As I said before – your mess, your problem."

Jack watches him walk away, Frank casually holding a head in a bag, which he places in the boot of the Range Rover before they drive off.

He exhales, his shoulders slumping as he turns back to what used to be Tweak and his entire body starts to shake from the inside out. "You shouldn't have skimmed, you little bastard."

Unsure where to begin, Jack takes the pallets off the empty oil drum Frank had set them on, then grabs both legs and drags the body beside it. He tries lifting him inside, but dead weight, even with his fathead gone, is still too heavy. So, he lays the drum on its side and rolls it into place where his ugly mug used to be, pushing his shoulders in. It takes every bit of strength he has to shove the uncooperating, limp fuck into the cylinder.

"Even dead, you're a right pain in my arse, you fuck. Get... In... There!" he grunts, shoving in bursts, moving him into the rusted-out barrel, inch by inch. It's nearly half an hour before he has the torso in and realises the legs just won't fit. Unless maybe...

Walking around to the other side, he hooks his fingers on the lip, pulling up towards him as he pushes down on the bottom with his foot. It takes him a few tries but somehow manages to get the barrel upright again, but now the legs are sticking almost straight up out the top.

"Damn you, Tweak!" Jack bends over, hands on his knees, trying to catch his breath as his nose drips fat drops of sweat onto the dusty, cracked concrete floor.

From this position, he tilts his head to glare at the offending legs, and his eyes catch the gleam of the axe, leaning against the wall. A chill passes through him, but he stands, resigned. He's got no other choice, does he?

With a loud huff, he hoists the heavy axe over his

shoulder with both hands, then swings it down hard on Tweak's leg where it sticks up over the lip of the barrel, just above the knee. He swings it, again and again, blood droplets splattering over him like spray paint, covering his clothes, his face, his hands. He swings until the leg is holding on by nothing more than a thick fold of flesh, then he drops the axe and bends the leg backwards on itself, stuffing it in with the rest of the body.

He slumps down onto the stack of pallets, leaning forward, elbows propped on his knees, as he inspects the bloody palms of his hands.

He takes a few minutes to catch his breath, then quickly demolishes the second leg in half the swings it took for the first. He's exhausted, covered in sweat and blood, and wants nothing more than a bath, a brew, and his bed. The second leg falls with a thud at his feet – he stares at it in disgust for a minute before picking it up and tossing it in with the rest, then lifts the lid onto the drum and seals it on with the locking band.

His shirt is completely drenched with Tweak's blood and his own sweat. He grumbles under his breath the entire way to his office, longing for the bath he was so rudely pulled from for this. Heart beating like the devil in his chest, pounding out a rhythm he couldn't tap a toe to if he tried, he strips off the rest of his soiled clothes, leaving them in a bloody, sweaty heap by the office door. He shoves them into a little pile with his shoe before letting himself fall into his chair with a breathless huff.

In his underpants and string vest, he leans back, staring blindly into the space as he waits for his heartbeat to come back to normal before picking up the phone, dialling from memory.

"Hello, is this Pat? It's Jack." He pauses, listening. "Yeah, fine, thanks. Is Arthur 'round?" He changes the receiver to the other ear, sweat still slick on his skin.

"Good, good. Tell him to get to the yard, sharpish, will you? Yeah, thanks."

He sets the receiver back in the base with a loud click, then slumps forwards onto his desk, cradling his head in his hands.

Chapter 31

When George opens his eyes, the house is pitched in darkness, except for the thin beam of moonlight squeezing through a crack in the transom window. He's pressed close against Val at the bottom of the stairs, terrified of the dark, but she's still sleeping.

"Mummy? Mummy, wake up." He nudges her shoulder, but it only makes her head fall to the side. With a gasp, he quickly stands and carefully lifts her head back up, leaning it against a cushion he finds nearby so it won't fall again. "Is that better, Mummy?"

George's lip trembles when she doesn't answer. Gently, he moves the matted hair from her face and kisses her lips. "Love you, Mummy," he whispers, the way she does to him most nights when she isn't sleeping on the sofa.

"Night night, see you in the morning."

He turns to look up at his dad, hanging there, his feet firmly on the floor, his knees slightly bent, motionless.

"Daddy?" A car passes by outside, the headlights flashing through the window, reflecting in Graham's eyes, making them dance.

With a gasp, George jumps up. "Daddy!" he grabs his cold hand. He tries to hold it, but his dad's fingers won't bend. "Daddy, talk to me." But his dad doesn't talk, either.

A cry bubbles out as he runs to fetch his doll, hugging him close to his chest. "I'm scared, Raggy," he whispers to the doll, on a hiccup between sobs. Careful not to look at his dad again, he keeps his face turned away as he goes back to curl up beside his mother, sticking close to her side so he can feel what little heat is coming off her. He lays his head on her chest, crying himself to sleep to the faint beating of her heart.

Chapter 32

"Took you long enough, didn't it?" Jack scowls as Arthur and Tony amble in thirty minutes later. "Sorry, had to pick this one up," Arthur motions to Tony with a shake of his thumb, then frowns at Jack's strange appearance. "Where're your clothes, boss?"

Jack looks down at himself, remembering he's standing there in his underpants, hands still stained with blood. He points to what looks to be a soiled pile of rags in the corner by the door. "Don't mess about, I'm not in the mood," he looks at Arthur's companion. "Tony, get rid of those straight away. Burn them, every bit, yeah?"

"You got it, boss," Tony picks up the pile, wrinkling his nose at the stench and the smear of blood that gets on his hand. "Don't like the look of this one," he mumbles as he passes Arthur in the doorway.

Arthur looks down at the stained bundle Tony is holding, cringing, taking a small step back. "Me neither," "Quit your yacking," he storms past the two dumbfounded men. "Arthur, follow me."

He's already halfway around the corner when Arthur snaps out of it and follows, picking his way along a floor soaked in blood. Rounding the corner, he sees the biggest of the mess and stops dead, staring up at Jack. "Fuck me, boss, what's gone on here? You hit dog or soma?" Jack stops and turns, looking almost comical in his underpants and sweat-stained vest, a deep scowl etched on his face. "Double-dealing. That's what's gone on here," he motions with both hands to the floor. "I need you to clean up this blood, every trace. Can't have the crew seein' this mess. Then get rid of this," he points to the old drum on the left as Tony walks up to them. He

stops short, jaw going slack as he stares at the floor. "Woah…"

"What's in it?" Arthur interrupts Tony. "Tweak." Jack tells him, point blank.

Tony's eyes go wide as saucers as he looks up at Arthur, then back to Jack, his mouth still hanging open. "That's right," Jack continues. "Tweak. The dirty, double-dealing sack of shit. And if I find out the pair of you knew about this and didn't say soma, I've got a couple more drums rustin' away in the back of the yard. We

clear?"

"Crystal, boss. Tone and me, we didn't know. Swear it," Arthur lifts a hand to some imaginary Bible.

"Right, then," Jack turns to Tony. "Did you get rid of them clothes?"

"They're gone, boss. Burning as we speak in the wood burner."

"Good. Get to work." Jack storms back off to his office, slamming the door behind him, wishing he'd had

the mind to ask Arthur to bring him a clean pair of trousers and a jumper.

Tony eyes the closed door suspiciously, keeping his voice low. "Errol won't be pleased, his mate being topped, will he?"

Arthur shakes his head, kicking at a rare spot of unstained dust on the concrete floor. "Fuck Errol has an account; probably he is doing all this. Right? I'll get what's left of him hosed off. Go back, make sure those clothes are good an' burnt, yeah? Then bring the van 'round."

"Right."

With the nozzle on the highest power, Arthur tries to get every single spot off the concrete, knowing if he doesn't, he could be in the next drum. He's watching the last of it swirl down the floor drain when Tony backs the van into the yard, all the way to where the drum is.

"Clothes gone?"

"Yeah." He hops out, shoves the keys into his pocket. "Nowt left but a pile of ugly-jumper-ash. Bet Barbara's gonna be glad to see the last of that one," he chuckles.

"Right, good. Don't tell that to Jack, you'll end up dead." He wipes his hands on the arse of his trousers. "I reckon the quarry is a good place for this," he kicks the drum lightly with the tip of his wet trainer.

"Good idea. Fill it full of those big rocks they got, drill a few holes in it, he ain't coming back up. Job's a

good one," he nods. "Jack will have our heads if we fuck this up."

Arthur grins. "Yeah, literally," he opens the back door of the blue transit van, tossing things aside to make space for their precious cargo. "Let's get the mangy bastard in here and get it over with."

"Hefty bastard!" Tony grunts as they lift the drum in and he shuts the door. "Let's get out of here, yeah?"

"Hang on." Arthur walks over to Jack's office, knocking lightly before pushing the door open just enough to poke his head in. "All done, boss. Floor's sparklin'. Gonna get rid of the drum."

Jack doesn't look up, only nods slightly. "Cheers, Arthur. See you tomorrow."

Arthur shakes his head as he closes the door softly, leaving Jack to stare at a half-empty glass of whiskey, the open bottle clutched in his other hand, sat behind his desk.

Chapter 33

George floats in and out of sleep throughout the next hours. Once, he opens his eyes, everything is dark, except a glow coming from the toilet, where someone's left the light on, and the television in the next room, with its fuzzy salt and pepper screen, as Mum always calls it. But the sound is turned all the way off, so it's silent as a graveyard. George doesn't like the dark, so he shuts his eyes tight again, pressing into his mum.

The next time he opens his eyes, he can see streaks of light coming through the boards over the living room windows, reflecting in the big mirror with the big piece missing. The television has gone off. The smokey grey screen is covered in dust and finger marks, and he can see where someone's traced the outline of a smiley face with their finger – he wonders who it was.

Hunger and the desperate need to wee make him peel himself away from Valerie. The light is off in the toilet now, but it was on the last time he'd woken up. He tries flipping the switch up and down, but nothing happens, so he has to wee in the dark. A few minutes later, he returns to his mum, holding a half-empty tin of Twiglets he's found in the kitchen, and finding she's wee'd all over the floor.

"Mummy, Are you hungry, Mummy? I have

135

biscuits." She doesn't answer, but her eyes flitter half-open for a second and her head shifts, her lips parting, but no sound comes out. He looks up to his dad but finds him still staring off. He doesn't want to think it, because thinking it makes him too sad, but he knows his dad is dead. Errol killed him. He heard his mum scream it at him yesterday.

Nipper is dead. His dad is dead. And his mum looks dead, but she's not. He knows she's not because she moves a little. She's still too tired to get up, that's why she's wee'd on the floor. Sighing heavily, he puts the red tin on the bottom step and runs to the loo to pull some of the towels from the basket. They're dirty, but he can't reach the clean ones.

As best he can, he tucks them up around his mum, soaking up the mess, then lays one over her lap.

He sits beside her with his tin of biscuits, eating the lot of them, stale as they are. He tries to give some to his mum again, but she doesn't want any. She only groans once, the small sound coming from cracked lips. He tries giving her water from the bathroom tumbler, but it just spills all over the front of her, so he drinks the rest himself. It tastes like toothpaste.

Hours pass; he sits by his mum, with his back against the wall on the bottom step of the stairs, telling Raggy stories about the last time his dad took him to the funfair, and how he loved the candyfloss. He picked the blue one because he likes blue better than pink. Blue is for boys, and pink is for girls. That's what his dad said. Maybe his mum can go with them next time, and she can have the

136

pink candyfloss because she's a girl. He falls asleep, leaning against the wall holding Raggy doll talking to his mum.

Hours later, George is woken by the growling noise coming from his tummy, and his bum hurts from sitting so long in the same place. He carefully steps around his mum, going into the kitchen. Back in the kitchen, he pulls open the fridge, but the smell makes him recoil. The meter must be empty like he's heard his mum complain about sometimes. The stench of turned milk and rotten meat make his stomach churn, but a bit of red catches his eye. Holding his breath, he reaches to the back, pulling out a big tomato. It's a tad warm but doesn't have any fuzz growing on it.

Sitting at the cluttered kitchen table, he bites into the soft red flesh, enjoying the tangy sweetness as the juice runs down his chin and onto his striped shirt. He devours every morsel, except for the green bits on top, then pushes the chair to the sink to get a drink of water that doesn't taste like toothpaste.

The light coming through the cracks is getting dimmer, so it's probably close to his bedtime. George has always liked bedtime because he doesn't have to listen to Errol and his mum fighting or making other strange noises behind the closed bedroom door. He doesn't like those noises. Last time, they were really bad, and mummy screamed a lot.

Pulling a tattered cushion from the couch, he goes back to his mum's side, tucking in beside her on the floor and taking her hand in his. She squeezes back this time, and a soft, ragged sound still comes from her mouth every few seconds.

When George opens his eyes the next morning, there are no more ragged sounds coming from his mum's mouth. Her hand still gripped in his, is cold and stiff, and he has to pull hard to get his hand out of hers.

"George, you need to escape. You have to get out of the house."

Startled, George sits up fast, his little heart beating out of his chest. His eyes dart around the dim room, trying to find who had spoken. He sees no one, but his eyes land on the bottom stair, where Raggy is sitting propped up in the corner. He doesn't remember putting him there; didn't he go to sleep holding him? He never goes to sleep without his doll.

"You have to get out, George."

George gasps, the voice obviously coming from Raggy. *"How can you talk? Dolls can't talk!"*

"Of course, we can. That doesn't matter, does it? You have to get out of here. Bang on the wall and shout so someone will hear you."

George frowns, matching Raggy's sad upside-down smile. *"What about Mummy and Daddy?"*

"It's okay, George. Someone will come help if you bang on the wall. Look! Use the empty Twiglets tin and bang and shout really loudly." Raggy points to the discarded red tin near Graham's feet.

"You can move!"

"Yes, of course, I can. Now, go!"

George scampers up, picks up the tin and runs to the

138

living room, hitting the wall repeatedly with the red tin until his arm feels too heavy to keep going.

"Shout for help, George!"

George bangs the tin with his other hand, whilst shouting as loud as he can. "Help! Somebody help me! I'm in here, Mummy and Daddy won't wake up! Help!"

Annie turns the television set off, frowning. "Fred, d'you hear that?"

Fred walks in from the kitchen, a lit Capstan dangling from his lips, steaming cup of tea in his hand. "What you sayin', love?"

Annie points to the wall adjoining the neighbour's house. "Do you hear that banging? Could have sworn I'd heard Georgie shouting, banging' on the wall. Have you seen him recently?"

Fred puts his cup down on top of the television, pulling the cigarette from his mouth. "Can't say I have, no." A deep crease forms between Fred's thick brows.

"Okay, love. I'll pop 'round and have a look. Hope that gob shite isn't in."

Annie follows Fred to the door, seeing that Graham's car was parked out front. She watches Fred shuffle to the neighbours in his worn house slippers, leaning on her walking stick, she waits on the front step.

Fred bangs the door with a closed fist, taking a long drag of his cigarette before tossing it onto pavement. "Valerie, you in there, love?"

The small voice answers through the thick wooden door. "Help, Mummy's on the floor, she won't wake up. Daddy is here too, but he can't move."

Annie gasps, a fluttering hand covering her mouth. "Dear God, Fred!"

"Call 999, Annie. Quickly!" Fred pushes against the door with his shoulder as Annie rushes back in to call the police, but it doesn't budge. "Can you open the door, George?"

"I can't reach; Daddy's in front of it. Is that you, Uncle Fred?"

"Yes, it's me, George. Don't worry, son. We'll have you out of there in a minute. Move away from the door."

Fred hurries back next door to make sure Annie's calling for help.

Annie is on the phone, waiting for the operator *"Police please."* She waits a moment, until she hears a voice on the line. *"Hello, I think someone is dead next door, and a small child is locked in with her."*

"Can you give me the address?" the police operator asks.

"Yes, the address is 64 Kenilworth Road, Manchester." Annie grips the phone tightly, her heart racing.

"Right. Keep a look out for the police car, we're sending someone now."

"Please, hurry."

"They're on their way, ma'am." the operator tells her.

"Thank you." Annie places the receiver back on the phone before turning to Fred. "They're on their way." Her hand flutters to her chest, cheeks flushed. "Do you need a hand?"

Fred shakes his head. "Sit down, love. You wait 'ere in case they ring back. I'll wait with Georgie." He walks back next door, pulling out another Capstan, striking a match with shaking fingers. This isn't how he'd planned to spend Monday morning.

Chapter 34

WPC Cooper knocks on the door, Doonan pulls the cover back over the evidence board hiding the contents from prying eyes.

"Come in."

"What is it?" Doonan asks her, annoyed. "We're a bit busy."

"Sorry. We've just had a call from a hysterical woman about a child in danger."

Doonan raises an eyebrow, frowning at her. "What the fuck has that got to do with us? Toddle off and ring social services. There's a good girl."

"Okay," Cooper starts. "But we were told to let you know; the call is for 64 Kenilworth Road, sir."

Doonan stops flipping his notepad and looks up at the other detectives, then back to Cooper. *"Erm,* good work, love. We'll take it from here."

"Thanks, sir." She turns to leave, but Doonan stops her. *"Oy,* love. What's your name?"

"Cooper, sir. Alison Cooper."

"Right, Alison. Get your bag and coat, love; you've pulled. You're comin' with us. If there's really a kid involved, we might need someone to look after him."

Cooper smiles, nodding. "Yes, sir." She closes the door behind her.

"Right, boys," Doonan addresses the detectives. "That's Errol's gaff. Mercy, you're with me. Jackson, you and Burns get the gun and follow us down, on the double." He stands, grabbing his jacket from the back of his chair. "Morrison, do some digging on that tramp you interviewed earlier who's fished a body out of the canal."

"Yes, boss."

Doonan, Mercy, Burns, and Jackson exit the incident room, leaving Morrison on the phone. Doonan and Mercy leave the station through the rear entrance. followed by WPC Cooper. They walk towards a black Ford Granada 2.8 Ghia .Doonan gets in the driver's seat as Mercy opens the rear door for WPC Cooper.

With Mercy sitting shotgun, Doonan manoeuvres the car out of the station lot. "When we get there, follow my lead. This Errol character's a fucking animal Cooper." He catches her eye in the rearview. "You stay in the car unless I give you the all-clear, okay?"

"Yes, sir." Mercy and Cooper answer in unison.

"Ah, for fuck's sake, call me Dan when we're not at the station, will ya?"

"Yes, Dan." They both answer again as Doonan flattens the pedal to the floor with the wheels spinning, he turns on the siren.

Chapter 35

Catching a glimpse of the Range Rover on the security camera, Pete looks up from the pile of paperwork that's been giving him a headache for the best part of an hour.

He pushes up from his chair and walks to the door. As he opens it, he watches Frank go around behind the Range Rover, opening the tailgate and reappear walking towards him with a brown box.

"What can I do for you, pal?" he asks as Frank stands in front of him holding the box with both hands.

"You Pete?"

"I am, who's askin'?"

A half smile tugs at Frank's mouth. "I have this parcel for a friend of yours."

"Yeah? What friend would that be, then?" "Errol." Frank looks at him, deadpan.

"Sorry." Pete glances around the busy yard, workers mulling about, getting ready for the next incoming barge. "I don't know anyone called Errol, so fuck off. As you can see, I'm busy."

The other side of Frank's mouth lifts in a full smile. "Quite the charmer, aren't you?" He moves forward, leaning against the doorframe and forcing Pete to take a step back into the security room. "Listen, I know Errol's your cousin. Tweak told me."

144

Pete feels his hands begin to shake, so he stuffs them in his pockets. "Well, you're wrong, mate. I don't know any Errol, and what kind of fucked up folks call their kid Tweak? Take off, yeah? You're wasting my time."

Frank's smile disappears. "Fine, you can play your little game if you want."

Pete opens his mouth to give him a sharp retort, but Frank interrupts him. "I know you're hiding him out here somewhere, just like I know where you live, Pete, and that your very pretty daughter Emma goes to Huyton Secondary School.

It's all Pete can do to keep his knees from buckling as he feels the blood drain from his face.

A new grin flickers on Frank's face at Pete's obviously visible reaction. He thrusts the package against his chest, forcing him to take it. "If, or rather, when, Errol gets back, make sure to deliver this parcel. It's important. Let's just say it's a little *heads-up* from his best mate, Tweak." He winks, clicking his tongue against his teeth.

Pete puts the surprisingly heavy parcel on the floor beside the desk. "I'm not admitting to anything, but seeing as you don't believe—" He stops short as he turns back 'round and sees Frank is gone and the door frame is empty. He watches the Range Rover drive off towards the gate, before shutting the door, locking it after him, eyeing the suspicious parcel with a side-eye.

Chapter 36

They're the first ones on the scene, but Doonan knows his other men will be there any minute. He looks at Mercy and Cooper as an old man stands from the steps and begins walking towards them. "Wait by the car, let me see what's going on."

"Detective Doonan." He extends his hand. "Did you call this in?"

"I'm Fred." He shakes the detective's hand. "My wife did. We live next door. I've tried to get in, but the door's locked. George is in there, he's only five."

"Anyone else in there with him?"

Fred shrugs. "I've not heard anyone, only George banging on the wall. He says his dad won't speak to him and his mum is asleep."

"Right. Go on back to your house for now, we'll come over later for a statement." Fred nods, joining Annie on their doorstep as Doonan walks back to his car.

"Find out where Jackson and Burns are," Doonan tells Mercy. "Just did. ETA's three minutes."

"Right. I'm going for a shufty 'round back. You go up to the door and listen, see if you can hear anything

inside besides the boy." Doonan takes off down the alley at the side of the house, leaving Peters to follow orders.

Chapter 37

Errol watches through a crack in the door, when the last car leaves the yard, he sneaks out, ambling over to the security office. He pulls on the door, but it doesn't budge. "What's going on?" He tries again, but nothing.

Looking around, he finds an old concrete block and drags it over to stand on it.

Through the dirty window, he sees Pete sat at his desk, bent over it with his head in his hands. "What now?" He taps the window with a finger and Pete's head snaps up, eyes wide and filled with a flash of terror. The fear is quickly replaced with what seems to Errol a mix of

a little bit of relief and a lotta bit of pissed.

He gets up so abruptly, his chair scuttles back on the floor and hits the wall. In two steps, he's got the door unlocked and steps aside as Errol walks in, then shuts the door again, turning the lock. "What the fuck have you got me involved in, eh?" He stands, practically vibrating, arms crossed in front of his chest.

"Calm down, cousin. What'd you mean?"

"I mean what the fuck have you got me involved in?

Had a visitor this morning."A visitor," Errol frowns. "What'd he want with you, then?"

Pete's face turned red. "Wasn't me, they were looking for, was it? It was you!"

"That's not possible." Errol shakes his head. "Nobody knows I'm here."

Pete shook his head so hard Errol thinks it might fly off. "Some fucker does, yeah. And that's not all! He knows where I live, knows my Emma's name, where she goes to school. Fuckin' hell, Errol, What the fuck?"

Errol swallows the lump that's suddenly stuck in his throat. "What did he look like?"

Pete throws his hands up, letting them fall again, his scowl deepening. "I don't know, man. Big Irish fucker. *Big.* Said Tweak sent him."

"For what?"

"For what? Does it matter? You said nobody knows you're here, mate. Last time I checked, Tweak wasn't nobody, was he?" Pete shakes his head, pacing the small office. "If they hurt my Emma..." he swallows the rest of the words on a curse. "There." He points to the box sitting on the floor. "He delivered a parcel for you. Said it was a heads-up from Tweak, whatever the fuck that means."

Errol eyes the package suspiciously, approaching it as though it might jump out at him. Picking it up gingerly, he sits it on Pete's desk and leans his head over it, frowning.

"What the fuck're you doing?" Pete looks at Errol like he's lost his mind. "Seeing if it's ticking."

Pete's eyebrows raise to his thin hairline. "You think Tweak's sent you a clock?"

"Yeah, maybe. Strapped to a load of dynamite."

Pete's eyes grow as big as golf balls as he makes a run for the door, but Errol grabs a fistful of shirt and pulls him

148

back. "Fuckin' stay here."

"There's no dynamite in there. Box has been here since the mornin'."

"Why'd you run, then?"

"Dynamite's not the only option, is it?" Pete plops down on the floor in the farthest corner he can find, hiding behind his hands like a little child as he watches Errol through his splayed fingers.

Taking the letter opener sitting on Pete's desk, Errol carefully cuts through the tape. "Could you go any slower?" Pete's voice catches, betraying his terror.

"Don't fuckin' rush me!" Errol growls, wiping at the sweat on his forehead. Once he finally has the tape cut, he lifts each flap painstakingly slow. Lifting the last one, he jumps backwards, a strangled cry dying in his throat.

Pete scrambles to his feet, pressing himself into the corner. "What the fuck is it?"

Breathing heavily, Errol tries to swallow but there's no saliva left in his mouth. He approaches the open box again, reluctantly. Staring back at him with one dead eye, and a glass diamond wedged into the empty socket where another eye used to be, is Tweak's horribly bludgeoned head. Stuffed in his open mouth is a folded-up envelope.

Errol grabs the corner of it, forcing himself to look away from his mate's blind stare. He rips the envelope open and pulls out a small note card.

"What's it say?" Pete takes a step forward, still not knowing what else is in the box.

"Return what you have stolen," Errol reads out loud.

Pete takes another step forward, tentatively craning his neck to see what's in the box, even though he really doesn't want to – curiosity always gets the best of him. It takes no more than half a second for him to realise he really shouldn't have looked, and he's out the door and tossing his supper all over the floor.

"Pete, fuck's sake, get back in here. Shut the door, you'll draw attention."

Pete wipes his mouth on the back of his sleeve, the front of his shirt covered in what used to be roast beef. "Sorry. Nobody's about anyway, couldn't hold it in."

Errol pinches the bridge of his nose, squeezing his eyes shut.

"Right, I need to think."

"Who is it?" Pete gives a wide berth, not wanting another glimpse of whatever poor saps' noggin is sitting on his desk."

"My mate, Tweak. Jack must have killed him. Guess that's what the fucker meant when he said it was a heads-up. Twisted bastard. Fuck!" He looks at his cousin, his frown deepening. "Sit down, Pete, just let me think for a minute, yeah?"

Pete plops down on his chair but rolls it away from the box, as far as it'll go, while Errol sits in the cracked vinyl and chrome chair across from the desk.

Leaning forward, elbow on his knees, he stares at the note as though it might hold the answers to all of life's deepest questions. After a long while, he jumps up as if he's been shocked. "That'll work."

"What'll work?"

He picks up a black pen from the desk, frowning at it and tossing it back down. "I need a blue pen."

Pete shuffles forward, rolling the chair up and keeping his eyes averted. He digs into the mess of a drawer until he finds a blue pen, hands it to Errol and quickly rolls back again.

With a flourish, Errol scrawls a J at the bottom of the unsigned note, then reseals it inside the envelope and stuffs it back into Tweak's mouth, where he'd pulled it out of.

"Let's see you get out of that one, you dirty prick." Pete frowns, thinking Errol's talking to him. *"Eh,*
what'd you mean?"

"Not you, Pete, relax. Never mind what I mean. Ring the pigs. Tell them you've got a delivery from a bloke with a Manchester accent, dropped off here for someone called Errol." He pushes the flaps back down.

Pete's eyebrows shoot up. "Are you sure, mate? You want me to mention your name to the pigs?"

"Yeah, man." He nods, grinning. "Tell 'em you've got a cousin Errol, but not seen him for ages. Didn't know how to reach him, so you opened the box." Pete's face goes grim. "Yeah, and shit myself."

Errol's grin turns into a full-blown smile. "Exactly right. They'll see the sick all over your jumper; they'll know you're not lyin'."

Pete nods, reluctant. "What if that driver comes back?"

"He won't." Errol shakes his head. "Too dangerous. He's gonna want to keep low." He stands, pulls a thick wad of twenties from his pocket and tosses it into Pete's lap.

"What's this for, then?" Pete picks up the bills, looking up in confusion.

"When the pigs are done doing whatever it is they're gonna do with you, take off. Go on the sick and disappear for a couple weeks. Take the family on a little holiday."

"Why?"

Errol walks to the door, looking back at Pete. "I've got a few loose ends need tyin'. These blokes are bad news, may come after you to try and get to me."

Pete stuffs the twenties into the pocket of his trousers. "Fuck. Yeah, okay. Wife's got a cousin in Sunderland; she's been after us to visit."

"That'll do. Good lad. I'll contact you when it's safe."

Pete watches Errol walk out, hopping over the splatter of vomit on the floor and lookin' 'round to make sure nobody's watching as he makes his way back to the unit. He rakes his fingers through his hair, trying not to think of what's sitting in a box behind him, not two feet away. "You fucking idiot. What the fuck've you got yourself mixed up with. Shit. Shit!"

He goes to the toilet, running the cold water and splashing it over his face, the back of his neck, swishing it in his mouth to clear up the sour taste of the sick, then dries up with the hand towel and goes back to his desk. He pushes the box away to the corner in case one of the flaps were to pop up again, then picks up the phone and dials 999.

"Operator."

"Hello, can I have the police, please?" He waits for the call to be transferred. *"Police department, can I help you?"*

"Yeah, uh, I'd like to report a suspicious package."
"What's suspicious about it, sir?"

"Well, it's, uh... it's got someone's head in it."

Chapter 38

Mercy Peters watches the street filling up with nearly a dozen police cars, an ambulance coming up behind them pulling up as close to the house as it can.

Peters keeps his post by the door, wondering how Doonan's doing in the alley.

For his part, Doonan manages to get through the overgrown alley, weeds and brambles clinging to his trousers, burrs sticking in big patches he knows will be hell to get out later. A bin sits against the wall, overflowing with rubbish, flies and wasps buzzing. He can see the edges of the bin crawling with maggots and thinks wryly, what lovely people must live here.

Swatting the pests away, he climbs up on top of the bin to peer over the wall, but from his vantage point, he can't see through the dingy windows into the house.

He hoists himself up and over the wall, dropping into what could be a nice garden if it wasn't covered with more rubbish and weeds nearly as tall as his knees.

He curses as thistle pokes through the fabric of his trousers. "You people ever hear of a lawn mower?" he grumbles all the way to the door, trying to avoid the worst piles of rubbish rotting like a poor substitute lawn ornaments.

Even from up close, peering through the window as

best he can, pushed up on his toes, the grease, dust, and grime are so thick, he can't make out anything in what he expects is the kitchen as these houses are pretty much all laid out the same.

Making his way to the door, he trips over a discarded tin, losing his balance and stumbling forward, smashing into the low concrete step. "For fuck's sake!" he hops, regaining his balance and grabbing at his throbbing ankle, before kicking the menace of a tin across the yard.

He bangs a fist on the door. "Police, open up!" Leaning in, he listens for any movement inside but hears nothing. He didn't think he would, but following protocol is important to him. He turns the knob, but finds that it's locked. "Of course."

If he didn't know better, he'd swear the house was empty. But he knows better, and it's almost making him dread what he has to do next as he ignores the churning in the pit of his stomach.

He shoulders the door, but it barely budges, so he shoulders it again. It gives a little this time, so he steps away a few paces, then rushes it, throwing his entire body weight against the panels.

The old wood splinters and cracks, giving way completely and landing him with a crash onto the kitchen floor. The smell hits him first, even from where he lies on what's left of the door. The sour stench of death permeates the air, assaulting his senses so violently he nearly vomits, but manages to hold it in.

Raising his head, he has the perfect view of the hallway from under the kitchen table. It's dimly lit from daylight pooling in behind him where the door used to be, but there's enough of it to send a fresh wave of nausea flooding through him.

In his many years in homicide, he's seen his fair share of horror and tragedy, but nothing he's ever seen has prepared him for what he's looking at now.

A man, appearing at first glance to be standing behind the door, but is actually hanging, feet flat on the floor but bent at the knees. Impaled on something, probably by the base of his skull. Eyes wide open, he's staring blindly down at a woman lying at his feet, at the bottom of the stairs. She's leaned back against the stairs, shirt ripped open and covered in blood, with bloody towels tucked all around her.

Even from this distance, Doonan can tell the woman is obviously dead – no living woman is that shade of grey. Beside her, curled up into her side and holding a strange-looking doll, is a little boy, maybe five or six. He's very much alive and staring at Doonan with wide eyes. He looks to be covered in blood, but from the looks of the scene, Doonan doubts any of it belongs to him.

He swallows the growing lump in his throat, blinking furiously against the dampness in his eyes as he stands, brushing off the dust and bits of slivered wood.

He walks carefully down the hall, looking up the stairwell and into the living room to make sure nobody's after jumping out at him.

"Hi son, are you all alone?" He keeps his voice low, calm, so as not to alarm the boy who's obviously already terrified.

The boy looks at his strange doll before looking back up at Doonan and nodding. "Is there anyone else in the house?"

The boy looks at the doll again before shaking his head. "Only Mummy and Daddy." His voice is small, and Doonan has to strain to hear him.

"Okay. I'm a police officer, my name is Doonan."

"That's a funny name."

Doonan gives the boy a little smile. "It is a funny name, yeah." He moves up but stops when the boy flinches back. "Don't be afraid, son, I'm just going to open the door a little, all right? Let a bit of air in, and I can talk to my officer. Okay?"

The boy just stares back at him, gripping his doll tightly, glued to his dead mother's side. It's all Doonan can do to stop from sniffling as he pries the door open a few inches – as much as he can, with the body hanging behind it, but just enough to squeeze through.

"*Oy,* Peters," Doonan calls out this constable.

Peters turns, seeing Doonan squeeze through the crack in the door. He walks up from the bottom step where he's been keeping watch. "All clear inside, sir? Can you open the door?"

"No, son. It's a right shit storm in here." He keeps his voice low. "Call Cooper up here." Peters waves Cooper over and she runs up the steps.

"Sir?"

"I need you in here. Quickly."

"Right, straight away, sir." She follows him back in the barely open door, stepping into the stomach-curdling stench. Her eyes immediately fill as she takes in the scene before her – a small boy clinging to his dead mother's hand, covered in what appears to be her blood. The mother's shirt torn open, a wide gash across her stomach. The father – obvious by his resemblance to the boy – seems to be hung from a coat hook, staring blindly at his family below him.

"Sweet mother of God." Her hand flutters up to her mouth as Doonan steps in front of her, gripping her shoulders and forcing her to look at him.

"Right, young lady, we can't have none of that." He keeps his voice low so that the boy won't hear them. "Can you take this young lad next door? We need to take him out of this house. God knows how long his folks have been dead."

Cooper nods, blinking hard at the threatening tears. "Good. And tell Peters to call for an ambulance."

"There's already one outside, sir. The paramedics are ready."

"Right, good. Let's get him out of here, yeah?" Cooper nods again, sitting on the step beside where

George is sat, still clinging to his mother. She keeps her voice soft, trying hard to control the tremors in it. "Hello, sweetheart, my name is Alison. What's yours?"

The boy looks down at his doll, as though intently listening to what it's saying. The doll is silent, obviously, but Cooper remembers being a young girl and believing her dolls and teddies could speak to her. She can't imagine what must be going through this poor lad's traumatised mind at the minute.

He looks up to her. "I'm George."

Cooper tries to smile. "It's nice to meet you, George. And who's this little man?" She motions to the doll.

"He's Raggy doll. He's my best friend." George grips Raggy more tightly.

"Well, he had better come with us, then. We're going to go next door, to the neighbours', all right?"

"To Uncle Fred's?"

Cooper looks up to Doonan for confirmation, which he gives her with a slight nod.

"Yes, that's right, to Uncle Fred's." She holds her hand open to George, hoping he'll come willingly – she can't imagine having to pry him away from his mother.

Doonan calls out to Peters from the slight crack in the door. "Send the paramedics in the same way Cooper came."

"Straight away, sir."

George puts his little dried blood-covered hand in Cooper's, looking up at her with sad eyes. "What about my mummy and daddy? Are they coming with us?"

She can't hold in the streaming tears now as she feels her heart shatter to pieces for this little orphan boy.

Doonan can feel it from where he stands – he's seen more horror in his career than he likes to remember, but this one... this one might just be the one that breaks him. He turns away quickly, pulling the handkerchief from his pocket and wiping at his eyes.

"In a little bit," Cooper tells George softly. "We need to get you sorted out first, okay?"

George breaks down into sobs, pulling his hand from Cooper's and turning to grip at his dad's leg. "Please,

Daddy! Daddy, I don't want to go with her. I want to stay with you and Mummy!"

Cooper rushes to kneel beside him, her heart in pieces. "George, look at me, sweetheart." When he doesn't, she gently turns his face to her. "Look at me, George."

Right on cue, two paramedics, followed by a young officer with a camera, come down the hallway.

"Look, these nice men are like doctors. They've come to see if they can fix your mummy and daddy, but we need to give them space, okay?" She opens her arms to him,

and after eyeing the paramedics with a mixture of distrust and awe, George runs to her, burying his face in the crook of her neck, bawling.

Cooper grabs Raggy from the floor where he'd been dropped, and stands, George wrapped around her like a vice. She stands back a bit as Doonan instructs the officer. "Take your pictures, quickly. I won't have this boy climbing over a wall to get out of here. We need to be able to open the door."

As she's waiting for them to move the man, Cooper takes in the rest of the space from her vantage point. Dull light from filthy windows casts a shadowy gloom into the living room to her right. Dingy furniture, and a dingier carpet, littered with spent syringes and other paraphernalia.

As her gaze drifts back to the hallway, they're caught by a horrific sight she'd missed until now. Swallowing the bile, she gives a small wave, catching Doonan's attention, then points to the corner where what appears to be what's left of a very small dog, large spike nails protruding from the little furry mass.

"Dear God," Doonan whispers. "Who would do such

159

a thing?"

George lifts his head, turning to see what Doonan is talking about. He sniffs loudly. "That's Nipper. Errol killed him because Nipper was scared and bit him."

"Where's Errol now, son?"

George only shrugs and lays his head down on Cooper's shoulder. She hands him Raggy and he hugs him close as the paramedics carefully shift the fathers's body enough to open the door.

"Let's go to Uncle Fred's." Her voice is low and soothing in George's ear, he nods, hugging her neck tightly.

Her tears are unchecked as she exits the house onto the cracked front steps. Peters steps aside to let her pass. "You okay, love?"

She merely shakes her head, unable to speak as she goes down the steps walking across to where an elderly woman is waiting for them.

"Hi love, I'm Annie."

Cooper walks up the steps to her and lets the woman pull them both into a hug.

"C'mon, George, let's get you and Raggy cleaned up. Then we can have your favourite – milk and cookies."
"Sorry, ma'am. We can't clean him up just yet,"

Cooper tells her with a shaky voice. "We need

S.O.C.O. to see him first. He can have the milk and cookies, though."

Annie smiles sadly, nodding as she leads them into the house, closing the door softly behind them.

Chapter 39

Constable Lloyd brings the police car to a halt outside the security office, lights flashing, siren blasting.

Pete opens the door, praying his obvious nerves will be attributed to his gruesome discovery, and not to any possibility of involvement, from the police's perspective. He watches as two constables exit the car and walk up to the door.

"Evenin', sir. Did you call in a suspicious package?"

"I did, yes." He steps back, making room for them to enter, cringing as they step over the splatter of vomit on the floor. "This way."

"I'm P.C. Lloyd," the first constable tells him. "This is P.C. Thomason. What's your name, sir?'

"I'm Pete. Pete Tetlow." Thomason walks up to the desk, taking the pen from his pocket and lifting the flap of the box, immediately recoiling. "Fuck me!"

"What is it?" Lloyd looks up, finishing writing down Pete's name on his notepad.

Thomason leans in again, a look of disgust on his face. "It's a head – badly burnt. There's a fat diamond shoved in where his eye should be, and a piece of paper sticking out his mouth."

Lloyd steps up, peering into the half-open box, then back up to Thomason. "You ever see anything like that before?"

"Can't say as I have, no."

"Right. Get onto the station. Tell them we need forensics out here."

"Got it."

Lloyd turns back to Pete as Thomason walks back to the car. "Right, then. Tell me exactly what happened." Pete nods, relieved when the flap falls closed on the box. "Got a knock at the door this mornin'. Fella said he had a package for Errol. I told him, nobody here by that name. He didn't take my word for it, pushed the box into my chest so I grabbed it. Then he gets back in the car and drives off. When I opened it, I chucked it up." He pointed towards the door, colour rising on his cheeks. "That's when I rang you."

Lloyd raises his eyebrows, looking up from his notepad. "You said you got it this morning. You waited all day before ringing us, then?"

Pete shakes his head. "No, sir. I didn't open it straight away. See, I've a cousin called Errol but haven't seen him in a couple years. Called 'round, tryin' to see if anyone knows where he is, no luck. Then had a few barges come in, got busy. I was gettin' ready to clock out and remembered the package. That's when I opened it."

"Right, right." Lloyd scribbles more notes. "Did you recognise the driver?"

Pete shakes his head again, starting to feel a bit nauseous and praying he won't vomit again. "Nah, never saw him before. But he had a Manchester accent."

"What did he look like?"

"I'd say six foot – maybe a bit more. Well built, dark hair." Lloyd nods. "What was he driving?"

"Dark-coloured jeep thing, not sure of the make. I didn't take much notice."

"Right, okay. You'll need to come back to the station with us. This place'll need to be sealed off whilst we wait for forensics to go over it."

"All right, yeah. I just let my boss know."

From the other side of the yard, Errol watches, perched on a stool to see out the grimy window at the top of the unit door, glad it's too dark for anyone to see him if they even looked in his direction, and hoping Pete stuck to the plan.

Chapter 40

The sky beginning to cloud over, Constable Mercy Peters walks into the house, unprepared for the literal horror show that waits for him.

He gasps loudly, both from the massacre and the stench. "Fuck me, boss."

Doonan turns, frowning. "Peters, outside." He points back to the door. "Send in Jackson and Burns. You're in charge of the logbook – make sure anyone who comes in and out of here is registered. Be sure to note down these three." He points to the constable and two paramedics working behind him.

"Yes, boss." Peters runs back outside and waves down Jackson and Burns who have just pulled up.

"Overshoes and gloves," he tells them as they walk up to him. "We need to protect the evidence – can't mess up the scene any more than it already is. And, *uh.*" He pauses, rubbing a hand over his face. "Prepare yourselves, boys. It's a fucking bloodbath in there."

Jackson and Burns frown as they don their protective gear before entering the house. Burns, the first one in, stops dead in his tracks, taking it all in "What the fuck happened here?"

Doonan turns to look at Burns, Jackson stepping in from behind him. "We'll have to ask the kid to know for sure, but it may take some time as he's terrified, and with good reason." He motions with his hands, encompassing the entire entry hall. "We have to find Errol before Jack Harrison does."

Jackson frowns. "Why would Jack Harrison want to get involved with any of this mess?"

Doonan takes a deep breath. "Because, sunshine, if you did your homework, you'd recognise the poor sod hanging from the wall behind you."

Jackson looks to the poor sod in question, hanging from a coat hook behind the door. "Nah." He shakes his head. "I don't recognise him, sorry. Who is he?"

"That, Jackson, is Graham Harrison. He's Jack Harrison's kid brother, and the boy is his nephew."

Jackson's eyes grow wide. "Holy fuck."

"My sentiments exactly." Doonan agrees. He points down to Val on the floor, where the paramedics have concluded she is in fact, quite dead, and there's nothing they can do to fix her, as Cooper had told George.

"Valerie Harrison. According to our sources, she's Graham's ex-wife. Errol was banging her – this looks like his handy work. Get an A.P.B. out on him and that waste of skin mate, Tweak."

"Right." Burns nods.

"Where's the kid now, then?" Jackson asks. "Can we speak with him?"

"Not a chance. He's next door with Cooper. You ain't seen the state of the poor little fucker." Doonan shakes his head, still seeing the boy's terrified eyes in his mind. "Just get social services down here straight away, and make sure

Cooper goes with them when they leave. He's taken a liking to her as I hoped. Don't want to traumatise the kid any more than he already is – for now, where he goes, so does Cooper."

"You got it, boss."

"Right, let's seal this place tighter than a nun's chuff until S.O.C.O. gets here."

"On it." Jackson nods. "Burns, you take the back."

With the kitchen door back up as best they can, and every exit taped up, they all exit the house. With quick work, Doonan has police officers guarding every access to the house, front and back, blocking the alley.

A small crowd has begun to gather on the street, teaming with police cars, flashing lights, and men in white coveralls. With the perimeter cordoned off with yellow police tape, the neighbourhood looks like something out of a crime film, Doonan thinks, as he walks into the next-door neighbours', where Cooper has been waiting with George for what feels like hours.

Chapter 41

Knowing he needs to disappear, Errol leaves Liverpool and makes his way back to Manchester, making sure not to be seen. He manages to get to Jack's builders' yard without anyone taking notice, after watching for some time ensuring nobody's about, he sneaks in through a break in the fence.

Making his way into the central area surrounded by buildings, he makes his way to the old shed where he's been stashing the drugs. He needs to get them, then grab his diamond, and high tail it out of here.

Making sure again that nobody's around, he starts stacking pallets under the old duct. Grabbing the one on the bottom, his hands slide in something wet and sticky, which he wipes on the legs of his jeans, taking no notice of it. There's always something wet and sticky in builders' yards.

He frowns when he notices the old drum is gone, but quickly finds another, and stacks it on top of the pallets, climbing up to retrieve his loot. But peering into the shaft, he finds it empty.

"Fuck!" They're gone, which means Tweak's a rat.

He's the only one who knew where he kept them.

Jumping down from the barrel, he notices his pants are covered in red paint, and shakes his head. Jack's gonna have someone's head for spilling paint all over his floor. But when he looks back at the stack of pallets, then back down at his stained hands, bile pools in his throat as he realises the congealed, sticky substance is not paint at all. "Shit. Shit!" He tries to wipe his hands clean but there's no getting the blood off.

Looking around again, he notices the old tipper van is parked over a very clean section of the yard. A small puddle has formed under the end of the hose where it hangs – it's been recently used.

"Sneaky bastards," he growls. "So, this is where they fucked you up, init, Tweak?" He walks over to the hose, turns it on slightly and cleans the red from his hands. "Well, Jack, let's see you talk your way out of this one, then."

He leaves out the back fence break, the same way he came in. Maybe he'll have better luck getting his diamond back from that little bastard kid.

Chapter 42

The clouds have long passed, and daylight is quickly fading by the time the forensics van pulls up to 64 Kenilworth Rd.

Peters checks them into the log, then waits, pacing the front hard whilst they go through every part of the house, checking every corner, every cupboard, photographing and bagging everything that could be considered evidence, which, at that point, can be practically everything.

By the time they're done, hours have gone by, his feet are screaming as loud as his stomach as he watches the bagged bodies being loaded into the waiting mortuary vans. He thanks the heavens Cooper left hours ago with the boy and social workers – the kid doesn't need to be subjected to seeing his parents hauled off in body bags.

Spotlights are lit just outside the cordoned area, and every neighbour and onlooker is questioned and interviewed.

Finally, as the last of the police cars start dissipating, Graham's car is towed away, and Peters gets to go home.

Chapter 43

Father Willis watches from the front gate of the children's home as a dark blue saloon car pulls up to the curb.

Glynis steps out of the driver's seat, her hair perfectly coiffed as usual. She opens the back door and coaxes out a small boy, about five or six, clutching a burlap rag doll as though his life depends on it. "Come on, love, there's nothing to be afraid of, it's going to be all right." She motions with her hand.

George scuttles across the leather seat and slides out, staring at the gravel and sticking close to Glynis' leg. She takes his hand, shuts the car door, and leads him over to Father Willis just as Gina hurries past them.

"Gina!"

Gina stops in her tracks, closing her eyes for a moment—she'd hoped to get inside without being stopped.

"Where have you been until this time?"

She knows he's keeping his tone civil because the social worker lady is standing there watching.

"Just out. Why?" She starts walking again, but a strong hand grabs the back of her coat, yanking her back with a hard tug. She grabs at her throat, where the buttons are pulled too tight until he gives her a bit of slack.

"Wait here, young lady. I haven't finished with you just yet."

She glares at the hateful man, crossing her arms in front of her chest as she leans back against the garden gate post, scowling.

Glynis walks up to where she stands, holding a little boy's hand – he looks sad, and a little lost and afraid.

The social worker frowns down at her, seeing her bruised cheekbone and swollen, split lip. "What's happened to you, love?"

Gina knows there's no point in telling the truth, not with the old prick standing right there. Glynnis wouldn't believe her, anyway. She lifts her chin defiantly. "I fell out of a tree getting my ball back. Why?"

Glynis shakes her head, sighing, then looks back to Father Willis. "Right, well, this little fella's name is George. He'll be staying with you for a little while until we can locate any relatives."

Willis shakes his head in turn, frowning. "Glynis, I'm sorry. As I said on the phone, we've no room. We're full at the minute. No room at the inn, some might say." He smiles, but there's not an ounce of friendliness in the gesture.

"Don't quote the bible at me, Willis." Glynis lifts her chin the way Gina had. Something about the man demands assertion. "I know exactly what goes on here."

His smile disappears completely as blood rushes up his neck. "You'll watch your tongue, young lady."

She raises her eyebrows, putting a hand on her hip, daring him to continue. He clears his throat. "We're still full."

Gina watches George during the whole scenario,

noting how he seems so scared, lonely. So much like her when she first arrived here. She smiles at him.

"Father?"

Willis looks down at her, questioning.

"Father Willis, George can stop in my room, I don't mind. I'll look after him, it won't be a bother, I promise. We'll keep out of trouble."

His raised eyebrows turn into a deep frown as he listens to her offer, confused. Gina's a rebel child, never one to take part or be helpful in any way. Certainly, not one to pay any mind to other children. But it's late, and he knows Glynis won't take no for an answer.

"All right then. It's late, I'll allow it. Go on, then, take him in, Gina. Get him something to eat, and yourself since you missed supper... again," he adds, biting his tongue against the reprimand he swallows in Glynis' presence. "I'll be in shortly."

Gina smiles, taking hold of George's little hand as he looks up at her. "It's okay, George. Come with me. I'll protect you, I promise." She pulls him along beside her, chattering. "That's a nice doll you've got – what's his name? Do you like chicken legs? I can tell you a bedtime story..."

Glynis and Father Willis watch them disappear into the house.

"Two weeks, Glynis. That's it. Then he's gone. He can't be bunking with Gina for long, it won't do. What's his story, anyway?"

"I'm hoping it won't take that long to find his family. His mother and father were brutally murdered in front of him, not sure how he's made it out alive, but he has. From the sounds of it, he was left to fend for himself in the company of their bodies for days – I'm surprised he's speaking at all, poor lad."

"Horrendous. Have they caught the murderer, then?"
"Not yet, no. Horrible creature, whoever it is. Heard one of the coppers mentioning a name as I left, seems like he's the main suspect."

"What's the name?"

Glynis frowned, trying to recall. "I'm thinking Merryl, or maybe Harrold." She pauses, mouthing a few names quietly. "No, no, Errol. That's it, yeah. Errol."

Father Willis' eyebrows crease in a deep frown as he turns back to where Gina and the boy disappeared into the house, then turns back to Glynis. "His last name, it wouldn't be Harrison by chance, would it?"

Her frown matches his. "How did you know that?"

He rubs both hands up and down his face, shaking his head. "Errol was shagging Jack's brother's ex. Which makes this kid Jack's nephew."

Glynis grips the rail of the gate, gasping. "Oh, shit. Well, that complicates things."

He tips his head at her. "You don't say." His tone is slightly sarcastic, but she only rolls her eyes. "Does Jack know?"

"I don't think so," she tells him, pulling her coat tighter around herself. "Seems they're keeping it hush-hush at the minute. I would assume in hopes of catching Errol."

Willis shakes his head. "No, that's not it at all. If they're keeping it quiet, it's because they're hoping to get

173

to him before Jack. You, my dear" – he points a finger at her – "need to keep your lips sealed about George being here."

"Agreed, but I think the police followed me here."

Willis nods, having already noticed the car in question pass by after she'd pulled up. "Yes, possibly. They'll be using the boy as bait, without a doubt. Funny thing, though, Errol killing Mum and Dad, but leaving George alive. Would have thought he had a bit more about him."

Glynis' jaw slacks, her eyes boring cold daggers into the man. "How can you call yourself a man of God, saying horrible things like that?"

Willis smirks. "I go to confession." He winks at her.

"You're sick, Willis," she hisses, venom coating her words.

"If that's what you think, can I assume you won't be wanting this, then?" He pulls a thick wad of ten-pound notes from his pocket, waving it at her.

She eyes the money, biting the inside of her cheek to keep her retort to herself as she sticks out her open hand.

He chuckles humourlessly. "Be nice if you practised what you preach, eh Glynis?"

She presses her lips firmly together, stuffing the money into her coat pocket as she turns on her heel, but Willis grabs her arm and pulls her back, getting his face so close to hers she can smell the cheap Bourbon on his breath. "Not a word about the boy being here, yeah? Not to anyone. I'll let Jack know."

She gives him a single, curt nod as she yanks her arm free of his grip and walks back to her car, slamming the door a little too hard. She watches him stroll casually back to the house, hands in his pockets as though nothing's happened. She shakes her head, disgusted at the whole situation, and at herself for taking the money. Again.

Flooring the accelerator, she spits gravel at the garden wall as she drives off. Not for the first time, and not the last, she wishes she'd chosen a different profession. It's about a quarter mile up the lane before she passes the unmarked car that had followed her here, and watches it pull out behind her in the rearview mirror.

Poor George, she thinks. Born into the wrong family.

Chapter 44

Jack takes a sip of extra strong tea, squinting against the too-bright light of the sun beaming through the window, nursing a whiskey-induced headache. He's flipping through the day's job sheets when his office door bursts open without a knock, Jimmy rushes in, breathless.

"Boss, the police."

Adrenaline rushes through him, waking him up faster than any tea can. "What about the police, Jimmy?" He tries to sound calm, but feels anything but.

Jimmy points behind him. "They're on the way, up the lane, mob-handed." Jack stands, shoving his chair back abruptly. "Lock the gates – stall them." Jimmy nods as he runs out.

"Fucking pigs, why would they be coming here straight away?" He opens the safe and pulls out the bundles of drugs – they'll no doubt have a search warrant. Jack doesn't think they're onto him for Tweak, but if they're coming in mob-handed, as Jimmy put it, they're on some sort of mission. Better to take heed.

He moves a ledger from one of the carved oak bookshelves and pulls a hidden switch, making the shelf swing open. No time to waste, as he can already hear the shouting from outside, he tosses the packages into the empty space inside, shutting the shelf back up quickly. He slams the safe closed and sits back at his desk, taking a sip of tea, his hands shaking from the adrenaline.

The locked gate doesn't stop the police for very long. They easily bust through it, smashing in with brute force, swarming the few workers already milling about.

Monroe walks up to Jimmy, his face like stone. "Where's Jack?"

"In his office – where else would the boss be?"

"*Oy*, you!" Monroe calls one of the constables over to him, pointing to Jimmy. "Cuff 'im" Jimmy takes a quick step back. "What for, I've done nothing!"

"Obstruction, for starters," Monroe deadpans. "Then we'll see what else we can come up with."

"This ain't right; I've done nothing. I just work here!" Jimmy squirms as the PC slaps the cuffs on him, reading him his rights. "Why are you arresting me? Why are you lot here?"

But the PC ignores him, shoving him along in front of him towards the black Maria van. Jimmy stumbles as he's unceremoniously shoved in to find a couple workmates are already sat there, hands cuffed behind their backs, looks of confusion plastered on their faces.

"Get this lot back to the station," Monroe barks. "Then get back here."

Jack comes out of his office just as the van is leaving the yard. "Where the fuck are you taking my workers? They have jobs to do." He waves the pile of job sheets in the air.

"Not today, Jack," Monroe says with a patronising wink. "They're going for a nice little ride to the nick."

"What for? What've they been up to?"

"Oh, loads, I presume. But why don't we wait and see what they say when they're questioned, shall we?"

Jack scowls at the van turning out of the yard, and notices the mangled gates, hanging off their hinges. He can feel his pressure mounting and knows his face is likely the colour of the tomato sandwich he's had for breakfast. "What the fuck have you done to my gate, you arsehole?"

Monroe casually turns to look, as though he has no idea what Jack is on about, then smirks as he shrugs a shoulder, turning back to Jack without an ounce of remorse. "Oops."

Jack's fists clench as hard as his teeth, and he thinks his head might explode from the pressure. "Oops! You're a fucking—"

"The gates are the least of your problems, Jack," Monroe interrupts calmly. "You're not going to be thinking about them at all in a minute, I promise."

"They'll be *your* problem when I speak to my solicitor." He turns to walk back into his office. "Whatever will be, will be." Monroe's smug tone stops him dead, and

he turns back around. "Stop talking in riddles, ya prick. You come bustin' in here, breaking my gates, hauling my men off and pouncing about. What the fuck do you want?" Monroe smiles again. "All in good time, Jack. All in good time."

Before Jack has the chance to walk away again, he grabs him and spins him round, dragging his arms behind his back, job sheets flying all over the ground as he cuffs him. "I'm arresting you for the murder of Jerome

Campbell." He spins him back around to face him. "You don't have to say anything. But it may harm your defence if you don't mention when questioned, something which you later rely on in court. Anything you do say may be given in evidence."

Jack's eyes grow wide, his jaw-dropping but no words coming out.

"You're barking up the wrong tree, Monroe," Jack hisses. "I haven't murdered anyone. I don't even know anyone called Jerome Campbell."

"We had an anonymous call last night from someone saying you murdered one of your workers here – namely, Jerome Campbell."

Jack shakes his head vehemently. "I don't have any workers named Jerome Campbell. I don't know any Jerome Campbell. Your anonymous caller was obviously on drugs. Uncuff me, I've work to do."

"Ah, yes. Well, you may only know him as Tweak."

"I know Tweak, but haven't seen 'im in a couple days." Jack's heartbeat was threatening to break out of his ribcage. "Someone's feedin' you a load of horse shit. Why don't we call him right now, he'll tell you the same, yeah?

"He won't be telling anything to anyone, but you already know that, don't you?"

They both turn at the shouts coming from behind the office, and a PC comes jogging 'round the corner. "Over here, boss. Looks like blood, and a lot of it."

Monroe looks back to Jack, lifting his shoulder in another shrug. *"Oops,"* he repeats with the same casual smile on his face. "Looks like you're gonna need that solicitor, after all, Jack."

"It's a builder's yard, you prick. Someone's always cuttin' themselves. It comes with the job."

"Yeah, you're probably right. But we've gotta follow up on the allegations – you understand that, don't you, Jack?" He winks at Jack as he shoves him, pointing to a waiting police car. "Move." Jack shakes his head, the cuffs digging painfully into his wrists at his back. "This is fucking bullshit, Monroe, and you know it. You're fishing. So how about you cast your line elsewhere, eh?" He turns in time to see a pair of constables taping off the spot where Tweak's head rolled, and a sour taste fills his mouth.

Monroe shoves him again, moving him along to the car. "I like fishin'. It relaxes me." He pushes him down into the back of the police car, slamming the door after him. "Take him to Peter Street," he tells PC Davies. "He's not to see or speak with anyone until I get there. Understood?"

"Understood, boss." Davies pulls out towards the gate as Monroe turns to another constable walking towards him. "Get S.O.C.O. down here, straight away."

Chapter 45

Father Willis comes into Gina's room to find her and George fast asleep on her bed, the boy clinging to his ugly doll for dear life.

The creaking of the floor wakes Gina and she bolts up in bed, clutching the sheet up to her, weary-eyed until her gaze lands on Willis. George stirs beside her from the sudden commotion.

"How did he sleep?"

Gina frowns, clutching the sheet tighter. "Not very well. Been up most of the night with him. He was having nightmares." George shuffles closer to Gina, gripping her leg and eyeing Willis with distrust. "The noises coming from the other room didn't help."

Willis scowls at her, his eyes darkening. "Careful, Gina."

His tone leaves no room for guessing, and Gina is too tired to argue.

"Make sure he gets some breakfast but take him to get cleaned up first. I've left some clean clothes that should fit him in the shower room."

Gina salutes sarcastically as Willis turns his back on her to leave the room. "Yes, sir!" She sticks her tongue out at the closed door, taking George's hand. "Come on, George, let's go get some breakfast."

George sits up, his bottom lip quivering for a second before he starts to cry. "I want my mummy," he whimpers as Gina pulls him into a hug.

"I know. It'll be okay, promise." She scoots off the bed, holding out a hand. "Let's get Raggy doll something to eat, and clean him up a bit, yeah? He looks a little hungry."

George wipes at his eyes with the back of his sleeve, looking down at Raggy and listening, then looks back up at Gina, nodding. "Okay. Raggy says he's hungry. I'm hungry, too."

Gina gives him a reassuring smile as he takes her hand and jumps off the bed.

As they leave the room, Gina sees a man as old as Father Willis coming out of her friend Jill's room. When he notices them, he picks up his step, looking down at the floor as he walks away. George clings tightly to Gina's hand as they move down the hall by fourteen- year-old Jill's door. She's curled up on her bed, her nighty bunched up to her waist, sobbing.

Anger flaring up in her chest, Gina shuts Jill's door and quickly pulls George off down the hall, biting her cheek.

"Does she want her mummy, too?" George asks her in a small, timid voice.

Gina nods as they keep walking towards the stairs. "Yeah, she wants her mummy, too." Her voice is as low as George's but filled with quiet fury.

In the dining room, they walk past a group of young girls clustered together at the dining table, quietly eating their breakfast. Gina nods at them in greeting as they walk by, but they ignore her completely, as though she isn't there at all.

She brings George to the far end of the table, helping him up onto the chair. "George, what does Raggy want for his breakfast? We have porridge or jam on toast."

George looks at Raggy, listening. "Raggy wants porridge, please."

Gina nods, smiling at him and patting Raggy's head. "And what about you? What would you like?"

"I'll have some of Raggy's porridge. He doesn't eat much."

"Porridge it is." She smiles. At the counter, she fills a bowl to the brim with the sticky porridge, then spreads a thick layer of strawberry jam on two slices of toast, hoping the priests won't come in before George finishes eating.

"Here you go." She places everything in front of him, smiling when he looks up in confusion. "Just in case Raggy's still hungry and wants some toast," she explains. "Would you like a glass of milk?"

George nods as he dips his spoon into the bowl, taking a bite for himself, and a pretend bite for Raggy.

He's so famished, that he's nearly done with the porridge by the time Gina puts the glass of cold milk in front of him. He gulps down half of it in one go before moving on to the triangles of toast, then washes it down with the rest of the milk.

"Wow, you and Raggy must have been really hungry." Gina smiles at him, wiping the jam off his face with a napkin. "I've never seen a boy and a doll eat their breakfast so quickly."

George gives her a small smile as he slides off the chair and helps her bring the dishes to the sink.

"Come." She reaches for his hand again. "Let's go get a wash, then."

They walk by the group of girls again, unintelligible whispers sounding among them as they walk out of the dining room. "Ignore them, George. They're just little witches."

She pulls him down the hall to the shower room and shuts the door before turning on the water.

"Just a quick wash. You can take Raggy in with you – he looks like he needs a wash even more than you."

"You can get undressed, I won't look. I'll keep watch so nobody comes in. Be quick, there'll be others who need to wash, too."

George watches for a minute as Gina puts a clean towel on the bench for him, with the clean clothes Father Willis has found, then sits on the floor with her back to him.

He quickly undresses, leaving his clothes in a pile. Under the warm jet of water, he holds Raggy up, letting the stream wash over him. He's amazed at the way he changes colour, from the ugly, rusty colour he's been the past few days, back to the regular brown he's supposed to be.

George watches as the red water swirls down the drain between his feet, then sets Raggy down on the floor and scrubs himself off with the bar of soap, rubbing it all over, even in his hair, like mummy does, and then stands under the water, letting the dirty bubbles wash off.

He's afraid of someone walking in, so he quickly turns off the water and steps out, drying himself with the towel Gina's left for him and putting on the clothes. They're not his clothes, and they're a little big on him, but at least they smell clean and there are no tears. All his clothes have tears and stains.

All dried and dressed, he wraps his damp towel around a dripping Raggy. "Are you all done?" Gina asks, still sitting on the floor facing the door. "Yes, all done."

She stands, turning and smiling down at him. "Here, let me help you with Raggy, he's all drippy. We don't want to make a mess on the floor."

George looks at Raggy, unsure, before handing him to Gina. "Okay, Raggy says he likes you."

"*Aw,* well, I like Raggy, too." She squeezes the towel around the doll, trying to get as much water out of him as she can. By the time she's done, the towel is soaked, but Raggy's just a bit damp. She hands Raggy back to George and folds the towel over the edge of the towel bar to dry. "Come." She holds her hand out again. "We need to go see Father Willis now." She tosses George's dirty clothes into the wicker basket by the door on their way out.

George clings to Gina's hand, sticking close to her side as they walk down the hallway to Father Willis' office. The door is closed, so Gina knocks.

"Enter," he calls from inside.

Gina pushes the heavy wooden door open, and they step into a large office. George looks around in awe, having never seen anything like it. The walls are lined with bookshelves from floor to ceiling. The man, sitting in a carved, ornate wooden chair, looks up at them from behind a big desk, glasses perched on his large, hairy nose. George recognises him from the night before, and this morning, when he'd woken them up.

"Oh, it's you." He looks at Gina in disgust. "Has he eaten?"

"Yes, Father," she replies with an overly polite, sarcastically sweet voice.

Willis ignores her insolence, focusing his eyes on the boy. "Hi, George, my name is Father Willis. We're going to look after you for a little while until your uncle Jack can come pick you up."

George presses himself against Gina's side, partly hiding behind her. "I want my mummy and daddy."

Willis crosses his arms over the ledger he's been working on. "I'm sorry, son. Your mummy and daddy have gone to be with baby Jesus now. I'm sure they loved you very much, but you'll be staying here until your Uncle Jack comes."

George clings to Gina's leg, sobbing. "I want my daddy—"

"George," Gina interrupts, hugging him close. "You can stay with me. I'll look after you and Raggy. You won't be alone, promise."

"Gina," Willis starts, standing behind his desk. "That piece of rag needs to be tossed in the bin. It's a health hazard. I'm sure we can find him another doll." He looks at it, disgust plainly painted on his face.

George's whimpers are cut short as he stares down the

man with the hairy nose, gripping Raggy tightly. "He's mine!" he snarls, eyes blazing. He turns to run for the door, but Gina catches him, kneeling in front of the shaking boy.

"George, it's all right. Nobody" – she stares daggers at Father Willis – "is taking Raggy away from you." She holds both of George's hands, then looks back to Willis again. "Nobody," she emphasises.

He rolls his eyes, not in the mood for a battle with the little brat. "Right, whatever. Make sure it gets washed, then."

"Raggy's clean," George states boldly, holding him close to his chest. "He's had a wash with me in the shower room."

"He's—" Willis starts but is quickly interrupted by Gina.

"I'm taking him for a walk down the canal, if that's okay."

Willis waves them off, annoyed, as he picks up the phone. "Fine, Gina. Do *not* let him out of your sight."

Gina pulls a pouting George out of the room, shutting the door after them. "I don't like him," George tells her, gripping her hand.

"Nobody does."

In his office, Willis dials out a number, leaning back into his chair as he stares at the closed door, dreaming up a new punishment for Gina.

"Hello, Jack."

"The voice on the other end of the line isn't Jack's." *"Can you get him for me, please?"* he frowns in annoyance. You call a man's personal line, you expect

him to answer.

"Who's calling, please?"

"It doesn't matter who I am," he barks into the telephone, anger rising. *"Who are you—"* The interrupting response turns his blood to ice as he feels the colour drain from his face.

Slowly, quietly, he replaces the receiver on the base and leans forward, elbows braced on his desk, holding his suddenly pounding head in both hands.

Chapter 46

PC Davies pulls the car into the Peter Street station in Stretford. He gets out of the car and opens the door for Jack to get out.

Jack stares at the young man, chest puffed with undeserved power, as he slowly gets out of the car, sauntering as lazily as he can towards the door.

Davies shoves him forwards roughly. "Get movin'. We haven't got all day." Jack stops, looking over his shoulder. "I'd be careful if I were you, son."

Davies twists Jack's cuffs, pinching his wrists and making him wince. "I said move, and I'm not your son, old man."

"That's no way to treat a prisoner, is it?"

Davies shoves him again, stopping at the back door.

From the corner of his eye, Jack watches as Davies punches in the security numbers to unlock the door, before he's once more shoved by the brassy young constable. He'll get what's coming to him, Jack thinks, as he stumbles forwards into a long, glass-panelled corridor.

Looking through the glass panels, he sees most offices are empty, most pigs haven't made it into work yet. Movement catches his eye, and he looks to see a familiar face. The young girl cleaning the glass as they pass locks eyes with him for a moment before quickly looking away and picking up her duster from the floor.

Jack smiles to himself as he's pushed along into an interview room, where he plops down onto a cold metal chair while Davies stands by the open door, leaning against the door frame.

"I'll be out of here before you know it." He pauses, staring at him. "Son," he adds, condescendingly.

Davies ignores him, only smiling as he turns his head to look out the door.

Returning the smile, Jack closes his eyes and leans against the wall, pretending to be comfortable whilst his wrists throb from the too-tight cuffs at his back.

Liz glances into the open room as she walks by, noting that Jack is sat leaning against the wall with his eyes closed.

PD Davies nods as she walks by – she nods back, continuing down the hall and past the Custody Sergeant. "See you tomorrow, Liz," the sergeant calls out to

her. "Yep, see you tomorrow, Sergeant. Have a good day."

Chapter 47

The door firmly shut behind her, Liz looks around to make sure nobody's looking before she half- walks, half-jogs towards the phone box at the end of the street. She drops a coin in, dialling a number from memory.

"Hello?"

"Barbara, hello. It's Liz. I've just seen Jack – he's been arrested."

"Jack, arrested?" Barbara's voice rises in confused panic. *"Are you sure you're not mistaken?"*

"No, it's definitely Jack." "Did he see you?"

"He did, yes."

"And you're positive it's my Jack." "Yes, positive."

"Where is he being held, then?"

"Peter Street police station in Stretford."

"That's where that Monroe works out of, isn't it?" "It is, yes."

"Right. Thank you for letting me know, Liz. I appreciate you calling me."

"No problem, Barbara. I thought you'd want to know in case they don't let him call you."

"I'll see you Thursday, then?" "Yes, see you Thursday. Bye."

Liz hangs up the phone, looking around again to make sure she isn't being watched. Confident nobody's noticed, she leaves the phone box, wiping her ear with a tissue where the telephone touched it, and continues walking home down Beaumont Terrace.

Chapter 48

Billy blinks against the sun as he walks from his car to the front door of his club. O'Leary's already waiting there for him, as usual. For whatever fault he can find in that lad, lack of punctuality isn't one of them.

"Mornin' Boss." O'Leary holds the door open for Billy, following him in. "Nice mornin', init?"

Billy inhales deeply, relishing the scent of stale tobacco and ale. *"Ah,* nothin' like the smell of a good, old-fashioned strip club, first thing in the morning, *eh,* Feargal?"

O'Leary cringes at the use of his given name. "Could think of better things to smell, boss," he wrinkles his nose at the smell he can never seem to wash off.

"And what would that be, then?" Billy opens the door leading upstairs. "Francine's crotch?"

Watching from the bottom of the stairs, O'Leary's glad Billy can't see him as he walks up the dimly lit passage. "Don't know what you mean, boss."

"She's a good girl," Billy calls over his shoulder. "Don't fuck her about."

"I would never, boss."

Billy rolls his eyes, not believing a single word rolling off O'Leary's silver tongue. Unlocking the door, he pushes it open just as the telephone begins to ring. He closes the distance to the desk in three strides, picking up the receiver.

"Billy here, who is it?" "Billy, it's Barbara."

Billy frowns – it's unusual for Jack's wife to be calling him, especially at this time of the morning. *"Barbara, good morning. What can I do for you?"*

"It's Jack, Billy. He's been arrested. I didn't know who else to call…"

Billy tucks the receiver into his neck, holding it up with his shoulder as he reaches for a pen and notepad. *"It's all right, Barbara. Don't worry, it's probably all a big misunderstanding. Which nick have they taken him to, do you know?"*

"Liz said he's at Stretford, on Peter Street."

"Right, got it. Don't worry, love, I'll take care of it." *"Thank you so much, Billy. I appreciate it."*

"Don't mention it. I'll call you later." "Do you need me to come down there?"

"No, you stay home in case he rings you. I'll get Archie."

"All right, thank you, Billy."

"No worries, Barbara. We'll talk soon." Billy scribbles down 'Stretford' and 'Peter Street' on his notepad before sitting down behind his desk.

"O'Leary!" he shouts, the lad's footsteps quickly sounding on the stairs. *"Yeah, boss?"*

Billy looks up at him as he picks up the phone again. *"Jack's been lifted – the filth might come here. Check about, make sure everything's sweet. Get Francine to give you a hand."*

"Sure thing, boss. What about—"

"Feargal." He stares at him pointedly, gripping the phone. "I need to make this call. Bring my car 'round'."

"Yeah, okay, Boss." O'Leary disappears back down the stairs as Billy dials another number.

"Hello?" The slurred greeting comes from the other end of the line, telling him the man was still in bed.

"Archie, is that you?

Archie clears his throat, and Billy hears the rustling of sheets, the squeezing of old mattress springs. *"Yeah. Yeah, Billy. What is it?"*

"Jack's been lifted." "Ah, shit."

"Yeah, my feelings exactly. Are you dressed?" Billy knows full well Archie isn't dressed.

"Pulling my pants up as we speak, Billy." "Good. I'll pick you up in twenty."

Billy hangs up the phone, rubbing both hands up and down his face. He hates starting the morning off with problems – hasn't even had a cuppa yet. He grumbles as he storms out of his office, slamming the door after him, and lumbers down the stairs.

Downstairs, he sees that Francine is already hard at work, cleaning rags in hand, sleeves rolled up. Good girl, that Francine. He hurries out the door to find O'Leary already has the car ready for him. He's stood by the car, the driver's door open and waiting.

"Thanks, son." He slips behind the wheel and is off before the door slams shut, accelerator pedal pressed to the floor as he spins gravel down the wrong side of the road. Temper flaring at the mess he's being made to clean up this early in the morning, he narrowly avoids colliding with the milk float coming in his direction.

"Shit!" He swerves back onto his own lane, causing the truck to also swerve, crashing into a parked car. Billy watches in his rearview as dozens of crates slide off the back of the float, crashing onto the street in a mess of milk and shattered glass.

Seeing Billy's car disappear around the corner, O'Leary swears under his breath as he quickly runs back inside, ignoring the sea of white flooding down the road — he wants no part of that questioning. He locks the door after him and heads off to help Francine with the cleaning. She's bent over, wiping down a table, her short skirt hiked up and not leaving much to the imagination. If he's lucky, he smiles, he might have time for some of that fucking around Billy warned him against.

Chapter 49

Detective Inspector Doonan bursts into the incident room, walking into a blue haze of cigarette smoke and a mess of constables and detectives milling about, chattering and drinking coffee. Not a single one notices him walk in, all too busy gossiping.

"Right, quiet, please."

The room quiets down, except for a pair of constables deep in conversation at the back of the room.

"I said, quiet," he repeats, more loudly, as everyone turns to look at the chattering constables who quickly stop talking.

"Right. I assume you're all up to speed on yesterday's discovery of two bodies at 64 Kenilworth Road."

Everyone agrees with nods, keeping quiet.

"Good. What some of you might not know, is that our victims are Jack Harrison's kid brother, Graham, and his ex-wife, Valerie. We've got a couple of suspects." He walks up to the board, pointing at a couple of the mugshots pinned up. "Namely, Errol and Tweak."

"Any news on either of them, yet?" PC Mercy Peters asks, downing the last of his coffee. "Not yet," Doonan

tells him. "We have a circulation out to all forces in the north of England.

Hopefully, someone will get a hit on one or both of

them sooner rather than later."

"Any connection with these two and the kid that homeless bloke pulled out of the canal the other day?" Peters flicks ashes from his cigarette in the overflowing ashtray on the table, taking a long drag.

"Can't rule anything out." Doonan walks back to the middle of the room and leans on the desk. "We're still waiting on forensics – we should have their findings today."

A soft knock sounds at the door, and WPC Cooper walks in, handing Doonan a slip of paper. He reads it quietly and gives it back to her with a nod. "Tell him I'll be there in five. Thanks, love."

Cooper nods. "Yes, sir." She walks back out, the rest of the officers watching her leave and salivating at the sway of her hips in those uniform trousers.

"Yes, up here, you bunch of pervs," Doonan grumbles at them. "Right. I want you to focus on Errol Tansey our main suspect for the Kenilworth double murder. I want you all out there, shaking trees, putin' pressure on your snouts, knocking shops, bookies, the lot. Let's find this bastard."

"What about this Tweak fella?" Peters asks as everyone stands.

"Forget Tweak for now." Doonan looks at him, pointedly. "Right," he tells the room. "You lot, let's get to work. Peters, my office, now."

Peters follows him across the hall to his office as the rest of the constables disperse. "What is it, boss?

Doonan sits behind his desk, writing an address on a slip of paper and handing it to Peters. "You're going on a little field trip to Liverpool."

Peters takes the slip, frowning as he looks at the address.

"What's in Liverpool?" "Tweak's head."

Peter's own head snaps up from the note to catch Doonan's eyes. "His head, boss?"

"Yep." Doonan nods. "Got delivered to someone called Pete, a relation of Errol's, yesterday. Works security at the docks – address is on the slip." He pointed to the paper Peters is holding. "We're hoping the person who delivered it might have an inkling Errol may be hiding out at the docks. Get there as fast as you can, have a nosey 'round the docs, ask a few questions. If Errol's been there or is still there, someone's bound to have seen or heard something."

Peters nods, slipping the paper into his trouser pocket. "Right. If he's there, what do you want me to do?"

"Ring me." "Right. Is that it?"

"One more thing" – Doonan looked at him – "pick up the head on your way back from Port. I'll ring Liverpool police and let them know you're coming."

"Got it."

Doonan watches Mercy leave the office, closing the door after him. He pulls his pager from his pocket, punching in a quick message as he stands, walking to the window behind his desk and looking out onto the street below.

Chapter 50

Back in Ireland, Joseph Brayden is sat having his breakfast with his family. The long, sixteen-seater dining room table gleams with fresh lemon polish and is laden with bowls of fresh fruit and pastries. Sunlight is beaming through crystal clear windows, the ocean sparkling in the distance.

He takes a sip of tea as he watches his children pick at the warm biscuits and sausages, thinking of how perfect his life is.

A vibration in his pocket brings him back to the present, and a wide smile spreads across his face as he reads the message on the pager.

"Good news, love?"

He raises his smile up to Louise, the morning sun catching her fiery hair as she returns his smile, plucking a juicy strawberry from the bowl in front of them.

"Aye, quite good, love. Things are moving in the right direction." He stands, bending forwards and dropping a kiss on her offered lips. "You'll have to excuse me – I need to make a call."

Chapter 51

O'Leary has Francine pinned between him and the bar, hands up her jumper, tongue down her throat – the cleaning rags sitting forgotten on top of the bar.

Francine pulls away slightly, turning her head to the side. "Feargal, Billy's phone is ringing upstairs."

He buries his face in the crook of her neck, nipping at her vanilla-scented skin. "Let it ring, love. I'm not Billy's keeper." He lowers his hands from her breasts, reaching round back and lifting her skirt, hooking his thumbs in the waist of her knickers and pulling them down an inch as she grinds up against him, then stops again.

"I can't concentrate with that thing ringing, Feargal. It's not stopped for five minutes," she whines.

O'Leary huffs, pulling away. "For fuck's sake, Francine. Look at me." He points down to the bulge in his pants, then pushes it against her, making her whimper in pleasure.

She pushes him away as he dives for her neck again. "Go answer the phone, then you can have your way with me." She reaches down, squeezing his bulge firmly as she licks her lips seductively. "Hurry up." She runs her fingers through his hair, bringing her knee up slightly between his legs until he groans.

"Tease." He grins, running hell for leather up the

stairs to Billy's office. He barges in, lunging for the phone that's still ringing off the hook.

"Hello," he barks, out of breath.

"Where's Billy?"

"Fuck me, Willis. What do you want? Billy's not here, he had to go out."

"Where's he gone to?" *"Jack got lifted, why—"*

"Yeah, I know that. I need to tell him something." *"Tell him what?"*

"Jack's kid brother, Graham—he's been murdered. And his ex-wife, Valerie. I've got his nephew George here at the home."

"You're fucking joking! Does Jack know?" *"Doubt it. Need to get to Billy first."*

"Shit. Right—he's gone to pick up Archie. If I hurry, we can catch him there. I'm on my way now." O'Leary slams the phone down and runs back down the stairs, heading straight for the door.

"Where you going?" Francine calls out to him.

He turns back, the mood killed. *"I need to go, love. Emergency. Lock up and don't let anyone in until I get back."*

"For fuck's sake." She walks towards the door as he opens it. "Okay, but hurry back, yeah?" She locks the door after him, watching from the window as he runs to his orange Ford Capri.

He turns right, having to go the long way round due to the road to the left being closed off to clean up the sea of milk and glass. She watches as he speeds down the road until he disappears around the corner.

Aigburth Liverpool

Father Willis slams the phone down, running both hands through his hair and leaving it in a wild mess. This is the last thing he needs, as he stands and rushes out his office door, slamming it shut behind him. He takes off down the hallway at a full run, not stopping until he gets to his Zephyr parked in the yard.

Not bothering with the safety belt, he guns the engine down the road, tyres squealing as he rounds the bend, swerving like a drunken man as he passes Gina and George walking on the pavement.

"This life's more trouble than it's worth," he growls to himself as he takes the next bend on two wheels.

Chapter 52

All is quiet on Kenilworth Road as Errol slinks towards the house. Nosy crowds have long left, as have the police cars and forensics vans. All that's left is the yellow police tape blocking off the front door.

Errol moves quickly, quietly, careful to avoid any windows as he hurries past Fred and Annie's window. The curtains are drawn, but he can't take any chances of being seen. "Nosy fuckers," he mumbles under his breath as he ducks, staying close to the wall.

He manages to make it to the alley without being seen, and climbs over the wall of the back garden, landing hard on a patch of bramble.

He swears under his breath as he shakes the thorns from his pants and makes his way to the kitchen door. It's taped off as well, but nobody's going to see him back here. It doesn't take much to move it out of the way, but he does it carefully. Any noise and those pricks next door will be calling the pigs again.

Inside, he listens to make sure nobody's waiting to ambush him – there are no sounds, he makes his way slowly to the hallway, taking in the carnage he left behind.

The only proof left of his crimes are the pools of dried blood covering nearly every inch of the floor in the entrance, and a long, dark rusty trail going down the wall from where the coat hook has been removed, to the baseboard.

"They even scraped off the pile of fur." He chuckles to himself as he steps over the dried puddle at the bottom of the stairs, taking them two at a time up to the attic. In George's room, the wardrobe is pulled away from the wall, revealing a little door behind it.

"So that's where you'd hide away, you sneaky little fuck."

He pulls the wardrobe aside completely, ripping the little hatch right off its hinges. The space is much too small for him to fit through, so he flashes a torch down the tight corridor under the chimney down to where George's safe space was tucked in, at the end. "Little fuck," he repeats through his teeth as he flips off the torch and goes back down to the second floor.

He stops dead when he enters his bedroom, surveying the mess the pigs left behind. Every drawer has been pulled out and overturned, clothing strewn all over the floor. They've even pulled the piss-stained mattress off the bed – it's stood up, leaning against the chimney breast, covering the old, broken fireplace.

Stepping over piles of clothes, Errol shoves the mattress aside, laying it onto the mess on the floor.

Kneeling, he reaches a hand up into the chimney, feeling around and praying the nosy pigs didn't look up there.

He smiles when his fingers grip a cloth-covered bundle. "Jackpot." He pulls it out and lays it open on the stained mattress, untying the dirty rag he's got wrapped around his treasure.

His smile grows even wider when he picks up the loaded revolver and a rolled-up bundle of ten-pound notes. He stands, tucking the revolver down the front of his pants, covered up with his shirt. "Fucking wankers couldn't find their own arseholes with a map."

He stuffs the money into his pocket and leaves the room, heading down the stairs. "Right, me boyo. Let's find out where they're hiding you and my diamond."

He sneaks back out the same way he came in, not bothering to put the kitchen door back where it was. He won't be coming back here, anyway.

Chapter 53

Walking down the familiar towpath she could walk blindfolded, Gina holds George's hand tightly as they make their way towards John's tent.

George pulls Gina to the edge so he can look down at the water. He stares at his rippled reflection as a barge goes by, sending small waves against the edge of the towpath. When the waves settle, he steps back, lifting Raggy up to his face, staring intently at him.

"George." Gina's voice is soft. "Are you okay?"

George looks at his feet, clad in tattered shoes. He shakes his head. "Do you want to talk about it?" she asks gently.

He shakes his head again, lower lip quivering. "Okay, that's all right. You don't have to if you don't want to. I know all about secrets." She pauses, looking at the doll's stitched face. "What about Raggy, how is he feeling? Does he want to talk today?"

George turns Raggy to face Gina, using his fingers behind the doll's head to make him nod.

Gina crouches down beside George so she can be at face level with Raggy. Looking at the doll instead of George, she speaks to it as though it's a real person. "What happened at the house, Raggy?

George brings Raggy up in front of his face, hiding

behind him. "A nasty man killed George's dog, then he hurt his mummy and daddy, and they went to be with Jesus."

Gina startles at the strange, growling voice that comes from the small boy, but she smiles when he lowers the doll and grabs her hand. She squeezes it. He gives her a small smile in return. She looks down at the doll. "Thank you for telling me, Raggy. I hope the police find the nasty man and lock him up."

She turns her eyes to George. "Do you want to meet my friend?" George nods, his smile growing a little.

"C'mon, he lives this way."

They walk for a few more minutes before coming to a small encampment with a tent. "John," Gina calls out. "John, you in?"

The big man's head pops out of the tent, a big grin on his face for his little friend. "Hi, Gina." George squeezes Gina's hand in a vice grip, hiding behind her back.

"Oh, sorry little man, I didn't mean to startle you. I'm not used to Gina bringing company."

"It's okay, George," Gina coaxes softly. "John's my friend. He's a nice man, you'll like him, promise."

He pokes his head out a little from behind Gina, eyeing John suspiciously. John winks at Gina, then sticks dirty fingers in his mouth, pulling the corners out and making a funny face, flashing tobacco-stained teeth and wiggling his tongue.

George giggles and comes out from behind Gina, still sticking close to her side, not letting go of her hand.

John points to Raggy, clutched close to George's

chest. "Who's your little mate, son?"

"This is Raggy doll." George turns Raggy to face John.

"I see." John nods, smiling. "Pleasure to meet you, Mister Raggy."

George looks down at Raggy and back to John. "He says hello, John."

"Well, ain't that somethin'?" He flashes a yellow smile. "Is he hungry?" John asks George. "I've got a bit of chocolate if he fancies some."

George doesn't need to check with Raggy this time; he just nods vigorously, his smile widening. "Raggy likes chocolate a lot."

"Ah, that's what I figured." John winks at him as he pulls out a piece of Cadbury chocolate from his bag, breaking off two squares. "Here you go, lad." He handed the pieces to George. "One for you, and one for your little mate."

"Thanks." George smiles as he takes the pieces, stuffing one into his mouth straight away, whilst pretending to feed the other to Raggy.

"I don't think Raggy's very hungry right now, George. Why don't you wrap it up and he can have it later?"

George nods, accepting the small piece of foil John hands him and wrapping it around the tiny square of chocolate before dropping it in his pocket.

John leans back on his elbow, looking up at Gina. "To what do I owe the pleasure then, young lady? Just out for a stroll?"

"I wanted George to meet you." She pauses, smiling down at George, then hesitates for a moment. "And, *uh...*"

"And what, love?" A strange hardness fills her eyes. A determination, maybe fear? John isn't sure – the girl can be a bit hard to read.

"And ask you for a favour."

He pushes himself up to standing, getting out of the tent. "Go on, then?"

She lifts her face up to him. "I might need a way out in a couple weeks." She grips George's hand tightly as he turns to look at another barge going by on the canal. "They're up to sommat."

"Planning somethin'?" John frowns, not liking the sound of it.

Gina nods slightly. "Yeah. I heard Willis tell Reid – they're savin' me for sommat special." She puts her free arm 'round her waist as she glances quickly at the ground then back up to John. "A lot of the older girls are leaving next week. They're shippin' them off to some sort of club in Leeds. I don't know what they want me for, and I don't want to, but..."

She looks away, averting her eyes. "There was a man walked out of Jill's room this mornin' – she was cryin' and her nighty was lifted."

John feels the blood burning in his veins. "How old is Jill?"

"Fourteen."

Gina turns her face back up to him and she suddenly looks every bit the ten-year-old lass that she is. "Don't worry." He kneels down, looking into her eyes. "I'll speak with a mate of mine in Newcastle – see if he can help us. But it'll take some money."

Gina nods. "I'll see what I can find. Few silver candlesticks knockin' about. They won't miss 'em." She looks down when George tugs on her hand.

"I don't want you to go," he whispers, his eyes large and pleading.

"Don't worry, George." She smiles down at him. "I won't ever leave you behind, promise. I promised I would take care of you, didn't I?"

George returns her smile and throws his arms around her waist, hugging her tightly. "We should get back," she tells John. "George, say bye-bye to Uncle John."

"Bye-bye, Uncle John," he responds timidly.

"See you tomorrow, then," Gina tells John as she turns, pulling George after her. "I'll try and bring something."

"You be careful, lass. Keep your eyes open and your wits about you." He watches the children walk back down the towpath until they disappear 'round the corner, then makes his way to the telephone box at the end of the path.

Chapter 54

The Custody Sergeant watches Monroe walk in about an hour after Davies. "What room is Jack Harrison in?"

The sergeant follows him down the hall. "Room seven. Can I help you?"

"No, thanks. Just watch." He walks into the room, closing the door after them, noting that PC Davies is stood leaning against the wall by the door.

Jack opens his eyes from where he's leaning against the wall, staring a hole into Monroe's head. "I want my phone call."

Monroe sighs patiently, turning to the sergeant. "Get me a cup of tea, will you, lad?"

The sergeant looks from Monroe to Jack, then back again, nodding slightly. "Okay." He hates being patronised just because he's younger, but his dad always told him it's better to pick your battles, and this isn't his interrogation. Seething quietly, he leaves the room, closing the door softly as Monroe turns back to Jack with a smile on his face.

"I've got you bang to rights this time, Jack." He motions to the table, prompting Jack to return to his seat. "There's blood all over the place, and when we match it to

Tweak, you're going down, for a long time." He slowly walks around the table to stand behind Jack, Davies watching on.

"The only person going down will be your missus, on my cock, when I get released later—"

Munroe's fist cracks against the back of Jack's skull, sending him crashing into the table, then sprawling onto the tile floor face first with a grunt. He doesn't give him the chance to get up before landing his foot hard into the man's stomach.

Jack empties the contents of his stomach all over the floor and the front of his shirt as he struggles to get back up onto his knees. "You've always been a prick, Monroe, but you've just crossed the line this time, pal."

The sergeant walks back in with a steaming cup of tea, just as Monroe is looking to land another punch to Jack's already bruising, vomit-covered face. "What the hell is going on here?" He puts the cup on the table, scowling at the scene and looking to Monroe for answers.

Monroe flushes. "He went for me, so I hit him," he answers, matter-of-factly.

"His hands are cuffed behind his back, Monroe. What did he do – try to bite your fuckin' nose off?"

"No, he tried to headbutt me. Isn't that true, Davies?"

Davies nods, but the sergeant pays him no mind as he looks down to where Jack is kneeling, looking rather dazed. "Is this true, sir?"

Jack scowls up at him. "I was sat on that chair." He motions with his throbbing head. "Kinda hard to headbutt someone whilst sitting down, don't you think?"

The sergeant looks at Davies, a deep frown creasing his brow. "Davies, go get a cup of tea."

Davies opens his mouth to argue, but the look on the sergeant's face makes him think better of it. "Yes, sir." He leaves the room, flashing Monroe a glance.

"Monroe, I suggest you leave this to me." He grabs a hold of Jack's arm, helping him up to his feet.

"I don't think so," Monroe growls. "Go do your own job – I'm questioning my suspect."

"Not like this, you're not." He leads Jack to the door. "We do things by the book here. Until the doc's seen 'im and he's properly booked in, you ain't talking to him."

He pulls the door open. "Now, fuck off, and let me do my job," he frowns down at Monroe's bloody knuckles in disgust. "And clean yourself up." He walks out, leading a quietly grinning Jack down the hall to the doctor's room.

Chapter 55

Archie's stood on the curb, waiting when Billy pulls up. He walks up to the door, but stops short, hand on the handle, as another car comes barrelling towards them, blaring on the horn.

His temper already at the end of its rope, Billy gets out of the car and pops the boot, pulling out a wooden cricket bat. Both men stand behind the car as they watch the speeding Zephyr scratch to a halt about sixty feet up the road.

Billy swears under his breath when he sees Father Willis get out of the car and half-jog towards them. He tosses the cricket bat back into the boot and slams it shut, turning to scowl at Willis as he walks up, breathless.

"What the fuck you playin' at, Willis? You nearly got snotted, then." He looms, fists on his hips, waiting for the man to answer.

"Sorry." Willis bends forward, trying to catch his breath. "I needed to tell you before you go see Jack."

"Tell me what?"

The roaring of another engine has all three men turning as a flash of orange comes careening 'round the corner sideways, speeding towards them. Billy swears when O'Leary sends gravel flying as he comes to a hard stop a few feet away.

"Fuck me, the whacky races have come to town," he growls. "What the fuck are you doing here?" he asks as O'Leary comes out of the car. "I told you—"

"I didn't think Willis would make it in time." O'Leary interrupts him. "Graham, Jack's brother, he's been killed by Errol."

Billy's eyebrows shoot up as he turns to Willis, his fists dropping from his hips. "Is this true?" Willis nods, still catching his breath. "Yeah, couple nights ago. Police've been keepin' it on the quiet-like. Jack doesn't know." He takes another breath before continuing. "Social Services brought Jack's nephew to me a couple days ago – kid's proper fucked up. Was in the house and left to his own devices with his dead mum and dad for a while before they found 'im."

"Billy," Archie speaks up. "I need to get into the police station straight away."

Billy rubs his hands over his face, trying to take it all in. Things just keep getting worse, don't they? "Right. O'Leary, back to the club, and don't breathe a word of this. It's business as usual."

"Got it, boss."

O'Leary gets back in his car as Billy turns to Willis. "You make sure that kid's properly looked after – keep them fuckin' nonces away from him."

"Don't worry," Willis tells him. "He's safe. Police are watching the place – it's just us and the kids there."

"Yeah, that's what worries me, you sick fuck. It's your lot I'm worried about – you make sure no grubby hands get on that boy, understood?"

216

Willis nods, his face darkening from the rushing blood, as he watches Billy and Archie get in the car. He barely moves out of the way in time and nearly has his foot crushed as Billy turns the car out and speeds off.

Chapter 56

Errol is lying in wait. It didn't take much to find Glynis Tyler – he just had to follow her to Davey Hulme, Manchester, to her fancy little terraced house. Well-to-do people make him sick, he thinks, as he watches from the outside toilet in her backyard.

He smiles as he sees her come out the kitchen door holding a bag of potato peelings. She's humming softly as she walks up to the bins next to the toilet – he waits until her back is turned and jumps out.

The potato peels scatter to the ground as she's startled. Eyes landing on his, she screams and runs back towards the house, but Errol grabs a fist full of her hair and yanks her back against him, pressing the blade of his pocketknife to her throat.

"Be quiet, you little bitch, or I'll cut your tits off."

Glynis cuts her scream short as tears flow down her cheeks and Errol marches her back inside. Through the kitchen door, she smashes her leg on the front of the cooker, crying out in pain.

"I told you to be quiet." He shoves her down into a kitchen chair as he slams the door closed with his foot, then turns the lock. "Don't move."

He rummages through the kitchen drawers until he finds a roll of cooking twine. Dragging her back up off the chair and down onto the floor. Pulling her hands up over her head, he wraps the twine around her wrists and ties her to the cooker door handle, her back pressed to the door. Tossing the rest of it aside, he leans into her, and she flinches back, bracing for the blow she's sure is coming. But instead, he turns one of the cooker knobs, the heat quickly beginning to rise. She tries to pull away, but he's secured her too firmly.

He presses his face in close to hers – she gags at his rank breath. "I'm gonna ask you some questions, and you're gonna answer them. Understood? If I think you're lyin', I'm gonna turn up the heat in more ways than one." She whimpers, nodding as she tries to pull her face away from his, but he grabs her by the hair again, holding her firm.

"You took a kid away from my house yesterday, didn't ya?" She nods, squirming as she feels it getting hotter.

"Where did you take him?

"The children's home." She sniffs, unable to stop the tears. "Which one?" he barks. "There are quite a few."

"F-Father Willis."

Letting go of her hair, he turns and paces the small kitchen, a deep scowl on his face. Glynis' eyes grow wide as the oven as it keeps getting even hotter.

"Any of Jack's men there?"

She shakes her head. "I don't know, I only dropped him off. I didn't go inside."

He turns back to her. "You must've been back to check on him, you dumb bitch. You're lying!" He turns the heat up higher.

"P-please, I don't know! Willis told me not to tell anyone, not even Jack."

"I don't think he knows anything. P-please, let me go, I'm burning!"

"Anything else I should know?"

She feels her back blistering as sweat pours down her face, mixing with the tears as a sob bubbles out. "P- police. There are police w-watching the home. P-please, let me go! I won't say a word, please! I promise!"

Errol stares at her silently, walking slowly to the sink to pick up the tea towel draped over the edge of the counter. He takes his time walking back to her as she squirms from the burning pain in her back, turning the heat off. He wipes the sweat and tears from her face with the towel.

"Didn't wanna do that, love, but I had no choice. You can understand that, eh?" She tries to smile, but it doesn't quite work.

Errol walks back to the refrigerator, tossing the tea towel onto the stove in a heap. He pulls out a pint of milk, chugging it down until it's empty as he stares at her over the glass bottle, then slaps it down on the counter hard and wipes his mouth with the back of his hand, never taking his eyes off her.

"Sorry, love. Forgot my manners. D'you want a drink?" Glynis nods, not trusting her voice.

He fills a tumbler with cold water from the sink and kneels in front of her, bringing it up to her lips, tipping the water into her mouth and then placing it on the counter. He takes the tea towel, dabs at her forehead. "If I let you know, you promise you won't tell anyone I was here?"

Glynis nods vehemently, fresh tears pouring down her cheeks. "I need to hear you swear it."

She takes a shaky breath. "I swear to Almighty God, I will not say a word to anyone."

A wide smile spreads on Errol's face, so she tries to return it, but then he buries his fist violently into her stomach, stealing the breath from her lungs. While she fights for air, he shoves the soiled tea towel into her mouth and reaches up, turning the knob on high as he stares into her eyes.

"Sorry, love. I don't believe in God."

Muffled cries through the towel barely reach his ears as he walks out the door, the cooker door burning through cloth and flesh.

Chapter 57

"I think you'd better wait in the car, pal," Archie tells Billy as they pull up outside the police station.

"Yeah, all right." Billy nods, waiting for Archie to get out. "I'll park 'round the corner." He watches until Archie disappears inside the station before moving the car around to the far side, out of the street. He turns off the ignition and pulls out a newspaper – he's not planning on reading it, but it won't look as suspicious, should anyone spot him.

Marching up to the front desk, Archie gives the woman a hard look. "I'm Archibald Devenney. I'm here to see my client." He leans in, making a show of staring at the woman's nametag. "Maureen."

"What's your client's name?" Maureen asks him. "Jack Harrison's his name."

She pulls out her ledger, scanning down the list. "When was he brought in?"

"About an hour ago."

She shakes her head as her painted fingertip makes it down to the bottom of the list. "Sorry, nobody brought in today called Jack Harrison."

Archie leans forward, folding an arm on the counter and speaking slowly. "I think you need to check again, love."

She lifts her chin defiantly. "I've been on since

half five. There's no Jack Harrison been brought into this station."

Archie takes a deep, dramatic breath, drops his briefcase onto the counter with a clang and leans in closer, staring directly at her, unblinking. "Right, love. I know he was brought in no more than an hour ago. Now, toddle off and find out where he is."

Maureen's perfectly plucked brows arch up high on her wide forehead. "Excuse me, sir, but nobody talks to me like that."

"Well, they do now," he retorts. "C'mon, then. Be a good girl, do as you're told." Maureen's mouth opens in shocked indignation, her eyes wide. "Well, I never—"

"Archie Devenney, as I live and breathe."

Archie turns at the familiar voice, to see PC Monroe walking up to him. "What are you doing here?"

"Did you hear what he said to me?" Maureen whines behind them.

"Yes, love," Monroe says to her patronisingly. "Go and make a brew. I'll deal with this."

She huffs, muttering under her breath as she stalks out of the room, slamming the door behind her.

Monroe turns back to Archie, shaking his head with a half grin on his face as though they've shared a joke over a stupid woman. "What can I do for you, then, Archie?"

Archie isn't laughing. "That's Mr Devenney to you, Officer. And you know right well why I'm here. Jack Harrison."

Monroe flinches at the slap down. "Sorry, *Mr*

223

Devenney, Jack Harrison isn't available at the minute. He's being looked after by the doctor."

Archie picks up his briefcase from the counter, eyebrows raised. "Why's he seeing the doctor? What's happened to him?"

"He slipped while resisting arrest. Banged his head. He'll live."

"I need to be in a room with him, now," Archie growls.

Monroe stares at Archie quietly for a moment, as though trying to decide whether he's a threat or not.

"Wait here," he tells him. "I'll get an officer to take you to the custody suite, soon as the doc's finished looking him over."

Monroe walks off before Archie has a chance to argue, so he just sits in one of the cracked vinyl chairs behind him, grumbling. He pulls a manilla folder from his briefcase, flipping through papers as he waits.

At one point, he looks up to see Maureen has returned to her desk. He chuckles when she makes an obvious point to ignore him.

"Mr Devenney?"

He looks up to see an officer approaching. "Yeah, that's me." He stands. "Follow me, please."

Archie follows the man into a sparsely furnished room with a metal table and two chairs. "Wait here, your client will be brought in."

He nods as the officer leaves, and sits on one of the chairs, dropping his briefcase on the table.

Within minutes, the door opens and another officer

escorts Jack into the room.

"Archie," Jack smiles, walking up to him and pulling him into a hug. "Am I ever glad to see you, pal. Get me the fuck out of this shithole."

Archie thumps his back before pulling away. "Let's see what they've got on your first. Have a seat." He looks up at the officer. "Thank you, officer. Could we have some tea?"

The officer nods. "You got it, sir. I'll be a minute." He walks out, closing and locking the door behind him.

Archie turns back to Jack who's now sat in the other chair. "What the fuck happened, Jack?"

Jack throws both hands up in the air, shaking his head. "Fucked if I know, mate. Jimmy comes running in sayin' the filth's on the way down the lane, the next thing I know, Monroe's reading me my rights and he's got me cuffed and thrown in the back of a car. Busted up my gate, arrested my workers, the lot."

Archie frowns, looking at the door and back to Jack. "He must've charged you with somethin' if he read you your rights."

"He did, yeah." Jack nods. "Suspicion of murder, he says."

Archie exclaims. "Whose?"

"Murder, yeah. Tweaks. Monroe says an eyewitness called them, told them I killed him in the builder's yard."

"Somebody called them?"

Jack sighs. "That's what he said, yeah. Thought he was having me on at first, then he cuffed me."

Archie shakes his head. "They can't arrest you based

225

on an anonymous call, mate. They need corroboration."

"Is loads of blood corroboration enough?" "What'd you mean?"

"They found blood stains in the yard. S.O.C.O. was on the way when they dragged me out of there. Oh, and so it goes, Tweak's head showed up in a box in Liverpool for some reason."

"Blood stains in a builder's yard doesn't sound so uncommon – could be anyone's. Who's to say Tweak didn't cut himself?"

Jack rolls his eyes at Archie, leaning back in his chair with a loud exhale. "Quite a *lot* of blood stains, Archie.

He taps his finger on the desk, thinking. "Right. Okay, listen to me, Jack. Unless they can physically put you at the scene of the crime, or this supposed witness comes

forwards and identifies you openly; they haven't got a pot to piss in. Just hang on a minute, sit tight."

Jack looks at Archie with his head tilted, rolling his eyes. "Funny, that. What else am I supposed to fucking do?"

"Sorry." Archie grins as he stands, banging on the door.

The officer who had escorted him unlocks the door. "All done, then?"

"Not quite," Archie tells him. "I need to speak with Monroe, immediately."

"Right, follow me." Archie follows him out and waits as he locks the door. "This way, sir."

The officer leads Archie down a long hallway, past several closed doors. When they get farther down, Monroe can be seen through an open door facing the hallway. He's leaned back in his chair with his feet up on the desk, the telephone cradled over his shoulder.

He catches Archie's cold stare over the officer's shoulder. "I'll call you back," he says into the telephone, quickly hanging up as they enter his office. The officer nods at him and leaves as Monroe shuts the door. "Have a seat, Archie." He drops the privacy blinds and returns to his own chair. "What can I do for you, then?"

"First things first." Archie sits. "Why hasn't Jack been told his brother's dead?" Monroe doesn't flinch. "We're still collecting evidence from the crime scene."

"That's bollocks, Monroe, and you know it. Keep your fairy tales for whatever gullible sod gonna believe them – that ain't me. What are you up to?"

"We're trying to catch the killer, *Mr Devenney*. Jack would just muddy things up and complicate it."

"How would Jack knowing his brother's dead complicate it?"

"You know exactly how," Monroe barks.

Archie shakes his head. "No. He's got every right to know, and you know it – you should've told him straight away. You need to tell him before he leaves here. If you don't, I will, and I won't be blamed for the fallout it causes."

"Don't come marchin' in here thinking you can tell me how to do my job, Devenney. Don't work that way."

"Someone needs to," Archie tells him, which earns him a dagger's stare from Monroe.

"Where's George? Is he okay?"

"Kid's all right, he's in a safe place. Under police watch until Errol's found."

Archie leans back in his chair, a half-grin wrinkling his cheek. *"Ahh* and there it is, then. Errol. It's all fitting now, innit? You need to get your hands on him before Jack does so you can bribe him to roll on his mate with the promise of a reduced sentence – that about the gist of it? Clever, that."

"There you go makin' assumptions and an arse of yourself in the process." Monroe spits. "We did it to protect George – he's the only witness."

"Bollocks!" Archie sits up in his chair, pointing an accusing finger at Monroe. "You know as well as I do, the only evidence you have is a bloody head that's turned up in Liverpool. In case you can't read a map, I can tell you that's miles from Jack's yard."

"We found—" Monroe starts but is immediately interrupted.

"Yeah, you found blood, I know. Blood at a builder's yard, shocker, eh? Even if it's Tweak's blood, he works for Jack and could easily have cut himself. And besides that, there are twenty- plus employees with a key to the gate – seems to me you're narrowing down your list of suspects without a motive."

"We've an eyewitness who saw him commit the crime."

"I'd like to see this witness's statement."

Monroe stares at him, unsure what to say. "Figures. You don't have one, do ya?" "He, *uh,* rang it in."

"He rang it in. I bet you didn't even get a name, did

you?" Archie stands, shaking his head. "Stop pissin' about, Monroe. You've got a man in custody on bogus charges with no evidence to speak of. You've beat the shit out of him – and don't even try to deny it, I ain't daft – you've busted up his gates, locked up his workers,

all on the word of some ghost witness. I'm walking out of here with my client, and there's shit you can do to stop me. This is a fishin' expedition. He needs to be grieving his dead brother and takin' care of that boy."

Monroe stares at him hard, knowing full well he doesn't have a shot at winning this argument. "Right, I hear you. Now fuck off. You'll both be back here at nine tomorrow morning." He stands and walks to the door.

"We'll be here." Archie follows Monroe to the door, preceding him out. "But now you're gonna tell him his brother's dead. Tell him I'm waitin' for him outside. You've got ten minutes."

He stalks off down the hallway towards the door, grinning as he hears Monroe slamming the door behind him.

Chapter 58

The sun is starting to set as Errol creeps about through the bushes near the children's home. He's glad he had the foresight to grab a few clothes back at the house.

He pulls the black hood up over to cover his face as he sneaks past a pair of pigs sat in their car chatting' and sipping on tea from a canteen. They're so enthralled in their own conversation they aren't paying attention to anyone else. "Plastic coppers." Errol chuckles under his breath as he hops over the wall of the home without being seen.

Scuttling across the grass, he tucks himself in between bins under the fire escape, leaning against the wall whilst he waits for night to fall. He can hear the clinking of dishes inside; his stomach reminds him how hungry he is.

Gina keeps her eyes on Father Reid and the two strange men on either side of him as she sits at the dining table waiting for supper, George at her side.

"Right, children." Father Reid scans the room. "All stand for prayer."

Echoes of chairs scraping against the floor are the only sounds that fill the room as the children obey silently. George still sticks close to Gina, gripping Raggy tightly.

Gina flinches as one of the men beside Reid motions towards her and leans in to speak in the priest's ear, the latter nodding at whatever he's heard.

"Bless us, oh God. Bless our food and our drink. Since You redeemed us so dearly and delivered us from evil, as You gave us a share in this food, so may You give us a share in eternal life. Amen."

"Amen," the children all reply in monotone unison. Father Reid crooks a finger at Gina, calling her over.

George grabs her hand and walks over with her, unwilling to be any distance away from her.

"When George is asleep, you're to come to my office straight away," he tells her, looking down his nose at her.

"What for?" She lifts her chin defiantly. "I've done nothing wrong, and I've been told not to leave George alone."

"Do as you're told, girl," he hisses, gripping his napkin in a white-knuckled fist. "Father Willis is away until tomorrow, so I'm in charge until then." His smile, matched perfectly by the man next to him, holds no humour, sending chills rippling down Gina's spine.

She nods slightly at Reid, ignoring the man completely as she takes George's hand and pulls him back to the table. "C'mon, George. Let's go eat."

They do so silently, the only sounds are the occasional clinking of forks on plates, and the murmur of the men's conversation with Reid and the other priests sitting around the main table. When their plates are empty, Gina sneaks a handful of biscuits from the basket on the table stuffing them into her pockets, whispering down to George so only he can hear. "Let's go, George. We need to leave, now. The bad men are coming."

He looks up at her, his head bent close and matching her quiet tone. "It's okay, Gina." He brings up Raggy between them. "Raggy won't let the bad men hurt us. Isn't that right, Raggy?" He moves the doll's head in a nod with his fingers. "See?"

She smiles, taking his hand as they slide off the chairs. "Come." They run up the stairs in a commotion of other children doing the same, nobody wanting to stick around with the priests and the men for a minute longer than they need to.

They make it into Gina's room quickly; she shuts the door behind them. "We need to hurry, George," she whispers. "We really need to get out of here, I—"

A click sounds behind her, cutting off her words as Father Reid turns the key in the lock. "I'm not as stupid as you think, girl." He laughs. "I'll be back for you later."

She runs to the door, pounding and kicking at it as she turns and shakes at the knob, to no avail. "Let us out, you can't lock us in here!" She gives a final kick with everything she's got as she hears him laughing down the hall.

Turning, she sees George cowering in the corner by the bed, face buried into Raggy. "Oh, George." She runs to him, kneeling. "George, I'm so sorry. I didn't mean to scare you. Look at me."

He lifts his head, red cheeks wet from the tears, sniffing loudly.

"I'm sorry, George, I'm sorry." She sits beside him in the corner, pulling him close to her side. "Nobody will ever hurt you again, that's a promise. Me and you, we're leaving this place tonight, and we're never coming back."

Chapter 59

"It's gonna break him, this," Billy says as Archie gets in the car. "I hope we find Errol before the cops do."

Archie lifts up a hand, shaking his head. "Not in front of me, Billy. I can't know. Don't wanna know." He nods towards Jack who's just come out the door. "You can talk about it later."

"*Ah,* fuck," Billy whispers as they see Jack crumble onto a bench and bend forward, head hanging between his knees, shoulders heaving from the wracking sobs.

"Give him a minute." Archie advises as Billy goes to get out of the car. After nearly five minutes when Jack doesn't appear to be in any hurry to move, Billy gets out and walks over to him, draping an arm over his back.

Jack looks up from his hands, face red and wet from crying, searching Billy's eyes. "Did you know?" His voice is hoarse, raw.

Billy nods slightly. "Found out just before we got here. Willis met me at Archie's place as I went to pick him up."

A deep frown creases Jack's brow. "Willis. How did he find out?"

"George is there, at the children's home, he's been there for a couple of days. Apparently, the place is under police watch."

Jack's grief turns into burning rage in an instant as he pushes to his feet, glaring. "A couple of fucking days!" he growls. "Why didn't he tell me?"

Billy stands, putting a hand on Jack's shoulder. "Jack, c'mon. Let's get you back to my place. Get you cleaned up, have a pint, cool your head a bit."

Jack shrugs off Billy's hand as Archie walks up to them, motioning to the station at their back and keeping his voice low. "Jack, we've got an audience, mate. Let's be off, right?"

Jack turns to see a small crowd of uniforms gathered outside the entrance, watching them as though they're the day's attraction. "What the fuck are you smiling at, you cunts?" he growls at them as Archie grabs his arm, stopping him from running back there.

"Jack—"

I'm gonna fuckin' kill them smug cunts. Every fucking one of them." He tries to pull away from Archie, but Billy gets behind him and stops him.

"No, you're not, and you're gonna keep your voice down or they'll have the cuffs back on you for threatening police officers. Use your head, mate." He pushes him forwards towards the waiting car. "Let's go back to mine, we'll get this all sorted."

They manage to get Jack to the car; Archie starts driving off just as Billy slams the door after Jack, making him run to get into the passenger seat.

"Laugh now you cunts, you won't be laughin' later!" Jack shouts through the back window as they drive off. He turns and falls into a sitting position, staring at Archie's eyes in the rearview mirror. "I want everyone looking for Errol. Put a price on him, but I want him alive—"

"Easy, Jack. You can't be saying all that shit in front of me." Archie interrupts his rant. "Fuck off, Archie," Jack barks. "You know what we do."

"I do, yeah," Archie shouts back. "But it doesn't mean I should be hearin' about it."

"Jack." Billy turns in his seat, looking at him. "Let me drop Archie off home, and we'll go back to mine."

"Faster if I drop you both off, Billy," Archie tells him as they round a bend. "I'm in court in an hour. I can bring your car back 'round later." He looks back in the rearview at Jack. "Jack, don't you think you should go home and let Barbara know what's happened? I'm sure she's been worried sick about you."

Jack doesn't answer, just stares straight ahead blindly.

"Maybe not, then." He pulls up in front of the club, turning to Billy. "Don't let him do anything stupid."

"Yeah, no stress." He gets out of the car, opening the door for Jack, who gets out without a word and bursts into renewed sobs as Archie speeds off, Billy unlocks the door.

"C'mon, you can cry over a pint or ten."

Chapter 60

Father Willis frowns at the two strange cars as he pulls into the car park in front of the children's homes. "Reid, what are you up to?"

He walks in, not bothering to take off his jacket before storming into the dining room and straight up to the main table where Reid is still sat with two men Willis has never met. "Father Reid." He eyes him with a telling look. "Would you mind telling me what these two men are doing here? You know everything's been put on hold for the time being."

Reid looks up at him, feigning innocence. "I thought it would be all right, seeing as they've arrested someone."

Willis raises his eyebrows, looking down at Reid. "Well, it's *not* all right, so you thought wrong. Kindly escort these gentlemen to the door. Now."

The taller of the two men stands up, puffing out his scrawny chest. "I've paid good money for tonight's entertainment. I won't leave until I've had my money's worth."

Willis cocks an eyebrow at Reid. "Who is he talking about?"

Reid stands, dusting the biscuit crumbs off his shirt. "Gina. About time she starts toeing the line."

"Gina belongs to Billy, Reid. Are you out of your mind? Give the man his money back and get them out of here," Willis hisses. "Now!"

The man props fisted hands on his hips, planting his feet. "I've paid for her, I want her. I'm not leaving until I have my time with her."

Willis notices the room behind them has grown completely quiet – the staff and straggling children have all fallen still, staring at the commotion as the noise of the argument mounts.

"Father Reid, kindly escort these men to my office straight away. We'll continue this meeting in private." He storms off, feeling every pair of eyes boring into his back as he leaves the dining room and marches to his office.

"This way, gentlemen, please." Reid motions for the men to precede him down the hall, leading them to Willis' office, where he follows them in and closes the door.

Willis stands in front of his desk, facing the men and staring daggers into Reid. "You've got some nerve, Reid, going off the minute my back's turned. Give these men back their money immediately and escort them off the premises."

"I told you." The tall man steps forward. "I don't want my money back. I want the girl."

"Fine." Willis nods at him. "Let me just ring Billy Gilmore and tell him you want one of his girls, right?"

"I don't know any Billy Gil—"

"Terry." His shorter friend steps up, grabbing his arm and shaking his head. "Let's just go, yeah? You don't wanna mess with Billy."

Terry frowns, looking from Willis back to his mate. "Oh, that Billy." He nods, pretending to know who they're talking about. "Nah, fuck that. Just give me my money back, then."

"Right, then." Willis shoos them off by wagging his fingers like he's swatting at flies. "Fuck off."

Reid goes to follow Terry and his mate out of the office, but Willis stops him. "Reid, once they've gone – proper gone, I mean – fetch me Gina and the boy.

Reid nods, colour rising on his cheeks as he bites his tongue and shuts the door behind him.

Willis walks to his chair, letting himself fall into it with a huff, and leans back, closing his eyes.

Chapter 61

"Special delivery, doc," Mercy Peters tells the doctor as he drops a large box in the medical room refrigerator. "I wouldn't look in there if I were you."

"You're stinkin' up my refrigerator, Mercy."

"Take it up with Doonan." Peters winks as he leaves the room and makes his way to Doonan's office. He pokes his head into the open door to make sure Doonan's in before entering. "Got the head, boss. Doc ain't happy it's stinkin' up his fridge." He chuckles. "Had a wander 'round the docks. Few spots look lived-in, handed out Errol's mugshot, told 'em to keep an eye out." He sits in the chair facing Doonan's desk. "Didn't bring back the security lad, Pete. No point."

Doonan puts his pen down, leaning back in his chair. "Why's that, son?"

"I think he's been coached. Definitely covering for Errol. Might be a good idea to get eyes on him by the Liverpool lot."

"Right, okay." Doonan nods. "I'll ring them. We'll have to wait for the lab to get back to us with the results from the blood found at the yard, see if they're a match to the head."

"Can't see it, myself." Peters shakes his head. "Would be a bad move on Jack's part – he's a smart man, don't think he'd get into that sort of mess."

"Maybe," Doonan says, unconvinced. "Monroe rang a couple minutes ago – Jack's been released, on promise to be back here in the morning. He had to tell him about Graham's death."

"Oof." Peters leans back, raising his eyebrows. "Shit's gonna hit the fan, now, innit? It's a race now, who gets to Errol first."

"Yeah, sure is," he agrees. "Keep it to yourself, lad. Ears are everywhere." Peters nods as he stands, mimicking zipping up his lips and turning a key.

"Good lad," Doonan tells him, picking up the phone and dialling out as Peters leaves the office.

Chapter 62

"We have to get out of here," Gina tells George as she gets up from the corner to rummage through the cupboard drawers under the window. "We have to hurry."

"But the door's locked," he replies, getting up to help her rummage.

Gina finds a couple of hair slides and a ruler. "There's nothing to use as a weapon," she laments as George's eyes grow wide. He knows what weapons can do, so Gina must be really scared. Crawling around, he looks under the cupboard and finds nothing, then moves to look under the bed, where he finds a pencil and a few scattered papers.

There's nothing else to find, so he lies on the floor, drawing his version of Gina on the blank paper.

They both jump, gasping, when they hear the key in the lock. "George," she whispers. "Come here." She motions frantically for him to get up, they both cower in the corner, the half-finished drawing forgotten on the floor.

She pulls him close as they watch the door open slowly, George gripping Raggy and the pencil to his chest as he presses close to Gina, hoping to become invisible.

With one eye peeking out from behind Gina, he sees Father Reid enter the room with a nasty smile on his face – the kind of smile Errol gave when he looked at his mum after watching the naked people on the telly. He fists a hand in Gina's shirt, whimpering.

Reid closes and locks the door after him, staring at Gina with a widening grin, walking towards them. "Right, you cocky little bitch. I'm to take you brats to Willis, but first, I'm gonna show you what girls like you are put on this Earth for."

George can feel Gina trembling beside him, and with his head pressed against her, he can hear her heart racing like a drum.

"Come here, or your little mate's gonna get hurt." Gina grabs George's hand, looking down at him.

"George, stay here and close your eyes. Everything's going to be all right, promise."

George's lip quivers as Gina steps away from him, but he does as he's told, shutting his eyes tight.

"I'm going to enjoy this," Reid hisses as he grabs Gina's arm.

Gina tries to twist away as he pulls off his cassock belt, but he's too big and too strong. She opens her mouth to scream, but he stuffs the belt into her open mouth before she can get a sound out, then tosses her onto the bed and ties her hands to the brass headboard.

She tries to kick and squirm, but it's no use, so she closes her eyes tightly as Reid tears away her blouse and pulls off her blue jeans.

Hearing the scuffle, George can't help but peek through his fingers, his eyes grow wide as he sees Reid pull his cassock up over his head. Fury boils up inside him as he remembers all the times he heard his mum screaming and crying in the bedroom underneath his. He looks down at Raggy and nods as though he is being told something by the doll

He jumps onto the chair beside the bed, waiting for Reid to pull his cassock all the way off, then with every ounce of strength and the power of sheer fury, he thrusts the pencil up and straight into Reid's right eye.

Screams of agony fill the room as Reid stumbles, clutching at his face, dropping his cassock in a forgotten pile on the floor.

George jumps off the chair, avoiding the wavering priest, and rushes to unlock and open the door, filling the hallway with Reid's harrowing screams.

In moments, the hallway is congested with a congregation of children and priests. Reid falls to his knees just as Father Willis comes rushing into the room. One look at the scene tells him all he needs to know.

He quickly shoos the children out of the doorway and closes the door, walking first to Gina, who's naked but for her underpants and thin camisole. He unties her hands, pulling the gag from her mouth, and she

immediately scuttles off the bed and runs to George, who's returned to his spot in the corner. She pulls him close as they watch Father Willis kneel in front of the screaming Reid. "This is gonna hurt you more than it hurts me, you fucking wanker." He grabs the pencil, twisting as he pulls out, taking ungodly amounts of pleasure in the additional pain he's inflicting on his subordinate as Reid's ear-piercing shrieks echo throughout the home.

"Serves you right." He stands, pulling Reid up with him. Picking up the discarded cassock, he throws it at Reid's chest. "Anybody asks, you slipped. Now get dressed and go see the matron."

He watches as Reid slips his cassock back over his bloody face then wavers out of the room. "Are you all right?" he asks Gina. "Did he touch you?"

Gina shakes her head slightly, wide-eyed and still trembling as she cowers near George. "What about you, George? Are you all right?"

The boy doesn't look up, intent on that burlap doll of his, seemingly in deep, silent conversation.

"Right, then. Let's forget this whole thing ever happened, shall we?" He walks towards the door. "Gina, get dressed, and then bring George down to my office." He ruffles George's hair as he walks out of the room, calling out to the other children as he shuts the door. "Right, c'mon, you lot. Back to your chores, show's over."

Gina sits on the edge of the bed, hugging her arms around her waist. "Thank you for doing that, George."

George looks up at her, suddenly looking a lot older than his five years. "He was going to hurt you like the bad man hurt my mummy. Raggy told me to do it."

"Can I see him for a minute?" Gina holds her hands out, accepting the doll as George nods. He stands and comes to sit beside her, handing Raggy over.

She gives Raggy a big kiss on the head and a tight hug. "Thank you for telling George to do that, Raggy. You both saved me." She hands him back to George and kisses his cheek.

They curl up together quietly.

Already on edge from the terrible screaming that just sounded from somewhere above him, the sound of sirens approaching has Errol scrambling off over the back fence and into the small, wooded area.

Chapter 63

"Thanks, mate." Jack closes the door without so much as looking at Billy before shuffling over to the front door. On autopilot, he unlocks the door and walks in, locking it behind him. He hangs his coat and just stands in the hall, staring vacantly at nothing, and that's where Barbara finds him.

"Oh, Jack, you're home!" She runs to him, wrapping her arms around him.

He hugs her back numbly for a moment, then breaks down into body-wracking sobs, holding on tightly.

"Oh, Jack, love, it can't be that bad, can it? They've let you out, must've all been a big misunderstanding?"

He shakes his head, face buried in her shoulder. "It's not the police, love. It's Graham."

"What about Graham," she asks, rubbing his back. "Has he been arrested, too?"

"No, love." He sobs. "He's dead. Murdered."

She steps back from him, searching his eyes. "What'd you mean, murdered? Don't be daft, love, he was only just here a few days ago. Surely, you've misheard."

Jack wipes at his face, fury filling him. "No, I haven't misheard. Monroe, that pig cunt, found great pleasure in telling me before I got released. Graham's dead, Barbara.

Him and Valerie, both murdered."

Her eyes grow wide with disbelief. "I don't understand." She shakes her head, her eyes filling. "Who killed them? Where? Jack, tell me—"

"I'm sorry, love," he interrupts. "I need to get my head 'round this myself. I'm going upstairs for a bath, see if I can…" He shakes his head again, lost. "I'm not sure what, to be honest." He calls back as he starts up the stairs. "Would you bring me a brew, love? I need to wash off the stench of them coppers off me."

Barbara watches him walk up the stairs as though he's in a daze, her heart sinking, as she's never seen her Jack look so defeated. Her heart breaking for him, and for poor little George, she walks into the kitchen and fills the kettle, putting it on to boil.

Chapter 64

"Look, George." Gina looks up at the night sky. "If we're lucky, we might get to see a shooting star. We can make wishes on them, you know."

"Are we allowed out here?" George asks her, looking out at the back garden from their perch up on the flat roof. Sat on the blanket Gina's brought out, they're eating the biscuits she's nabbed from the dinner table.

"I come out here all the time, they'll never know." She smiles at him.

A silver flash moves across the sky, catching her eye. "Oh! George, look, there's one!" Seeing the bright trails, George jumps to his feet, jumping up and down as he clutches his doll.

"Raggy! Raggy, look! It's a shooting star!"

From the back of the garden where he's been squatting for hours, Errol smiles as he looks up to the roof of the house. "There you are, ya little freak," he whispers to himself. "Errol's comin' to get ya."

He keeps the shadows as he moves quietly across the garden to the back of the house until he reaches the fire escape ladder. Without a sound, he pulls himself up and begins to climb up towards the children.

PC Wilcox is making the rounds about the children's home when an excited shout reaches his ears. "What on earth…" A second shout echoes, and he takes off towards the back of the house, following the sound.

As he turns the corner, the first thing he sees are two children standing on the flat roof, jumping and pointing excitedly at the sky. The next thing his eyes land on is the lone figure creeping steadily up the fire escape towards them.

As the man turns his head slightly, the light of the moon lights him up. Wilcox is able to see him clearly for a moment. "You've got to be joking," he mumbles to himself as he runs back out to the car, banging on the bonnet of the police car. "Mark!"

Bolton opens the door. "What's the matter?"

"Mark, call for back-up, straight away," Wilcox tells him, out of breath. Bolton frowns. "Back-up for what?"

"The bloke we're looking at for the double murders, I'm certain I've just seen him climbing the fire escape. He's looking for the kid. Just call them!" He doesn't wait for Bolton to reach for the radio before he's running back to the garden.

"Emergency assistance needed at the Rushiefold Lane children's home. Suspect from murder enquiry on site, heading up to the roof. Wilcox is already in pursuit to apprehend the suspect. Over." He hooks the radio back in its caddy and rushes off after Wilcox.

John, out for a nightly stroll, hears the commotion and sees the officer run out of his car and to the back of the home, right before he hears Gina shouting. Without a second thought, he runs back along the track by the boundary wall on his left and jumps over into the garden easily.

Errol reaches the roof, quietly climbing up off the ladder and sneaking up behind the children, keeping to the shadows. "Boo!"

Gina turns, unstartled, staring at Errol. "What are you doing here?" she demands. "This is private property."

Errol ignores her completely, his wild eyes dancing over the small figure clinging to her side. "Georgie, porgy, puddin' and pie, I've found ya now, it's time to die," he sing-songs as he slowly creeps forward.

Gina pushes George behind her, staring Errol down. "I don't know who you are, mister." She leans down, pulling out the large kitchen knife from her bag, pointing it at him. "But I suggest you fuck off before I—"

"You've got some balls, lady." He smiles at her. "I'll give you that. Just give me the kid and the doll, and I'll be on my way." He creeps forwards a little more.

Gina stands her ground. "You're not having either, you perverted freak! Has Reid put you up to this?"

Errol just smiles, shaking his head as he keeps moving towards them.

George tugs at Gina's jumper from behind. "It's him, Gina. He's the bad man, he hurt my mummy and daddy, and Nipper."

Gina's eyes grow wide as she keeps staring at Errol. Keeping George behind her, she takes a step back for each step forwards Errol takes, her hand shaking as she grips the knife with white knuckles. "You killed his family!" she accuses with a trembling voice.

Errol's smile grows wider as he nods and takes

another step forward. "They had it comin'" He advances, pushing them back towards the edge of the flat roof.

Gina hears George mumbling something but can't make it out for the buzzing in her ears and her focus on Errol. "Get back, or else!" she shouts, jumping forwards and thrusting the knife in the air towards him, causing him to take a jump back.

"You're a brave kid." He laughs. "Why ya protecting the runt, he's nothing to you. Hand 'im over, I promise I won't hurt ya."

Gina shakes her head, waving the knife in front of her as she catches a glimpse of a police officer slowly creeping forwards over Errol's shoulder.

Wilcox steps on a small fallen twig, snapping it; Errol turns, reaching for his revolver. *"Oy,"* Wilcox shouts. "Put the gun down!"

"Why would I do that, ya pig bastard?" Errol chortles. "Get your fuckin' hands up where I can see 'em!"

Raising his empty hands, his eyes locked on Errol's, Wilcox takes a careful step back. "Do yourself a favour, mate, and give me the gun."

Errol smiles, cracking his neck as he points the gun straight at Wilcox's chest, finger tight over the trigger.

Seeing her chance, Gina runs forward, sinking her knife into Errol's left buttock.

Crying out, Errol pulls the trigger, burying a bullet in Wilcox's chest and sending him tumbling backwards off the roof.

PC Bolton hears the gunshot half a second before he sees his partner career off the roof, landing in a broken heap on the ground below.

"Look what you made me do, you stupid little bitch!" Errol growls, pointing his gun at her, face contorted in fury as he limps forward.

Having seen the entire scene from the back wall, John runs to the fire escape and rushes, passing PC Bolton who's frozen in fear.

Gina holds the bloody knife, her hand shaking like a leaf as George clings to her legs behind her. She shuffles back some more, the blood dripping from the blade onto the roof.

Errol flashes a grin, rotten teeth making Gina want to vomit as the scent of urine reaches her nose from where George is cowering behind her.

"Make him go away, Gina! He's the bad man!" he shouts, terror sending his voice to a high- pitched shrick.

Errol steps closer. "Put the knife down, princess."

"Why?" Gina barks, enraged and terrified. "You're gonna kill us anyway!"

"Tell that whining little fucker to give me that doll, or I'm going to shoot you the same as I shot that dirty pig." He seethes, his eyes wild.

She backs up a bit more, still holding the knife up at arm's length, her breath ragged.

"I'm gonna count to five, love," he tells her calmly. "If I ain't got that doll, it's bye-bye and good riddance to the both of you." He aims the gun, raising it to point directly at her head.

"George." She blindly reaches for George behind her. "George, give me the doll."

"Raggy's mine!" George screams savagely at Errol. "You can't have him!"

"Please, George," Gina begs in a shaky whisper. "I'll get him back, promise."

"Five, four…"

Tears streaming down his cheeks, George hands Raggy to Gina. She turns, staring daggers at Errol as she reaches out her hand, dangling Raggy over the edge of the roof. "What do you want this horrible-looking thing for, anyway?

"Three, two…"

"Grown men don't play with dolls!"

John reaches the top just as he hears Errol cock the gun. He doesn't stop running when his feet hit the roof –

he's just about to tackle Errol when the latter turns and pulls the trigger, hitting John square in the shoulder.

Already in motion, John continues his tackle, ploughing straight into Errol and narrowly missing the children as they both tumble over the edge of the roof, landing with a loud thud on the grass below.

"John!" Gina cries out, running to the edge and peering down at the tangled mess of arms and legs, tears pooling out of her eyes, onto the roof. She watches, holding her breath, as George picks up Raggy where she's dropped him and joins her to look down.

John grunts loudly, shifting on top of Errol.

"John, I'm coming!" She grabs Errol's gun where he dropped it and runs for the fire escape. "George, hurry!" He runs to her, clutching Raggy close and gripping Gina tightly with shaking fingers. "C'mon, we have to make sure John's all right." They hurry down the stairs as sirens blare around the corner, running past PC Bolton who's still frozen on the spot until they reach the bottom. Police officers are rushing from the front of the house, running towards John and Errol just as Gina and George reach them.

The big man rolls over off of Errol, screaming in pain. Seeing Gina, he stops, taking a shaking breath, he winks at her. "You kids okay?"

Gina runs to him, throwing her arms around his neck and smacking a loud kiss on his cheek as tears stream freely down her cheeks. "Please don't die, John. Please— "

"Woah, woah, there." He raises weak hands up to her shoulders, pulling her away slightly. "I'm not intending to. We've got plans, remember?" He winks at her just as a police officer rushes over and pulls her off him, moving her and George off to the side roughly.

Father Willis rushes towards them from the house in time to see the officer's hands on the kids. *"Oy!"* he shouts. "Leave those kids alone!"

He runs to the children, kneeling beside them. "Are you two all right? Did he hurt you?"

"No." George shakes his head, holding Raggy tightly. "The bad man did."

Father Willis frowns, not understanding.

"The man who killed George's parents," Gina explains, pointing to Errol. "He tried to get George, but John saved us."

"John, of course." He looks up at the police officer.

"Get a doctor over here, this man needs help." He grabs Gina and George's hands, pulling them away. "Come on, let's go in and get a glass of milk. Let the ambulance people do their job."

Gina tries to pull her hand away, tears still streaming down her cheeks. "I want to stay! He's my friend!"

"You can't," he pulled her on. "I promise, I'll find out how he is later. We need to get you both inside – George is freezing."

Gina watches through eyes glazed with tears as police and paramedics crowd around John and Errol. The garden is flashing with white and blue lights as they walk towards the house, people buzzing around like it's a fete. Gina reaches a hand towards PC Wilcox as they walk by where he lies on a stretcher, a man in uniform holding an oxygen mask to his face. Everything feels like it's in fast- forwards and slow-motion, all at the same time.

Chapter 65

"Things are turning to shit, O'Leary," Billy says to the lad, standing in the doorway. He takes another sip of his best whiskey, putting the glass down on the desk. "Tell the blokes in the club, five hundred for Errol's whereabouts."

O'Leary's eyebrows shoot up. "For that kind of money, I might have a go at it myself."

"No, you're not," he tells him. "I need you here, keepin' an eye on the place. There's somewhere I need to be."

"All right, boss. Where're you going?"

Billy doesn't answer, merely picks up the telephone and stares at O'Leary until he leaves, closing the door behind him.

He dials, waiting for the voice to pick up.

"Yeah."

"Hi. I'll be there in twenty minutes. Usual place." He hangs up the phone.

Chapter 66

Coronation Street is playing on the television, but Barbara isn't really hearing the words as she sits, knitting a pair of gloves for George. Blue, because it matches his eyes.

She hears the splashing of Jack getting out of the bath, and the creaking of the pipes as the water drains from the tub. Jack starts opening and closing doors and drawers, then the soft cracking of the stairs as he makes his way downstairs.

Silently, he sits in his chair in front of the fire and stares at the dancing flames, though Barbara knows he isn't really seeing them.

Without a word, Barbara puts her knitting down in the basket beside her chair and goes to the kitchen to put the kettle on to boil, then comes back with a cup of tea and places it on the side table beside Jack.

As she puts the cup down, he grabs her hand, squeezing it as tears stream down his cheeks. "Jack, you're scaring me, love. Can you please tell me what's happened?" She goes to sit in the matching wingback chair beside him. "Please, talk to me."

He takes a shuddering breath as he looks at her, making no attempt at stopping the tears. "They're dead." She nods slowly, swallowing the lump in her throat. "Yes, you said Graham's..." she can't finish the sentence.

"Please, God, tell me George is okay. He's not
    dead, too, is he?"

"No, love." He shakes his head, looking back to the fire. "Graham and Val. That bastard Errol's murdered them." Errol's name hisses out through clenched teeth, leaving a sour taste in Jack's mouth.

"When?" Barbara's bottom lip trembles, her voice unsteady. "Monroe said five days ago."

Barbara's hands flutter up to her chest. "Five days! Why've they waited so long to tell you? Where's George?"

"They don't need a reason, do they? Pricks make up the rules as they go. George is at the Children's home."

"Dear God, not Willis', I hope." Barbara clutches at her throat, worry and grief painted on her face.

"Yes, that's where he is," he tells her numbly. "He's safe there for now. We'll get him tomorrow, bring him home. You can make up the guest bed for him, God knows the boy needs a stable place."

"I'll make it up with fresh sheets. We'll get him first thing. I'm not having that little boy spend another day in that horrid place. You know well as I know what goes on behind those walls. Him being a boy won't deter them."

"Yeah, you're right. We'll get him first thing, love." He takes a sip of his tea. "I need to focus, my head's a mess. That murderous cunt is still on the loose. Need to find him before the police do."

"It's late, Jack. Nothing you can do about anything tonight. Why don't you finish your tea and go up to bed. You look shattered. I'll be up in a minute."

Jack sighs deeply, nodding. "Yeah. Yeah, you're

258

right, love." He gets up, ignoring the tepid tea, and makes his way up the stairs slowly, as though in a daze.

Barbara waits until she hears the bed springs squeak, then goes to the kitchen. She dumps the remains of Jack's tea down the sink then picks up the telephone, waiting impatiently for a voice to pick up.

"Hello?"

"Can I speak to Father Willis, please?"

"I'm sorry. Father Willis is indisposed at the minute. Would you like to leave a message?"

"What do you mean, he's indisposed? What's he up to?"

"I'm very sorry, I'm afraid I can't—"

"I need to speak with him now." Barbara feels her temper mounting as she grips the receiver.

"As I said, he isn't availa—"

"Right, fine. Get him to ring me straight away." "Who should I ask him to ring?"

"Tell him to ring Barbara. He knows who I am." She hangs up the telephone in a huff, before flipping off the kitchen light and heading up the stairs to bed.

Chapter 67

In a car park on the outskirts of town, Billy drums a finger against the steering wheel to Abba's latest hit as he waits, his Luger tucked safely on the passenger seat under an old copy of The Sun.

He sees the headlights shine through the trees as a car weaves its way towards him, he tucks the gun into his jacket pocket, cutting the engine. He gets out and walks to the front, leaning back against the bonnet as the car turns into the car park and stops twenty yards away, facing him. "For fuck's sake," he mutters, raising his arm against

the blinding glare of the high beams. "Cut them fucking lights."

As though the driver hears him, the lights turn off.

Billy tries to blink away the light spots as Brayden gets out of the car.

"Sorry about that, Billy," Brayden says as he walks closer. "Can't be too careful these days, can we?"

"Yeah, sure." Billy nods, his vision clearing. He frowns at the Irishman. "What'd you want, then? I'm not very comfortable talking to you behind Jack's back. Couldn't we have done this over the telephone?"

"It's Jack. I'm worried about a lot of shit's going down. Too much shit, as I'm sure you've gotten a whiff of. Making me nervous."

Billy walks up as Brayden does the same, meeting him halfway between the two cars. "Can't say I know what you're on about, mate. What shit do you mean?"

Brayden raises his eyebrows skeptically. "I think you *do* know, Billy. The old bill's all over Jack like a bad rash."

Billy tilts his head. "We have a few local issues we need sorted, yeah," he admits, shrugging. "Last I checked, that's nowt to do with you, though."   .

Brayden shoves his hands into his jacket pockets, rocking on his feet. "That's not entirely true, is it?"

"I don't know what you're gettin' at, mate."

"I'm still down a diamond, mate," Brayden tells him, matching his stance, emphasising the last word.

"Thought that was all sorted with Jack the other night."

Brayden shakes his head. "Nah. That was only a bit of compensation for my time and patience, which I've been more than generous with. Jack knows that."

"Pretty sure that's gone with Errol, can't imagine we'll be laying eyes on that prick again, especially once he hears about Tweak." Billy shifts his weight, the gun weighing heavy in his pocket. "What's it gonna take to make this right, then?"

Brayden tilts his head the other way, waiting a beat before speaking. "I want in on your operation."

Billy stares at him, nearly laughing before shaking his head. "A single diamond's not worth that, sorry. What makes you think we're in the market for another partner?" Brayden smiles at him, holding up a finger before walking back to his car and pulling something out of the back and coming back to him. "This," he tells Billy, handing him a file folder.

Brayden frowns at it, reaching to flip it open but Brayden slaps a hand on his shoulder. "Not now." He smiles again. "Wait until you get back to the club. Have a chat with Jack in the morning. I'll be waiting for your answer." He winks at Billy then walks back to his car and drives off, leaving Billy standing alone in the empty car park.

As Brayden's car disappears down the road, Billy goes back to his car, slamming the door shut as he tosses the gun back onto the passenger seat. Turning on the overhead light, he flips open the folder, and a deep crease forms between his brows as he thumbs through the pages, each one more incriminating than the last. Detailed accounts describing meetings of undercover police officers with members of the gang. His frown deepens as he sees some of the members' names.

Cursing, he tosses the folder on the seat with the gun and peels out of the car park.

Chapter 68

Given the all-clear by the paramedics, cleaned-up and showered, Gina and George are back in their bedroom, cosy in their pyjamas.

"Right, that's enough now, George," Gina tells him. "You need to go to bed."

He doesn't answer her, just raises his doll up to the glass as he keeps looking down at the police still swarming on the lawn below. "Look, Raggy. They're taking the bad man away, now."

Gina walks up to stand beside him, pulling him close to her side as she looks down. Lights are still flashing, and policemen are everywhere.

They both turn at the knock on the door to see Father Willis come in.

"I've good news. John's going to be okay. He'll have to be in hospital for a few days as he broke a few ribs when he fell off the roof. But lucky for him, he fell on top of the other man and broke his fall.

A relieved smile spreads on Gina's face, and she feels she can finally take a full breath again. "What about the other man? The bad man. Is he dead?"

"Don't think so." Willis shakes his head. "But don't worry, Gina. If he survives, the only place he's going is prison."

George turns to look at them, hugging Raggy tightly. "The bad man is gone, now."

Willis nods, giving a small smile as George turns back to the window. "Keep an eye on him tonight," he tells Gina.

Gina nods as he pats her on the head and leaves the room, closing the door softly. "George." She turns back to him, staring at his reflection in the glass. "Why did the bad man want Raggy?"

George keeps staring at the garden, transfixed. "Because Raggy saw him hurt Mummy and Daddy."

"Oh. Right." Gina rolls her eyes as she pulls him by the shoulder, away from the window. "C'mon now, it's time for bed. Raggy's tired."

George turns a beaming smile at Gina for the first time since she's met him, then runs to his bed, launching himself onto the mattress with a giggle. "Night night, Gina." He burrows under the covers, tucking Raggy in beside him.

"Night night, George." Gina turns off the lamp and climbs into bed. "Don't forget Raggy," he tells her.

Gina smiles in the darkness. "Night night, Raggy. Sleep tight."

"Night night," sounds Raggy's strange, raspy voice.

Cuddled up with Raggy, George is asleep within minutes, his breathing soft and steady, echoing in the quiet of the room.

Gina stares at the ceiling. She can't stop replaying the night's events in her mind. She keeps seeing Errol's face, sneering at them. Keeps seeing the police officer get shot and falling off the roof. And John, tackling Errol, and them both tumbling off the roof. She thought he was dead, that she'd lost her friend. Why did he want Raggy so badly he was willing to kill for it?

Unable to sleep, she pushes the sheets aside and gets up, padding barefoot to George's bed. She carefully pulls the doll from the sleeping boy's arm without waking him and takes him to the window, where the light of the full moon is shining through the glass.

The garden below is quiet, now – the police having gone. She lifts the ugly doll and stares at him, frowning. "What's your secret, Raggy?" she whispers. Turning him over, she examines every inch, squeezing every part. "What are you hiding, eh?"

She nearly drops him, but quickly grabs him before he hits the floor, holding her breath as George rolls over and whimpers in his sleep.

Exhaling in relief, she grips the doll tightly and frowns as she feels something hard in its neck. Flipping him over again, she pushes aside the tattered yarn hair and notices the stitches. They're not the right colour of thread, and they look like a child sewed them on, though she can't imagine George doing it.

Carefully, she pulls at the stitches with her teeth until one of them breaks, then pulls them out one at a time until she's able to stick her finger through. Feeling around the batting innards, she pulls out something hard wrapped in a small, stained piece of cloth, she gasps as a perfect, glistening diamond tumbles into her open palm.

"Oh, my God!" She turns the stone this way and that,

eyes wide as it catches the light of the moon. "This is what he was after."

She quickly wraps it back in the small piece of cloth and stuffs it into the hole in her mattress,along with her other treasures. Carefully, she pulls at the stitches on Raggy's neck, closing up the burlap wound as best she can, tying it in a knot, before slipping him back under George's blanket.

It takes her a while, but she's eventually able to fall into a fitful sleep.

Chapter 69

"Nowt in the paper, boss," PC Mercy Peters tells Doonan, holding up a copy of The Mirror. "Looks like they've not got wind of it, yet."

Doonan stops pacing for a moment, looking down at Peters where he's sat on the floor of the waiting room, leaning against the wall on the upper floor of the hospital. He rubs his eyes, looking at his watch – six a.m. "Good. Gives us a bit more time to sort this shit out. Any news on Errol yet?"

"No." Peters shakes his head. "Doc's not been in yet." "Well, go find him. There's a good lad." He turns and keeps pacing as Peters stands, rolling his eyes at the patronising words.

Walking up to Errol's room, Peters looks in through the glass at the side of the door. He watches as a nurse walks up to him, where he's hooked up to machines and wires from every angle.

He jumps when an alarm sounds, just as the nurse begins chest compressions.

"Out of the way!" The doctor rushes past Peters, pushing into the room and to Errol's bedside. The defibrillator quickly attached to his chest, they shock him once, twice, waiting a few moments in between, until the doctor shakes his head. But then the machine starts again as Errol's heart begins to beat again on its own.

Checking him over, the doctor says something to the nurse that Peters can't make out through the glass, before walking out.

"Do you think he's going to live?" Peters asks him as he walks past.

"Don't know. Touch and go for a minute then. Best guess is fifty-fifty at the moment."

Doonan turns, expectantly, as Peters walks back into the waiting room. "Well?"

Peters shakes his head. "Doc says it's fifty-fifty. Just watched them shock him back to life just now."

"Woulda been better if they'd just left him dead," Doonan grumbles. "Right, I'm off. Stay here – I'll have someone over to relieve you as quickly as I can." He points in the general direction of Errol's room. "Do *not* let him out of your sight."

Peters exhales an exhausted breath. "I've been on for ten hours, boss."

"Stop whining," Doonan tells him as he walks off down the hall. "Do your job."

"Stop whining, do your job," Peters repeats in a mocking tone as he makes his way back to Errol's room and slides down to the floor, leaning against the wall."

Chapter 70

"Morning, Jack," Billy calls as he gets out of his car, just as Jack and Barbara are getting into theirs. "How are you feeling this morning?"

"About as expected, mate," Jack tells him, weary. "What is it? We're just on our way to get George from the home."

"I think you need to hear what I have to say, first," Billy tells him, grimly. "Can we go in a minute?"

Jack sighs heavily, seeing the look on Billy's face. "Right, okay. But let's make it fast, yeah?" He walks back up to the house, Billy following as Barbara glares at him. "Sorry, love. It's important, or I wouldn't be here this early." He motions for her to walk ahead of him and shuts the door behind them.

"Be a love, Barbara," Jack tells her softly. "And make us a cuppa, please. Billy." He motions to the hall. "Let's go into the lounge."

Barbara watches them walk into the lounge before marching into the kitchen in a quiet temper. Jack sits on the settee across from Jack, who's sat forwards in his chair, waiting not so patiently. "Right," Billy starts. "You need to focus on what I'm going to say."

Jack raises his hands along with his brows. "Tell me, then." Billy keeps his voice low and even. "We know where Errol is."

The words are barely out of Billy's mouth before Jack is out of his seat. "What the fuck are we doing, sitting here drinking tea for, then? C'mon! Let's go get the bastard!"

Billy stands, both hands up in front of Jack before he can storm out of the room. "Jack, for fuck's sakes, calm down. He's on life support at Manchester General, under armed guard. We can't get near him."

Jack slumps back down in his chair, face red with fury, just as Barbara comes into the lounge carrying a tray with two cups of tea, milk, sugar and a plate of biscuits. She looks from Jack, to Billy, and back to Jack, whose face is growing redder by the second.

"Thanks, love," he says in a clipped tone, not bothering to look at her. "Shut the door on your way out." Barbara swallows her retort as she storms out of the room and slams the door behind her. "What'd you mean, we can't get to the fucker?" Jack seethes. "He killed my brother."

"I know, we—"

"Who got to him, then? Brayden?"

"No." Billy shakes his head, bracing himself for the next bit of news. "He went after George. Found out where he was – not sure how, and no idea why he'd go after the boy. Don't worry." He raises his hands again. "He's okay. A tramp tackled Errol and they both fell off the roof."

"The roof?" Jack's voice keeps getting louder with each new exclamation. "What fucking roof?"

"The roof at the children's home. Seems George and some girl were up there, playing."

Jack stands again, fists curled tightly. "What the fuck kind of children's home lets the kids play out on the fucking roof?"

"Jack," Billy tries to soothe. "George is okay. He's safe and sound now. But we have other problems. Something worse."

Jack shakes his head, stomping back and forth across the lounge, the tea completely ignored on the table. "What could be worse, eh?" he stares at him, eyes burning. "My brother's dead, the filth have got Errol, George is—"

"I was summoned by Joseph Brayden last night," Billy interrupts him.

Jack stops, turning to look down at Billy. "What? What do you mean, you got summoned. What does Brayden want with you?"

"He rang and asked for a meet," he tells Jack. "I told him I was busy, and that he shouldn't be ringing me directly, but he wouldn't take no for an answer."

"Why didn't he ring me?" Jack propped his fisted hands on his hips, his frown deepening. "Because it was *you* he wanted to talk about," Billy answered, standing.

"What? Me – why?"

"He thinks you're losing your grip on things, getting sloppy. The thing with Errol, and the diamond, and the fact you didn't know drugs were being skimmed…"

"I showed him with Tweak I wasn't weak!" Jack nearly shouted before remembering Barbara and lowering his voice. "If he wants a war, he can have a war." He sits back in his chair, picks up his tea and gulps half of it down in one.

Billy follows suit, taking a seat. He leans forward, elbows on his knees as he looks at Jack.

"Leave George where he is for now, yeah? Brayden doesn't know about him, so he's safer there, should everything go to shit with Brayden."

Jack shakes his head, putting his half-empty cup back on the tray. "All this over a fucking diamond."

"Nah," Billy disagreed. "That's just an excuse. He wants what we've got, and if we don't play ball, he's gonna take it."

"Over my dead body," Jack deadpans, unblinking.

"Let's not let it come to that, eh? We need to be clever about this, Jack." He picks up his cup, taking a sip. "Have a sit down with him, see exactly what it is he wants. Just like old times, Jacky Boy." Billy smiles over his cup. "Remember when the Yorkshire lot tried to muscle in? We dealt with them, didn't we? This Irish prick don't stand a chance."

Jack leans forward, sighing heavily as he recalled the incident Billy described. "Tell Brayden he'll have to wait." He grabs a biscuit from the plate. "I'm burying my brother before anything else."

"I'll ring him today." Billy nods. "Gives me a couple weeks to go through the folder he gave me, find out who his snitch is."

"Snitch!" Jack sits up straight. "This conversation just keeps gettin' better and better."

"Leave it with me, Jack." Billy put his cup down, standing. "Take a bit of time out. I can manage things."

"Okay, okay." Jack tosses the biscuit back down on

the try as he stands. "I need to speak with Barbara about George, then. Go on, fuck off. I'll call you later."

"Right," Billy turns to leave but stops, turning back. "Don't forget, you need to be back at the station for nine-thirty this morning."

"Fuck, I forgot." Jack looks at his watch, frowning. "Thanks, mate." He pulls Billy into a hug, slapping his back. "I'll see you out."

"See you later, Barbara," Billy calls out.

She pokes her head around the corner from the kitchen. "Bye, Billy."

Jack shuts the door after Billy and joins Barbara in the kitchen. "I'm sorry about that, love. Didn't mean to snap at you. Leave that," he tells her, pointing to the dish she's drying. "We need to talk about George."

"What'd you mean? Is he all right?"

"He's fine. Let's go into the lounge, I need to tell you something."

She slaps the tea towel down onto the counter with a snap, propping her fists on her hip. "I don't want to go into the lounge, Jack. You can tell me right here."

He sighs patiently. "I need to go back to the police station this morning. Completely slipped my mind."

"Ring them, love, tell them you'll be late."

"I can't, love." He lays a hand on her shoulder. "Archie's on his way. But I've a bigger problem now."

"What could be a bigger problem?"

"It's Brayden," he says, feeling his anger mounting again at the mere mention of the name. "He's blackmailing us. Has information that could take us all down. I feel

George will be safer at the home until I get this all sorted."

"Do you, now?" she bristles, shrugging his hand off her shoulder. "Well, listen to me, Jack Harrison, and listen good. I'm picking up George, and if it's not today, it's tomorrow, no later, whether you've got things sorted or not. That boy's not staying in that house a moment longer than necessary, d'you hear me?" Her face is growing hot as she lets her own temper flare. "I'm ringing Willis and letting him know. This *thing* with Brayden will keep until after the funeral. You have the undertaker coming this afternoon."

A wise man knows when he's beaten, Jack thinks as he watches the colour rise in Barbara's cheeks. Still… "I still think it might be a big mistake to get him just now, love."

She shakes her head, picking her towel back up. "The only person who's made a mistake is Joseph Brayden," she says, her tone much calmer than she's feeling. "Now, go upstairs and fix your hair. You can't go into the police station looking like you've been dragged through a hedge backwards."

He sighs. "Yes, dear."

Barbara waits until she hears the bathroom door closing before picking up the phone and dialling out.

"Hello?"

"Joseph, is that you?"

"Barbara, love. What can I do for you?"

"Jack wants to meet you. Nine p.m. tonight." "Right, okay. Where?"

"64 Kenilworth Road, Failsworth." She hangs up and

puts the kettle on to boil as she hears Jack coming back down the stairs.

"Was someone on the phone?" he asks, walking back into the kitchen.

"No, love." She glances back at him, smiling. "Your hair looks much better. Go and finish your tea whilst you wait for Archie.

He plucks a biscuit out of the biscuit barrel and walks off to the lounge.

Chapter 71

Parked down the street from 64 Kenilworth Road, Brayden pulls his Gloch from the glovebox, checking the magazine He stuffs it in his pocket, winking at Frank who's sat behind the wheel. "Feel better taking Daisy with me. Not quite sure how this meeting's gonna go – keep your eyes open."

Frank nods once. "Sure thing, but Jack's got other things on his mind, boss. Don't think he's gonna try anything stupid."

Brayden taps the gun hiding in his pocket. "You've heard the saying about a trapped rat, Frank – better safe than dead." He jumps out of the car, motioning to Frank with a nod. "Let's go." They walk quietly down Kenilworth Road, eyeing the derelict houses with disgust. When they reach number sixty-four, Brayden cringes. "Fuck me. How can anyone live in a shithole like this?" Frank looks up at the house with its boarded-up windows and remnants of yellow police tape blowing in the breeze. The front garden looks like it hasn't been cut since the house was built.

"Smackheads and prossies, boss. Scum of the Earth." "Suppose so," Brayden agrees. "But those scumbags keep us in business. They pay for our lives of luxury, Frank. We'd be fucked without them."

"Yeah, you're right." He trips on a broken flag as they keep moving up the pathway nearly falling on his face,

distracting both of them from the figure looking down at them from the second- floor window.

"Right clumsy arse." Brayden chuckles. "C'mon, let's get this over with. Put Jack and his business out of their misery."

Frank smiles at him in the dark as he knocks on the door.

Brayden keeps his hand on the Glock in his pocket as they listen to the footsteps on the other side, but immediately lets go when the door opens.

"Ah, good. You're on time. Good man."

"Barbara, hi." He stares at her in shock. "Thought I was meeting Jack?"

"Yes, I know." She smiles. "But plans have changed. Come in." She steps back, motioning for him to enter, but quickly steps back in front of Frank, putting a hand up on his chest and stopping him. "Sorry, Frank. This is a private conversation." Frank looks at Brayden over Barbara's shoulder.

She turns to smile at him. "Not scared of a woman, are you, Joseph?"

Brayden scans the hallway and the empty rooms behind him before turning back to Frank. "Wait in the car, I can handle this. Won't be but a few minutes."

"All right." Frank frowns, but leaves, a bad feeling creeping up his spine as he hears the soft click of the door closing after him.

"Right." Brayden turns to Barbara in the dark hallway.

"What's this all about?"

"What's the rush?" She smiles at him again, her voice soft. "Do you fancy a cup of tea?"

"In this dump?" He surveys his surroundings – the ripped, blood-stained wallpaper, flaking paints. The crumbling plaster and that smell… he wrinkles his nose as he realises it's the stench of death. "No thanks. Can we get on with this? I need to be somewhere."

"That's where Graham and Val were murdered," she points to the blood stains on the wall behind him. "I know you don't care, but Jack does, so you need to back off and give him time to grieve."

Brayden shakes his head. "Barbara, I'm sorry for his loss, truly. But he's losing the plot."

"He's burying his only brother next week, Joseph. He needs time to get his head straight. Have some compassion."

Brayden saunters over to the staircase, swatting the dust off the third step before sitting down. Leaning back, he pulls out a fat cigar from one pocket, a Zippo from another, lighting it in a smooth flick of his wrist.

Taking a long, slow drag, he inhales deeply, then blows out the sickly sweet cloud of smoke in Barbara's direction. "That's all well and good, Barbara," he says in a patient tone, as one would speak to a child. "But time waits for no man, and neither do junkies." He leans forward, looking up at her. "They want their fix, and if we ain't there to give it to them, some other fucker will step up. Don't give a fuck about politics of the drug game." He takes another long pull on his cigar, flicking the ashes between his feet.

"The only thing they're interested in, lass, is putting our shit up their noses or stickin' it in their veins. Some are so fucked up, they inject it into their eyeballs." He shakes his head as though it's the craziest thing he's ever heard of, but Barbara doesn't react, so he keeps going. "This is the service we provide for these poor, unfortunate smack rats – twenty-four hours a day, three hundred and sixty-five days a year. It would be rather unkind of us to put everything on hold because Jack's brother died, and upset their routines like that, don't you think?"

Barbara stares at him quietly for a long moment, her face void of any emotion. "Help me understand what that has to do with you, Joseph." She tilts her head to the side, raising her eyebrows. "You supply us with some of our product – that's it. Nowt to do with you if our clients go elsewhere. We're the only ones impacted."

Brayden spreads his hands, the big cigar tucked between two fingers. "That's my point, Barbara. You need my help."

"In what way?" she frowns down at him, crossing her arms.

He leans back again, elbows on the step behind him. "I take over the operation. Jack and Billy take a back seat and get a percentage of the profits every week." He pulls another drag from his cigar, smiling up at her smugly like he's just solved all the world's problems.

"No," she shakes her head slightly. "See, Joseph, I reckon you don't understand how things work over here." "Barbara." His smile wanes a bit. "I've done my due diligence. I've been working on taking over Jack's empire for months now. Has Billy not shown him the pile of evidence I have on them?" Barbara's eyebrows shoot even higher as she watches Brayden flick his ashes carelessly.

"Jack's empire?"

"Yes, Jack's," he frowns. "Never took you to be a stupid woman, Barbara." He stands, cigar tucked between his teeth as he steps towards her with his chest puffed but stops in his tracks when she plants her feet, hands on her hips.

"I think your due diligence is flawed, Joseph. It's not Jack's outfit."

He flicks a hand in the air, waving her words away. "Well, Billy's then. Don't matter which, really. I'm takin' over, and anyone who gets in my way will come—"

"It's not Jack's, and it's not Billy's, Joseph. It's mine. Always has been. Jack works for *me*, as does everyone else. Including *you*." She points at him for emphasis, staring him straight in the eyes.

"No way," he frowns. "You're a woman."

"Well, that's the first thing you've got right all night." She stares hard at him, her eyes cold. "Now, sit back down on the naughty step like Mummy made you do, and don't you start crying – it won't help you this time."

His frown deepens as he flinches, shocked. *"Eh,* how'd you know that?"

"Unlike you," he says, her tone clipped. "I know everything you've ever done. What, where, when, and with whom." She counts off on her fingers. "See, I did *my* due diligence on you years ago, Joseph, dear, just as I do everyone who works for me."

Face burning red, Brayden takes a menacing step towards her. "Fuck off, Barbara," he shouts, spittle flying from his mouth. "I'm takin' over, and your bullshit ain't gonna stop me!" He raises the hand not holding the cigar over his head, aiming it at her face.

"Oy!"

Brayden spins around at the shout behind him to see Alex Markey standing at the top of the stairs. He quickly reaches for the gun in his pocket.

"Wouldn't do that, if I were you, mate." Alex slowly makes his way down the stairs, his own gun pointed squarely at the centre of Brayden's chest.

"Alex Markey," Brayden hisses. "What the fuck are you doing here?"

"Since you ask so politely" – he shoves him aside as he reaches the bottom of the stairs – "I'm here for my brother-in-law's funeral." He pulls a smiling Barbara into a warm hug. He turns back to Brayden, pointing to the gun gripped in his hand with his own. "Now, big fella, I

suggest you put that gun down. You owe my sister an apology."

Brayden's face takes on a different shade of red as he stuffs the gun back into his pocket, flustered. "I, uh, I'm sorry, Barbara. Didn't know Alex was your brother."

"Seems there's a lot of things you didn't know.

Should've shown more compassion towards Jack instead of taking advantage of him in a weakened state, don't you think, Bray?" She tips her head again. "You don't mind me calling you Bray, do you?"

He shakes his head slightly, still in shock. "No. No, that's fine."

Well then, Bray." She smiles. "You crossed a line that shouldn't be crossed. I wonder, what should I do with you, then?" Her smile widens as she watches the blood drain from his face.

"Ah, stop fucking with him, sis. He's only done what we would've."

Brayden nods vehemently, agreeing with Alex. "I'm sorry, Barbara. Please tell me how I can make this up to you."

"All right." She crosses her arm over her chest, her smile disappearing completely. "First off, stop bleating about a fucking diamond. It's gone. Get over it."

He only nods, swallowing hard.

"Second, we also need to get Jack's name out of the frame for Tweaky Pie's murder, don't you think so, Bray?" Barbara says same sweetly, enjoying the visible chill it sends through him. "I can do that, yeah," he agrees. "I'll ring my man, get it done."

"That's the third thing," she continues. "I want the name of your inside man."

Colour returns to Brayden's face in a rush as he shakes his head. "I can't, Barbara. I swore I'd never give him up. He'll have my head."

"Sounds familiar." She stares hard at him. "It's not a request, Joseph. Either you give up his name, or my dear brother here will drop in and pay a nice visit to your pretty wife and those two perfectly sweet children of yours on his way home."

All the air leaves Brayden's lungs as though someone's gut-punched him. Seeing Alex's keen smile, he knows exactly what such a visit would entail. Trapped, he rubs both hands over his face. "It's Paul Tomlinson."

"The assistant Police Commissioner?" Barbara asks, surprised. "Yes." He rubs his face again, shaking his head. "Well, well, well." Barbara's smile returns. "Never expected *him* to turn to the dark side. I need to know everything you have on him. We'll call it our little secret."

She winks.

"Right, fine. Are we good, then?" he asks, eager to leave.

"Barbara." Alex puts a hand on her shoulder. "Are you happy to move on?" She nods, and some of the tension leaves Brayden's body.

"You're coming to the funeral?" It's Brayden's turn to nod.

"Right. Good. We'll talk about our friend the commissioner, then. Oh, and Brayden? This little chat we've just had." She wags her finger between them. "It stays between us. No one, and I mean *no one*, *ever* knows of this conversation, or of my involvement. Understood?"

He nods again. "Yes, ma'am."

"You continue dealing with Jack like nothing's happened, and everything will be just fine."

"Anything else?"

"No, I think we're done, here." She turns to her brother. "Alex, see Joseph out, please."

She waits until the door closes behind Brayden and a few moments longer to make sure he's left the front steps. "That went better than expected." She takes a deep breath. "The assistant Commissioner." She shakes her head. "Can't wait to see what Bray has on him."

"I think you handled this spot on."

She smiles at him. "Yeah, a bit like the old days, eh?

Quite enjoyed turning the clock back." "Dad would be proud of you."

Her smile fades a little. "Are you staying for a few days? You can meet George tomorrow."

"No, sorry, can't." He shakes his head. "Need to get back over the water. Meeting with the Dutch in the morning, about the tabs. Have you mentioned it to Jack yet?"

"Not yet, no. I'll wait until after the funeral. Let things settle down a tad."

"Right." He leans in, dropping a kiss on her cheek. "Give George a kiss for me, then? I'll be back in a couple weeks."

They step out on the front step just as Brayden's car disappears down the street. Alex winks at his sister, waving goodnight as a black Mercedes pulls up at the curb and he jumps into the passenger seat.

Barbara watches the car speed away as she closes the door, taking a deep breath of fresh air after breathing in the stench of death for the best part of the last half-hour. Seeing the lights are on next door, she walks over to the door and knocks softly – a kindly man opens it.

"Hello there. Can I help you?"

"Hi." She smiles at him. "My name is Barbara. I'm George's auntie, and I wanted to thank you for finding him, looking after him the other day."

"*Ah,* yes, poor lad. I'm very sorry for your loss, Barbara. Would you like to come in? Annie's just put the kettle on."

"Oh, no, dear. I would love to, but I need to go." She turns as she hears an engine approaching, just in time to see her car pull up to the curb. Jimmy Fingers steps out of the driver's seat and opens the rear passenger door for her, waiting.

"Hold on a sec, love." Fred holds up a finger then turns his head and shouts. "Annie, come to the door, love."

Barbara plasters a smile on her face as a woman limps towards the door.

"Annie." Fred puts a hand over her shoulders. "This is George's Auntie Barbara."

"Hello." Annie smiles at her. "How is the poor lad? Is he holding up all right?"

"George is coping, yeah. I just wanted to thank you both for all you've done for George. As soon as funeral arrangements are finalised, I'll be sure to let you know."

"I hope they get the fella that killed them." Fred's smile turns to a frown. "It was bloody awful what they put that poor lad through."

"Fred, *hush,*" she frowns at him, putting a hand on his arm, then turns back to Barbara. "That's very nice of you, thank you. Will be nice to see little George again. Such a sweet boy."

"He is, yes," Barbara agrees, pulling a brown

envelope from her coat pocket. "I'm sure he'll be happy to see you both, as well." "This is a thank you, for all you've done for him."

"Oh, no, no. We can't possibly take anything. We love that lad."

"I insist." Barbara pushes the envelope closer, pressing it into Fred's hand.

"Fred, give that back!" Annie hisses as Barbara turns to walk towards the car with a small wave.

Fred and Annie wave the car off until they can no longer see the tail lights, then Annie turns back to him. "I can't believe you took that off her, Fred. What she must be thinking!"

"She insisted, Annie," he tells her, opening the flap. "It would have been rude not to take it." His eyes grow wide as he pulls out a stack of fifty-pound notes.

"We have to give it back, Fred. It's too much!"

"Not a chance," he tells her, pushing the notes back into the envelope as she limps away with a huff. "We can get the new cooker you've been wanting, and a colour telly for when George visits." He shuts the door, smiling at his loot.

Chapter 72

"How are you feeling this morning, George?" Father Willis asks him as he's sat in a large wing- back chair in the priest's office.

George scowls, hugging his doll close. "Okay. But Raggy has a sore head."

"We'll have the nurse look at him, then. But first, I've some good news for you, lad. You're going home today."

George looks up, wide-eyed. "Is Mummy coming to get me?"

"No, George, I'm sorry," Willis answers softly. "Mummy can't come, but your Auntie Barbara is coming to pick you up. You're going to go live at her house now, with her and your Uncle Jack."

George hugs Raggy more tightly. "When is she coming?"

"She'll be here after lunch. Now, be a good lad, run upstairs, and ask Gina to help you pack your things."

He slides off the big chair and runs out of the room and up the stairs. "Gina!" His excited shout echoes down the hallway.

She slides off her bed when George rushes into the room, out of breath. "What is it? Is something wrong? What's happened?"

George jumps up and down, running laps around the

room, making Raggy fly like a superhero. "Auntie Barbara is coming to take me to her house!"

"When?" Gina asks him, smiling.

"After lunch." George stops in front of her, face flushed and heart racing. "Can you help me pack?"

"I can, yes." She guides him to his bed. "But first, I need you to sit down for a minute, whilst I tell you something." She pokes her head out the door to make sure nobody's about, then closes it and goes to sit on George's bed, holding out her arm. "Come, sit on my knee a minute."

He climbs up onto her lap.

"George, last night when you and Raggy were asleep, I gave you a kiss. Raggy wanted a cuddle because he was afraid the bad man might come back."

George squeezes Raggy close.

"I noticed he had a lump in his head, so I checked to see if he was hurt."

George nods. "Yes, he banged his head on the roof. He told me last night before I went to sleep."

"Oh, did he, then?" Gina smiles at him. "Well, I thought he might be, so I had a good look, and a big piece of glass fell out."

George gasps loudly as he looks down at Raggy. "Is he all better now, then?"

Gina nods, patting his hair. "Yes, I got him all fixed up. He's happy again, no more lump in his head."

He throws his little arms around Gina's neck. "Thank you, Gina." He slides off her lap. "Do you want to come live with me at my Auntie Barbara's and Uncle Jack's? Auntie Barbara makes Shepard's Pie and chocolate biscuits."

"I can't, George. I'm going to live with John when he's feeling better. But promise you won't tell, all right? It's our secret."

"I won't tell," he whispers.

"Good boy." She smiles, going to her own bed and pulling the diamond out from the hole in the mattress. She knees down, showing it to him.

"Ohhh! It's so shiny!" His eyes grow wide at the beautiful stone. "Is that the piece of glass that was in Raggy's head?"

"Yes," she tells him. "But it's a very special piece of glass. It's worth a lot of pennies. What do you want to do with it?"

George looks at Raggy and takes a step back, pulling the doll away from the diamond. "I don't want it. It hurt Raggy. You can keep it."

"Are you sure?"

He nods, protecting his doll.

"Okay, but you can't tell anybody, all right? Not even Auntie Barbara or Uncle Jack. It's a secret just between us, just like me going to live with John."

"Okay. Can you help me pack my things, now?"

Gina pulls him into a big hug, then drops a flurry of kisses all over his face, making him giggle. "I love you, George."

"I love you, too. Can we still be friends when I go to live with Auntie Barbara, and you go live with John?"

Gina nods. "Forever and ever." She puts the diamond back in its hiding spot. "C'mon, then, let's get your things packed up."

Chapter 73

Morrison knocks on Doonan's office door at the Peter Street police station.

"Come in," Doonan calls, staring out the window at the row of terraced houses in the distance. Morrison pokes his head in. "Everybody's here, sir."

Doonan nods as he stands and walks to the door Morrison is holding open for him. "Quiet," he tells them as he walks in, and the noise and chatter immediately grow quiet.

"Most of you will be aware of the incident that took place at the children's home on Rushie Fold Lane last night." He pauses as the majority of PCs and detectives nodded in agreement.

"PC Wilcox is going to live. Doctors were able to successfully remove the bullet, which thankfully missed all major organs. But the fall from the roof fractured his spine. At this time, it's too early to tell whether or not he'll walk again."

Cooper raises her hand, and Doonan nods in her direction. "Yes, Cooper?"

"Has anyone arranged a whip round for his family, sir?"

"No, love," he tells her. "Good idea. Can you sort it?"

"Yes, sir."

He pulls out his wallet and hands her a five-pound note. "This will get the ball rolling."

"Thank you, sir." She folds the note into her pocket.

"Right," he addresses the room again. "Let's get down to business. Our main suspect in the 64 Kenilworth Rd. double murders, Errol Tansie, is currently in critical condition. He might have information on Jerome Campbell's murder – that's Tweak, as most of you know him – so, hopefully, he pulls through."

He searches the room until he finds the man he's looking for. "Jackson, we're still waiting for forensics. Can you chase them up?"

"Yes, boss."

"Cooper, has the social worker on George Harrison's case been in touch?"

"No, sir," Cooper advises. "I spoke with Social Services yesterday, and it seems nobody's heard from her for a couple days."

Doonan frowns at this news. "That's odd. Nip by her house, see what she's playing at, yeah?"

"Yes, boss."

"Right," he tells everyone. "Let's get to work, then. We still need to locate Jerome's body. Reach out to your snitches, find out what the word on the street is. We need to close this." He walks back to his office as the officers scatter to their respective duties.

Chapter 74

"Are you looking forward to going home?" Father Willis asks George who's once again sat in the big chair in his office, clutching that doll of his.

"I'm not going home," George tells him innocently. "I'm going to Auntie Barbara's until Mummy and Daddy are all better."

Willis exhales slowly. "Your mummy and daddy have gone to Heaven, lad. They're with Jesus now – they can't come back. Your home will be with your uncle and auntie, now."

"Can I go visit them?" He hugs Raggy tighter.

"I'm afraid not, son. Auntie Barbara will explain it to you."

"Okay." He looks down, his bottom lip quivering. "When is she coming?"

"There she is now." Willis points to the window as Barbara's car pulls into the yard. "Right, let's get your things and go out to meet her."

George slips off the big chair and picks up the small bag filled with his clothes, following Willis to the door.

When they step out of the door, they nearly bump into Gina who's stood waiting on the other side. She quickly grabs his hand and shouts, "George, run!"

They take off towards the stairs and are already out of

sight before Willis has finished locking his office door, Barbara enters into the vestibule.

He gives her a small nod and a smile. "Good afternoon, Barbara. George is just off saying goodbye to his friends. Can I offer you a cup of tea while you wait?" "No, thanks," she tells him coolly. "The faster I get him away from this ungodly place, the better. Fetch him."

She tilts up her head in superiority as she turns her back to him, sitting on the bench by the door.

"Right." he grimaces at her turned head. "I'll get him now."

Chapter 75

WPC Cooper pulls her car to a stop outside Glynis Tobin's home. She frowns, seeing her car parked out front, wondering why she hadn't returned anybody's calls. She walks up to the door and knocks, waiting a few moments before knocking again. "Miss Tobin, it's Alison Cooper. Can you open the door, please?"

When there's still no response, she bends to try and look through the letterbox but quickly recoils at the strong smell of overcooked meat. "What on earth..." She holds her breath and looks again, seeing no movement inside. Trying the door, she finds it locked.

She makes her way to the back garden to find it empty and quiet. She knocks on the kitchen door, her intuition twisting in her gut. The handle turns when she tries it, so she slowly pushes the door open. "Glynis To— "

The stench hits her like a wave, sending her stumbling back a few steps, back out into the garden where she takes a few deep breaths of fresh air, instinctively knowing she's going to find something horrific.

Holding her handkerchief over her mouth and nose, she creeps back inside and quickly learns the exactitude of her instinct as her eyes land on what used to be George's social worker. The badly charred remains, with legs swollen and split like overdone sausages, are tied to the cooker that's been left on high heat.

"Dear God." Cooper coughs into her handkerchief as she reaches to turn the heat off. Glynis' hair has been burnt off, but her face, which was turned away from the heat, is still mostly recognizable.

Feeling the surge in her stomach, Cooper rushes back outside just in time to be violently ill in the petunias.

She wipes her mouth with the handkerchief and rushes back to her car on shaky legs. Her hand trembles like a leaf when she picks up the radio mic.

"Cooper to base." Her voice cracks, not sounding like her own.

"Receiving, go, Cooper."

She takes a steadying breath. *"Suspicious death at 32 Haydock Street, Davey Hulme. S.O.C.O. and ambulance required."*

"Can you confirm the cause of death?"

She clears her throat, trying to erase the image from her mind. *"I'm not a doctor, but from what I can see, seems she's been slow cooked to death."*

There's a long pause on the other end before base comes back on. *"I'm sorry, did you say slow- cooked?"*

"Affirmative. Patch me to Detective Inspector Doonan, please."

"Copy, ma'am."

There's a brief moment before the static returns to the line, and then Doonan's voice. *"Cooper, what is it?"*

"Glynis is dead, sir." Her voice still slightly higher pitched than normal. *"She's been burnt alive."*

"Fuck. Are you okay? Do you need backup?"

"A bit shocked, sir, but I'm all right. I've requested S.O.C.O. and an ambulance. I don't think backup will do any good at this point, sir."

"All right, I'm on my way. Don't let anyone in the house until I get there."

"Yes, sir." "Good girl."

She walks back to the gate, refusing to go back inside, as she waits for everyone to arrive.

Chapter 76

Gina pulls George into the first empty room they reach, she kneels in front of him. "George, I'm leaving here soon. When John's better. I'm going to live in Newcastle."

His eyes grow wide. "Where's that?"

"It's a long way away," she tells him. "But don't worry, I'll write to you every week, promise." She pulls him into a hug as he starts to cry.

"No, please don't go! Please!"

She squeezes him tight. "I have to, George. There are too many bad men here who want to hurt me."

"You're going nowhere, girl," Father Willis growls, glaring down at her from the doorway. "George, come now. Your auntie is waiting for you downstairs."

Gina gives George another kiss before he walks sadly to Father Willis, reluctantly taking his hand as he pulls him away down the hall.

Almost too late, Gina notices he's left his bag on the floor. Quickly, she picks it up and rushes down the hall, flying down the stairs as fast as she can and past Father Willis who's stood in the doorway watching Barbara walk George to the car.

"George!" she cries out. "Wait! You've forgotten your things!"

George runs off, launching himself at Gina as she has

just enough time to kneel and catch him in a hug.

"I love you," he sobs.

"I love you too, George. Now, go on, back to your auntie. I'll write to you, promise."

"Come on, love," Barbara calls to him. "Let's get you home. Your friend can come for a visit soon."

Gina can't contain her own sobs as she watches George trudge back to his auntie, head hung low. She waves to them until the car disappears down the road. Father Willis comes to her side where she's still kneeling. "Run away, will you? I don't think so." He grabs a fistful of her hair, yanking her up off her knees as he pulls her back towards the house.

She bites her lip to keep from crying out in pain as he roughly drags her all the way back to the house and down the stairs, throwing her unceremoniously into the punishment room and locking the door. "I'll deal with you later."

Gina listens to his footsteps receding down the hall as she curls up on the dingy old mattress she knows so well. She doesn't hear as Father Reid peeks through the spy hole before taking the key out of the door and dropping it into his pocket, smiling menacingly as he walks away.

Chapter 77

PC Mercy Peters lets John into the back of the car when he picks him up from the hospital. "Sure you're ready to come out, mate?"

"It's like a prison in there," he tells him as he slips into the back seat. "How you feeling?"

Peters gets in starting the engine, taking John to the station for a statement. "Fucking sore, that's how. The other fella – he dead?"

"No," Mercy catches John's eye in the rearview. "He's in a coma."

"Why was he after them kids?"

Peters turns onto the roadway towards the police station. "No idea, pal. Was hoping you might know."

John just shakes his head, looking out the window. "Just as well you were there, though," Peters

continues. "You're a hero, now. Newspapers have been wanting to talk to you."

John flashes him a dark look. "You keep those vultures away from me, don't want nowt to do with 'em." Peters turns the car into the police station and smiles. "Looks like you might not have a choice, pal." He pointed towards the small crowd of reporters gathered at the front

door. "Quick, put your coat over your head. I'll whizz 'round the back and sneak you in."

He speeds up, quickly moving past them, taking the corner tight, coming to a hard stop in the back parking lot. "Argh! Fuck me, son! I've got eight broken ribs!" John cries out.

"Sorry, pal, I forgot." Peters jumps out of the car, pulling John's door open. "Quick, jump out before they get here." He pulls him by the arm to help him out, John cries out again just as a reporter rounds the corner of the station. "Quick!"

They make it to the door just in time, the flash of the reporter's camera reflecting in the glass of the door as they hurry down the hallway to the interview room.

"Fuck, man." John hobbles along. "I'm in agony. Have you got my tablets from the hospital?"

"They're in the car," Peters tells him, opening the interview room door. "Let's get you sorted and I'll nip out and get them for you."

John sits gently down on the chair and leans on the wall, closing his eyes against the pain as Peters leaves the room.

Chapter 78

"I'm leaving you in charge tonight," Billy tells O'Leary, flipping through some papers on his desk.

O'Leary slouches in the doorway. "I was supposed to take Francine to the casino tonight, boss. She's been naggin' to go on a proper date."

"Sorry, mate." Billy shrugs. "You'll have to give her a proper date some other time, eh? Jack wants me at his hotel in Bolton. Gotta sort out the funeral arrangements for next week."

"*Ah,* that's right." O'Leary shakes his head. "Give him my condolences, yeah?"

"Will do, son."

"What time are you leaving, then?"

"Half an hour." Billy looks up from his papers. "Picking Willis up outside St. Mary's church in an hour."

"Anything planned here tonight?" O'Leary asks him.

"Nah." He shakes his head. "Nothing happening until after the funeral. Jack's orders. So, should be nice and quiet tonight for you."

"Hopefully." O'Leary sighs heavily. "Right, guess I'll go tell Francine she's working tonight." He turns to leave with another sigh. "Wish me luck."

Chapter 79

"Morning," Monroe addresses the full incident room, standing with Doonan at the front by the evidence board.

"Morning, sir," they answer.

"You'll all have heard – we have Errol in custody." He raises his hands as the officers start to cheer and holler. "Calm don't, too early for celebrations. He's awake, out of his coma, but saying he can't remember a thing."

"That old chestnut," Doonan grumbles. "He's faking it."

"Could be, yeah," Monroe agrees. "But we can't interview him until we can prove he's lying. Doctors won't let us near him, so we'll have to crack on with what we've got." He turns to Doonan. "Where are we with Tweak's murder?"

"To be honest, unless we find our mystery witness caller, the only evidence we've got are the blood stains in Jack's yard." Doonan shakes his head, leaning back against the desk at the front of the room. "Forensics confirmed he was killed there, but Jack's only one of dozens who have access to that yard twenty-four-seven, so—"

"We need more evidence tying Jack Harrison to the murder," Monroe interrupts. "We've Tweak's blood in the yard, and a head without a body…"

"Best go to the Nag's Head, sir. That's how they serve their beer." PC Lewis pipes up with a chuckle, sending the room into a chorus of laughter.

"Quiet!" Monroe barks then points to Lewis. "My office after." Lewis drops his head, his laughter cut short. "We might've caught a bit of a break, though," Doonan continues, ignoring the tension. "About time."

Monroe turns back to Doonan. "What've we got?" "Forensics took Errol's clothes for examination. Lot

of blood on 'em, too much to be his if he's still breathin'. Should have results back from the lab today."

"Good. Let me know, as soon as they're back. This might be the best chance we've had in years to shut this gang down, so let's not fuck it up. "Right, back to work." He points to Lewis, then to his office before walking out, Lewis following like a scolded puppy.

"Mercy," Doonan addresses PC Peters. "Get to forensics straight away. Push them along, we need those results yesterday."

"You got it, boss."

Doonan shuts himself in his office, making sure the other room is empty before picking up the phone and waiting three rings before someone picks up.

"Hello?" "Hi, it's me."

"Any news?"

"He's awake but claiming he can't remember anything."

303

"Can we get to him?"

"No, there's no way in, Monroe has it staked out."
"Take care of it."

"Yes, I'll sort it out."

"Where are we meeting tonight?" "The hotel."

"Seven?"

"Eight."

He puts the telephone down and leans back in his chair, feet up on the desk as he stares out the window and lights a cigarette.

Chapter 80

On the fifth floor of the hospital, Father Willis passes a few plain clothes coppers pacing up and down the hallway. He walks past them, not paying them any mind, on his way to the matron's room where he knocks softly on the door.

"Yes, who is it?" her voice calls from inside. "It's me, Marge. Father Willis."

"Yes, come in, Father."

He smoothes out his frocks and plasters the most pleasant smile he can muster before opening the door.

"What can I do for you today, Father?" she smiles back at him from behind the desk, glasses perched on her nose.

He holds his hands in front of him, as though in prayer – or maybe pleading. "I need to speak with Errol Tansie, Marge."

She raises her eyebrows slightly, sitting back in her chair. "You're asking a lot, Father. We've been advised, nobody in or out unless absolutely necessary."

"Surely a priest would be considered necessary, Marge? Tell them he asked to see me, for confession."

A slight frown dips between her delicate brows as she stands, dusting the wrinkles from her skirt. "You're putting me in an awkward position, Father. Wait here, please. I can't make any promises."

Marge leaves Willis in her office as she walks down

the hall to find the armed policeman. "Hello, officer." She gives him her best smile. "The patient has requested to speak with a priest who can perform confession. Ours is on site now.

The officer seems to deliberate for a moment, his eyes landing on the golden cross hanging around the matron's neck. *"Um,* I don't see why not. I have to check him first – standard procedure."

"Of course." She gives a slight nod, smiling. "This way, officer." She leads him to her office, preceding him through the door. "Officer, this is Father Jackson, our resident priest.

The officer gives him a polite nod in greeting. "Hello, Father. Would you follow me, please?" Willis grips his rosary in clasped hands as he follows the officer down the hall to Errol's room raising his eyebrows in surprise as he stops and pats him down. "Sorry, Father," the officer apologises. "Only procedures."

"I don't need any weapons, son when I've got God on my side." Willis smiles warmly at him. Uncomfortable, the officer clears his throat, pushing the door open for him. "Right, in you go." The door closes with a soft click after Willis – the officer waits outside the door. The room is quiet as Willis makes his way to Errol's bedside where he sleeps soundly. Looking over his shoulder to make sure the officer isn't watching, he pats Errol's cheek with the back of his hand.

Startled out of sleep, he opens his eyes, squinting at Willis. "Oh, sorry, Father. I was just nodding off."

Willis raises his eyebrows, not buying the act. "Cut the shit, Tansie. What are you up to?" A small frown creases Errol's brow as he stares at Willis in genuine confusion. "I'm sorry...

Do I know you?"

"What's your name?" Willis asks him, beginning to doubt his earlier belief.

Errol looks defeated as he shrugs. "Don't know, Father. I can't remember. Can't remember anything."

"You mean to tell me you can't recall brutally murdering your girlfriend and her ex-husband in cold blood?" Willis asks him.

Errol shakes his head vehemently, his eyes filling. "I'm sorry, Father. I wish I could help you. The police asked me the same question." He paused, swallowing as his eyes danced from one of his hands to the other, and back up to Willis' again. "Am I really that sort of person, Father?" He shakes his head, tears spilling down his bruised and swollen face. "If I am, I don't think I wanna remember."

Willis lets out a long breath as he stares at the sobbing mess of a man. He's seen many a liar in his day,

but Errol isn't one of them. He's done the crime, to be sure, but he truly doesn't recall a minute of it.

Rosary wrapped around his hand, he places it down on one of Errol's, bowing his head. *"Pater noster, qui es caelis, sanctificetur nomen tuum. Adveniat regnum tuum. Fiat voluntas tua, sicut in caelo et in terra. Panem nostrum quotidianum da nobis hodie, et dimitte nobis debita nostra sicut et nos dimittimus debitoribus nostris. Et ne nos inducas in tentationem, sed libera nos a malo. Amen."*

He crosses Errol's head just as the officer re-enters the room. *"Dominus vobiscum."* He nods at Errol who's still sobbing like a child, and leaves the room with the officer.

"Did he say anything?"

"Say anything?" Willis repeats, feigning incredulity. "Look at him – he's a complete wreck. He couldn't say anything if he tried." Willis nods at him as he turns to walk away. "Thank you for letting me see him."

Knowing his time is borrowed, Willis makes a hasty retreat to the lift and manages to get in just as Monroe exits the other.

"Anything to report?" Monroe asks the officer.

"No, sir. Only that a priest has just been in. The prisoner requested one with the nurse."

"You fucking idiot!" Monroe shouts at him, storming past to the door. "Nobody is allowed to see him, priests included!"

The officer watches from the open door as Monroe runs to Errol's bedside, grabbing at his wrist to check his pulse.

"Oy, that hurts." Errol pulls his arm away, frowning. Monroe releases a breath. "The priest – what did he want?"

Errol shrugs. "He asked the same questions you did about the people you say I killed. Then he prayed and left." Monroe curses under his breath as he drops Errol's arm and storms back out the door, past the officer. He turns to him, face red with fury as the door closes. "Nobody is to go into this room unless that somebody is

me. No-fucking-body! Do you understand?"

The officer nods silently as Monroe storms off.

Chapter 81

In the red telephone box outside St. Mary's Church, Father Willis dials the children's home.

"Hello?"

"Reid, is that you?"

"Yes, Willis. Where are you?"

"I'm away this evening. You'll have to take evening mass."

"Have you already prepared a—"

"Yes," Willis interrupts. *"The sermon is on my desk. I should be back around twelve-ish."*

"Right, I'll take care of things here."

"Oh, I nearly forgot – Let Gina out of the punishment room."

"Couldn't I just—" "No."

"But I think—"

"Just do as you're told, Reid." "Fine, I'll let her out." "Thanks. Bye."

Reid walks down to the punishment room. Opening the door, he smiles at Gina, she backs away into the corner. "Stay away from me, you freak," unfazed Reid taunts her.

"Scream all you want, ya little slut, no one can hear you down here, and Willis is in Leeds for the night."

He points towards his eye patch. "Tonight is a payment day, bitch." He closes the door as Gina screams. Willis jumps as Billy pips his horn. He hurries out of the telephone box and gets in the car.

Chapter 82

A soft tap sounds at Gina's window, startling her. She uncurls herself slowly from the bed, every inch of her body battered and bruised. Each step towards the window sends shooting pains up her legs.

Pulling back the curtain, she doesn't see anyone, so pries the window up as much as she can. A large face pops into the pane and she stumbles back with a scream, slapping both hands over her swollen and split-mouth as she recognises her friend.

"John." She comes close to the window as he tries to pry it the rest of the way up, but it's stuck. His eyes roam over her battered little body, angry, hand-shaped bruises on both arms and everywhere else he can see that isn't covered up with fabric. Fury fills his eyes. "Gina, what have them bastards done to you?" he whispers. "I'm gonna kill them."

"Shh!" She looks behind her, listening for footsteps. "They'll hear you."

"Come down to the front, quick. I've got a car ready to take us away." Her lip quivers. "I can't, they locked me in here."

"Right." John nods, his frown deepening. "Hurry and get your things packed up, I'll be back in a minute." He disappears from the window, Gina pushes through the pain as she shuffles around the room as fast as she can, stuffing her clothes in a rucksack, then pulls out her treasures from the hole in the mattress, taking extra care to tuck the diamond carefully into her jacket pocket, along with the gun Errol dropped on the roof that she'd picked up."

She's ready just as John reappears at the window, holding a large red brick. He points behind her. "Take the blanket from the bed, quick, and stand aside."

She rips the blanket from her bed as John smashes the brick through the window, making sure to get all the sharp points, then motions for the blanket.

He drapes it over the windowsill so she can crawl up and out without cutting herself. "Hurry, they'll have heard the window breaking."

Quickly, Gina scampers up the window, her bag hooked over her shoulder. John grabs her, lifting her the rest of the way as he cries out in pain from the broken ribs. "Quick, John, I hear someone coming," Gina whispers, pulling at his hand as they hurry down the fire escape stairs as fast as they can, reaching the bottom just as Father Reid pokes his head out the broken window.

"Where do you think you're taking her?" He cries out as they both look up. John grips Gina's hand tightly, urging her forward. "Away from here."

"I think not!" Father Reid runs out of the room and down the stairs to the front door. He pulls on it and curses when he remembers it's locked, the key sitting on Willis' desk. Rushing, he runs to get the key and unlocks the door, grabbing a steel poker from the umbrella stand as he runs out the door.

Gina and John are making their way up the driveway as fast as they can, which isn't very fast at all.

Reid runs towards them, poker in hand. "You can't have her, you vermin, she's mine! I haven't finished playing with her, yet."

John turns, hellfire in his eyes. "Come a step closer and you'll be meeting your boss sooner than you've planned," he roars, but then quickly drops to his knees, crippled with pain.

Reid smiles as he advances some more. "And how do you plan on sending me there in your state, *eh?* You're weak as a little girl, look at you."

Gina turns on Reid, the same fire in her eyes John had a moment before. "Get in the car, John," she says calmly. "Start the engine."

John pushes himself up painfully, her tone reverberating through him. *No longer the ten-year-old, scared child,* he thinks, as he manages to get himself behind the wheel.

"Gina," Reid taunts, walking closer. "You can't leave yet. We've got unfinished business, you and me. Come back, let's go inside, there's a good girl."

"I don't fucking think so." She levels her stare at him, unflinching as his face grows red. "Get over here, you dirty little slut!" he shouts, raising the poker and taking a run at her.

Calmly, she pulls the gun from her pocket, takes aim, and pulls the trigger, sinking the bullet in the part of him that will ensure he won't be *playing* with any of the girls, ever again. He drops to his knees, screaming in agony as he grabs at his crotch, a large red stain quickly growing on the front of his pyjama pants.

"Little girls aren't so weak now, are they?" she sneers down at him. "I hope you die, you fucking cunt!" She gets in the car as lights begin to come on in some of the windows upstairs, and they drive off quickly.

"Where did you get that from?" John asks her, speeding down towards the gate.

"The fella who shot you dropped it when you went off the roof." She turns and sees the house is now fully lit up, and people are running out to Reid where he's crumpled up like a rag doll on the driveway. "Quick, let's get out of here."

John speeds through the open gate and spins the tires as they round the bend onto the road. "What the fuck has he done to you?"

"It doesn't matter. He won't be hurting anyone now." She pulls the diamond from her pocket, unwrapping it from the little rag and showing John. It sparkles as it catches the glow of the streetlamps as they drive under them. "This is ours."

"Where'd you get that from?"

"A friend gave it to me." She smiles, tucking it back in the rag and into her bag as she thinks of George, his Raggy doll. "I know what I want to do now, John. Will you help me?" She looks at him, a serious look on her face that belongs to no child he's ever known.

He smiles at her. "You don't need to ask, love." He punches the accelerator pedal as they pass the M6 Motorway sign.

Chapter 83

Fifty cars inch their way up Kenilworth Road, following the two hearses. They come to a stop in front of the house, Jack and Barbara step out of the third car, George dressed to the nines, carrying a white flower wreath almost bigger than him. He walks between his uncle and auntie up to the steps and gently lays down the wreath before bursting into tears.

Auntie Barbara explained to him what Heaven is, and he understands now that he won't be seeing Mummy and Daddy again.

Jack picks him up, holding him close as George buries his face in his neck. "It's all right, son. Let it out." He rubs his back, kissing his cheek before passing him over to Barbara as they walk back to the car.

He can't help but stare at the two head vehicles, adorned with white chrysanthemum flowers – the first reading 'Daddy' and 'Brother', and the second reading 'Mummy'.

They get back in and Barbara taps the window, and the car begins to move forwards again, followed by Billy behind them, carrying Fred and Annie.

"Are you okay, love?" Barbara asks Jack softly, holding George close in her lap.

"Not yet, but I'll get there." He looks back out the

window at the house as they drive away. "I'm gonna tear that house down," he whispers.

She lays a gentle hand on his arm, her voice soft. "Let's just get through today, love. We can sort the rest out later."

From a respectable distance, Monroe, Doonan, and WPC Cooper stand under a weeping willow, watching the cortege pull up.

When they reach the southern cemetery gates at Heaton Park, Father Willis steps out of the first hearse and walks ahead, leading the procession down the laneway to the two freshly dug graves.

"Good turnout," Monroe says, arms crossed as he leans against the gnarled tree trunk. "Pity it's not Jack's."

"Have we got eyes on the mourners?" Doonan wants to know.

"Yeah, couple of police photographers dotted about," Monroe tells him.

"Great." Doonan nods, pulling his handkerchief from his pocket and handing it to Cooper as Jack steps out of the car, holding the door for Barbara and a still sobbing George. "Will be good for intel going forward."

"Oh, that poor lad." Cooper sniffs, her heart breaking for George as he watches the undertakers pull the coffins from the hearses and carry them to the graveside.

"He's the only one here who deserves your tears, Cooper," Doonan tells her, blinking a few away himself. "This place is teeming with scum. Drugs, prostitution, to name the tamer crimes." He shakes his head as he watches about three hundred people crowd around the site.

"The Lord is my shepherd, I shall not want." Father Willis' voice carries on the wind. "He maketh me to lie down in green pastures: he leadeth me beside the still waters. He restoreth my soul; he leadeth me in the paths of righteousness for his name's sake."

Jack looks up, locking eyes with Monroe across the crowd. Barbara grabs his hand, squeezing and shaking her head slightly, casting her own shadowed stare on Monroe who merely gives a small nod.

"We, therefore, commit these bodies to the ground," Father Willis continues as Graham's coffin is lowered down. "Earth to earth, ashes to ashes, dust to dust; in sure and certain hope of the Resurrection to eternal life.

Jack barely holds himself together as his brother's coffin disappears into the earth.

"May God give to you and all whom you love." Willis goes on as Valerie's coffin is lowered next to Grahams. "His comfort and His peace, His light and His joy, and this world and the next; and the blessing of God almighty, the Father, the Son, and the Holy Spirit, be upon you, and remain with you this day, and forever. Amen."

George pulls away from Barbara and runs to the edge of the grave, pulling Raggy from inside his jacket and holding the doll over the openings. "Say goodbye, Raggy. Mummy and Daddy have gone to Heaven now.

Barbara hurries to George's side, pulling him back for fear he'll tumble in. She kneels, hugging him close as her own tears fall.

George looks at her, patting her face gently. "It's

okay, Auntie Barbara. Raggy said we'll see Mummy and Daddy again."

Barbara gives him a small smile, picks him up and walks back to Jack's side as Father Willis approaches, offering Jack a box containing soil.

Jack takes a handful, tossing it down onto Graham's coffin, then does the same with Valerie's, and waits whilst Barbara does the same, allowing George to follow suit.

As a long line of mourners walk up to pay their quiet respects and Barbara speaks with Willis, Jack stands back with Billy. "Have you seen who's graced us with their presence?"

"Yeah," Billy says, disgusted. "Monroe probably has his filth scattered all over this place like lice, taking pictures."

"I'm taking Barbara and George to Spain for a couple weeks," Jack tells Billy. "You're in charge until I get back." Billy nods. "Let me know where you're staying, just in case."

"I will." Jack turns away from staring down Monroe. "Let everyone know it's back to Tommy Duck's pub for the wake."

"Sure thing, Jack." Billy looks over Jack's, shoulder seeing a long line forming. "I think you're wanted." He points behind him.

Jack turns, acknowledging the mourners. "Sorry to keep you waiting, friends. Just give me a minute to speak with my wife. I'll be right with you." He walks over to Barbara where she's standing with an older couple.

"Jack, this is Annie and Fred. They lived next door to

George, and they looked out for him." Annie steps forward, holding out her hand to Jack. "I'm so very sorry for your loss, Mr Harrison."

Jack takes her hand in both of his, smiling down at her warmly. "Please, call me Jack. It's very nice to meet you both. We're all headed to Tommy Duck's – will you join us?"

"We will, thanks," Fred agrees, shaking Jack's hand in turn.

"That's sorted, then." Jack smiles at them. "You came with Billy, yeah?"

"Yes, nice lad."

Jack nods. "Good. You can ride with him – we'll see you there." He turns to make his way to the waiting line of well-wishers.

"Jack." Barbara stops him, a hand on his arm. "I'm taking George back to the pub now. I want to make sure everything is running smoothly. Fred and Annie can come with me – it'll be nice for George to visit with them, see some friendly faces."

"Good idea, love," Jack agrees. "George doesn't need to stay here any longer than needed. Get Jimmy Fingers to drive you, he's just over there." He points to where Jimmy is standing beside his car, ever at the ready, then turns back to greet the crowd.

"Annie, Fred, you can ride with us."

"Thank you, dear." Annie smiles as they make their way to Jimmy's car. It takes them a while to get to the car, being pulled aside every few steps by people eager to offer their condolences.

"Jimmy, change of plans," Barbara tells him when they eventually make it. "Jack's going with Billy, so you'll drive us to the pub."

"Yes, ma'am." He nods, opening the passenger door for her, then letting Fred and Annie get into the back, George tucked in snugly between them.

"Hiya, Uncle Fred!" George smiles, giving them both a snuggle.

"Hello there, young man." Fred smiles back at him. "Are you and Raggy okay?"

Barbara rolls down the window as they drive close to Monroe and his team and Jimmy pulls the car to a stop. "Enjoying yourself, are you?" she asks him. "This is a private funeral – you're not welcome here."

Monroe smiles at her. "Public property, love. Just enjoying the view."

"Makes you happy, this sort of thing, I expect."

He leans in close to the window. "It would if it were somebody else in the ground." He winks at her.

He flinches when Barbara spits in his face, stepping back as he pulls a tissue from his pocket, wiping his cheek, Doonan and Cooper glance at each other, rolling their eyes.

"Let's go, Jimmy."

THE END

OR, IS THIS JUST THE BEGINNING?